I DO
SOLEMNLY
SWEAR

Text copyright © 2012 D. M. Annechino

Printed in the United States of America.

Published by Thomas & Mercer
P.O. Box 400818
Las Vegas, NV 89140

ISBN-13: 9781612184227
ISBN-10: 1612184227

I DO
SOLEMNLY
SWEAR

D. M. ANNECHINO

THOMAS & MERCER

ALSO BY D. M. ANNECHINO

They Never Die Quietly

Resuscitation

DEDICATION

In memory of my longtime friend, John Plakus, a jack-of-all-trades, race-car enthusiast, freethinker, and a lover of good bourbon. He was truly a nice guy who left us way too soon.

CAST OF CHARACTERS

Katherine Ann Miles – President of the United States (former VP)

Peter Miles – President Miles's spouse

David Rodgers – Former President

Elizabeth Rodgers – Former First Lady

Trevor Williams – President Miles's father

Charles McDermott – President Miles's Chief of Staff (COS)

Olivia Carter – Executive Assistant to the Chief of Staff

Walter Owens – President Miles's VP, former Speaker of the House

Victor Ellenwood – Director of Central Intelligence (DCI)

Carl Kramer – Deputy Director of Central Intelligence (DDCI)

Albert Cranston – Director of the Secret Service

Toni Mitchell – Secretary of State

Richard Alderson – Secretary of Defense

William Riley – Press Secretary

Guenther Krause – Villain

Jack Miller – CIA Special Agent

General Charles Kelley – Joint Chiefs of Staff

General Cumberland – Joint Chiefs of Staff

General Wolfe – Joint Chiefs of Staff

General Wallace – Joint Chiefs of Staff

Admiral McCormick – Joint Chiefs of Staff

Admiral Canfield – Joint Chiefs of Staff

Ahmad Habib – Iranian Ambassador

Dr. Weinberg – White House physician

Leonard LaPlant – Medical Examiner

Joseph Vitelli – President Miles's personal chef

CHAPTER ONE

"The president is…dead."

Kate recognized the voice on the phone; she spoke to the chief of staff regularly. She could even see Charles McDermott's squinty eyes and that nervous twitch. But his shocking announcement didn't immediately register. It was almost as if he were speaking a foreign language.

Gripping her stomach, she shuffled across the room and glanced out the third-story window, the cordless phone pressed to her ear. Except for the faint whine of a distant siren, the streets were still. There was a heavy fog in the air, and the halogen streetlights looked out of focus, like pale-yellow balls of cotton. Kate's legs were trembling, and her stomach—always subject to an unwelcome assault—felt as if it were ablaze. Her voice, barely a whisper, broke the early morning quiet. "What happened, Charles?"

"It appears to be a heart attack."

How could this be? Just yesterday she'd jogged with the president, and Kate's five-foot-ten frame could barely keep pace with him. "Are you sure?"

"That's what Dr. Weinberg suspects. We won't know for certain until they perform an autopsy."

The word *autopsy* drew a horrifying image in her mind: she could see President Rodgers's lean body lying on a cold stainless-steel table, a man in a white lab coat standing over him with a scalpel poised above his chest. Kate's sky-blue eyes blurred with tears.

Kate heard a woman's voice in the background. She guessed it was the First Lady. "Elizabeth must be a wreck."

"She's remarkably composed," McDermott said. "She asked to see you."

Kate glanced at the wall clock. "Tell her I'm on my way."

"A car should be there directly." For a moment, there was silence. "I expect complete chaos, Kate."

Yes, she thought, *complete chaos*. "Have you contacted Walter Owens?" Owens, Speaker of the House, staunch Republican, was Kate's most formidable political opponent. They'd had heated conflicts from the moment she'd been elected vice president. At the mere thought of his rotund body and that insolent smile, the muscles at the base of her neck twisted into a knot.

"It was my next call," Charles McDermott said.

"Tell him to meet me at the White House."

"Anything else, Madam Vice President?"

"Yes, Charles. Tell me this isn't happening."

Kate dropped the telephone on the end table and collapsed onto a chair. She combed her fingers through honey-blonde hair, recalling the long road to the White House. Former secretary of state Hillary Clinton had forewarned Kate about Washington politics. Clinton had told her in the most forthright manner that the male-dominated Congress would try to eat her alive. They had tried. Oh, how they'd tried. But somehow—either due to her midwestern stubbornness or her tenacious nature—she survived. Once deemed impossible, a woman had finally assumed the role as second-in-command, piercing through the impenetrable male fabric of Washington. She imagined how Congress might feel now that the former governor of Kansas would soon occupy the Oval Office.

Holy shit. I'm going to be president.

Peter walked into the den, mumbling under his breath. Obviously, she'd interrupted his sleep. Her husband didn't enjoy being awakened, except when Kate was feeling amorous, which lately wasn't very often. His robe was untied, and she could see his middle-age paunch. She looked at his red, swollen eyes. Another broken promise. Back in Kansas, he had been a brilliant litigator. But in DC, no matter how many opportunities presented themselves, none met Peter's standards. Alcohol was his convenient crutch for failure.

"Insomnia?" he asked. An appropriate question. Kate had always been a nocturnal creature. A copy of *Gatsby*, dog-eared on page 122, sat faceup on the ottoman.

"David had a heart attack."

Peter didn't even flinch. "How bad?"

She almost couldn't answer; the words hung in her throat. "He...didn't make it."

Perhaps because her announcement didn't quite register, Peter seemed to dismiss this consequential event as if it were an unpleasant weather report. But then it appeared that he was jolted by the reality of Kate's announcement. "I can't believe this. I'm so sorry, Kate."

The doorbell chimed.

Kate's head was spinning, but she managed to stand and negotiate her way to the foyer. When she opened the door, the ghost-white face of Albert Cranston peered at her. She looked down at him; she was a foot taller than the director of Secret Service.

Two agents stood behind him. One of them, Agent Tom Walsh, a young, sturdy African American, had been exclusively assigned to the president. What was he doing here?

Katherine Anne Miles, still disoriented and numb, had enough sense to realize that Tom Walsh was exactly where he was supposed to be.

***

The overweight security guard raised the gate and waved the black limousine forward. The driver pulled up to the front door of 1600 Pennsylvania Avenue. Dressed in government-issued black suits, crisp white shirts, and charcoal ties, a group of Secret Service agents teemed around the car like a pod of orcas attacking a blue whale. If they had been wearing sunglasses, they could easily have passed for the cast of the movie *Men in Black*. As Kate stepped out of the backseat, she noticed a group of people gathered in the section of Pennsylvania Avenue closed to vehicles. She could hear their melodic chants. Some carried signs, waving them in the air. Kate couldn't comprehend what they were doing at this early hour. Did they know about President Rodgers? She couldn't imagine that someone had leaked privileged information. But this was Washington, and the communication network was like no other. The president couldn't even get a haircut without it making the front page of every newspaper and blog across the country.

She looked up at the massive white pillars supporting the canopy roof of the White House entrance. They reminded her of the Pantheon in Rome, one of her favorite places in Europe. She hadn't vacationed in Italy in over a decade and couldn't believe it had been so long. Since entering the political arena, she had little time to do anything but focus on her career.

With a silent nod of acknowledgment, Chief of Staff Charles McDermott ushered Kate through the double doors. The White House had the eerie feel of a mausoleum, and Kate, sensing the poignant irony, felt a chill shiver through her body. The halls were dimly lit, and as they walked down the main corridor, it appeared endless, like looking through the wrong end of a telescope. With the exception of two janitors busily mopping floors and Secret Service agents hustling about, the White House was all but deserted.

McDermott and Kate passed four agents huddled at the foot of the stairway. As Kate walked past them, she felt peculiar. Their chatter tuned down to whispers, and they appeared to be sizing her up in a predatory manner. She couldn't decipher the garble but knew they were gossiping about her.

She walked swiftly, her long stride and rapid gait making her hair bounce on top of her shoulders. McDermott's five-foot-four frame had to jog to keep pace with her. And this amused Kate.

Press Secretary William Riley and Speaker of the House Walter Owens intercepted them in front of the elevator. Riley was wearing tan Dockers and a navy polo shirt—a drastic departure from his usual GQ ensemble. His caramel-colored hair looked like he'd just had an appointment with his stylist. She caught a whiff of his cologne and recognized the scent: Cool Water. One of her favorites. Considering the dramatic circumstances, she couldn't fathom that he'd taken the time to splash on cologne. Owens was as sloppy as ever, his portly body stuffed into slacks that hadn't fit him in years, and the buttons on his dingy shirt strained. What remained of his gray hair was strategically parted just above his left ear and plastered across his shiny head.

Riley nodded. "Madam Vice President. Charles."

"I'm horrified," Owens said. He stared at his scuffed shoes. "This is an unbelievable tragedy."

"We need to schedule a press conference," Riley offered, "as soon as possible."

"Don't do anything," Kate said, "until I speak to the First Lady. Draft a statement but no announcements until I review it."

"Where will I find you?" Riley asked.

Kate eyed McDermott.

"Before we do anything, Madam Vice President, you must be sworn in as president."

McDermott's words blindsided Kate. For a moment, she stood dumbstruck, staring at the chief of staff in disbelief. It all seemed so surreal—bizarre, actually.

"We will arrange an official inauguration as soon as possible," McDermott said, "but for now, Chief Justice Cambridge is waiting in the Blue Room."

Kate glanced at Walter Owens, feeling certain that his comforting smile was a hollow gesture. She suspected that he was already scheming for a way to make her transition into the Oval Office a difficult one. She'd likely live to regret what she was about to do, but turmoil and panic would surely grip the White House during the next few weeks, and she needed to keep Owens, her greatest adversary, harnessed. As Speaker of the House, he had free rein to use his political moxie to raise havoc and make Kate's life miserable. But if she appointed him interim VP, a decision certain to incite controversy and raise questions about her sanity, he'd answer directly to her, and Kate might be able to limit his subversive activities.

"Walter, the nation is faced with an unprecedented crisis. We haven't always seen eye to eye, but it's time we set our differences aside and unite for the sake of the American people."

She paused for a moment, still not able to believe that her first decision might one day result in her undoing. "Walter, would you consider assuming the role as acting VP until I have had sufficient time to select a permanent replacement?"

Owens's eyes narrowed as if searching for an ulterior motive. But Kate guessed that his massive ego would take control. "It would be an honor, Madam Vice President."

McDermott sighed deeply. "The chief justice is waiting, Madam Vice President."

One look in McDermott's eyes and, already, Kate regretted her decision.

***

After being sworn in as president, an event Kate felt certain would remain a faint memory, McDermott whisked her away, and they rode the elevator to the second floor. Four Secret Service agents were posted at the main entrance of the Presidential Suite. Recognizing the COS and the newly sworn-in president, they snapped to attention like boot camp recruits and stepped aside. McDermott rang the doorbell.

Elizabeth Rodgers opened the door. The moment she looked at the First Lady, Kate's heart felt like it shivered. Elizabeth's hazel eyes were red and puffy, and her usually rosy cheeks were chalky white.

"Thank you for coming at this ungodly hour," Mrs. Rodgers said, almost apologizing. Her voice was unsteady, but she was as poised as a gymnast on a balance beam. Elizabeth pointed to the pale-yellow Louis XVI couch facing the white marble fireplace. "Please make yourselves comfortable."

For years, Kate had admired fifty-eight-year-old Elizabeth Rodgers. She'd always been a stalwart woman, determined and outspoken. Since entering the White House just a short time ago, she had redefined the role of a First Lady. Always active and publicly visible, she'd founded several influential women's organizations. Today, Kate was looking at a woman with a broken spirit. Her shaky voice exposed a fragile side Kate had never seen.

As instructed, the president and chief of staff sat next to each other on the sofa. It reminded Kate of grade school, like sitting in front of the principal, waiting to be scolded for some childish misdeed.

Elizabeth sat adjacent to them. She folded her hands on her lap in a proper manner and sat upright as if she were overtly conscious of her posture. She was meticulously kempt, not a single blonde hair out of place, and if it weren't for the wounded look in her eyes, Kate might have thought the First Lady was on her way to the opera. Kate glanced at the Rembrandt Peale portrait of George Washington hanging above the fireplace. How she'd love to trade places with him right now. A rush of heat radiated from the fire, but Kate's stubborn goose bumps had no intention of going away.

"My husband was an extraordinary man," the First Lady began. "A man of great ideals." Her eyes did not meet Kate's or McDermott's; they focused on something across the room. "He believed he could make a difference, change the political structure of Washington, generate a new spirit of patriotism in both politicians and in his fellow Americans."

She hesitated a moment and forced a swallow. Her tone was formal. It sounded like a eulogy. Kate listened without comment.

"Eight months was hardly enough time for my David to have accomplished anything." She lifted a glass of water and took a sip. A few drops trickled down her chin and spotted her dress. "Who will fulfill David's dreams, Madam President? Will you carry on his legacy?"

Kate didn't know what to say. Rodgers and she had started out on the same path—or so she thought—but Rodgers had drifted from the intended agenda as soon as he'd entered the White House. How could she tell Elizabeth that she could not and would not continue with policies that contradicted her beliefs? She continued to listen intently but was distracted by McDermott, who incessantly cleared his throat, studied his Rolex, and twitched his neck as if his collar were over-starched.

"Mr. McDermott," the First Lady said, "may I speak to Kate privately?" Kate was uncertain whether Elizabeth had excused McDermott because of his obvious inattention or for a more significant reason.

McDermott sprang up, his face flushed with blood, his voice edged with tension. "I'll be in my office, Madam President. I'm deeply sorry for your loss, Mrs. Rodgers." Considering the situation, his words seemed insincere.

The First Lady remained silent until the door clicked shut. She sipped her water. "Tell me, Madam President, are you willing to risk your life for what you believe?"

Kate felt like a wad of peanut butter was stuck in her throat.

"If they got to David, they can get to you, dear."

"*They*?" Kate was sure her heart had stopped for a moment. "Who are you talking about?"

"If I had their names, they'd be dead. They're out there. Close to you."

"Elizabeth, David had a heart attack. Dr. Weinberg—"

"My David could have wrestled a grizzly bear. He'd had some blood-pressure problems, yes, but through a strict regimen of diet, exercise, and medication, he had the heart of an athlete."

9

Kate was unclear whether the First Lady was delirious or if there was basis for the warning. "You're talking in riddles, Elizabeth. Tell me what you know."

"I should have known something was wrong when David went to bed at eight thirty. I should have called the doctor. He was a creature of habit, you know. His routine was always so methodical. He'd never retire until after the eleven o'clock news. Then he'd read until he couldn't keep his eyes open. Sometimes until one thirty or two. When he complained of a headache and a queasy stomach, I thought it was a touch of the flu."

Kate had many questions to ask, and didn't want to postpone them, but she didn't feel Elizabeth could answer them with any certainty right now. The First Lady was clearly consumed with grief. She seemed beyond rational thinking. After all, David's body was still warm. How could she think clearly? The only logical course of action would be to arrange another private conversation after David's funeral. Given some time, the First Lady might untangle her snarled thoughts.

"You look terribly tired, Elizabeth. Why don't you get some rest, and we can talk again in a day or so? If you need anything at all, please don't hesitate to contact me."

Before she left the First Lady, Kate embraced her with consoling arms. They held each other firmly, and she could feel Elizabeth's body trembling. Kate wished there was a way to comfort her but understood that only time could remove the cold dagger twisting into Elizabeth's heart.

Before Elizabeth released Kate, she whispered in her ear, "Be careful. Things are not as they seem."

The riddles continued.

***

Kate sat in McDermott's lavishly appointed office, watching him fidget like a child waiting to see a dentist. She'd never seen him rattled—when they'd first met, she swore he was an android—but David Rodgers's death seemed to have exposed a more human side in him. She'd thought about meeting him in the Oval Office, but under the circumstances, she just didn't feel comfortable.

Kate had been trying to decipher Elizabeth's cryptic warning, uncertain what to make of it. Why had the First Lady concealed her words from McDermott? Questions rose in her mind. Did the First Lady know something about McDermott that Kate had yet to learn?

Contrary to numerous warnings from constituents, Kate had worked remarkably well with McDermott. During her brief tenure in DC, he had been an important ally. McDermott played the political game of chess like a grand master; every move was strategic. But that was how you survived in Washington. Relationships were *everything*. She was well aware of his egocentric reputation. But for some less-than-obvious reason—she had never quite figured it out—he had formed an alliance with her. She knew that beneath his supposed loyalty there existed a hidden agenda, a means to an end. Perhaps now that she was going to occupy the Oval Office, he would expose his secret side.

Her real nemesis was Walter Owens. As vice president, Kate presided over the Senate. And Speaker of the House Owens sat before the House. The concept that these two stubborn politicians could meet in the middle on any legislation proved to be hopeless. They found themselves gridlocked on every issue. Of course, it hadn't helped that Kate had run for office as an Independent candidate with no allegiance to any party, and Owens was a staunch Republican. Consequently, productive joint sessions of Congress had been all but impossible. These two bodies of authority couldn't agree on what time to adjourn for lunch. How could they possibly collaborate on legislation when their respective leaders argued every issue? There were few points on which Owens and she agreed, but Kate hoped that appointing him interim VP had not been a foolhardy decision and that she could find a way to keep Owens in check. McDermott could be an important advocate, so it made sense to approach him diplomatically rather than flex her political muscles. She needed to keep him on her team.

"So do we have a game plan, Charles?"

He loosened his tie, leaned forward in the leather chair, and looked at her with penetrating eyes. "The rules have changed for everybody, Madam President. They don't teach you how to handle a situation like this at Harvard."

Of course there were procedures to follow and protocol, but she knew what McDermott meant.

She watched him drumming a pencil on the yellow pad sitting on his desk. It was obvious he had something substantial to say but apparently hadn't yet composed his words. Perhaps this was why he'd been so anxious in front of the First Lady.

Until this meeting, Kate had never appraised McDermott with such discriminating eyes. If God had been just slightly more generous with McDermott's features, he could almost be attractive. But his face was two-dimensional—tiny nose, weak chin, flat cheeks—and his eyes were like tarnished pennies. An unremarkable face.

"Madam President, as you settle into the Oval Office, I would encourage you to be prudent and not do anything too drastic."

"You mean like appointing Mr. Owens VP?"

"Actually, I thought it was a brilliant strategy. Had you given me the opportunity, I would have advised you to do *exactly* that."

Kate recognized Charles's subtle message. She'd made the impulsive decision to appoint Owens as VP without consulting him. "So, if enlisting Walter Owens as VP wasn't drastic, what *is* drastic, Charles?"

He gave her a long, searching look. "Are you planning to replace any staff members?"

"Do you think I should?"

He shook his head.

"What makes you ask such a question?"

He lifted a shoulder. "It's no secret that you reorganized in Kansas."

Now she understood. "You mean cleaned house?"

"That's a less appealing way of putting it."

"The state was being run by incompetent fools. I had no choice."

"People are always replaced when there's a new captain."

"Charles, I thought you had a little confidence in me. David's body isn't even cold yet, and you're worried about a *bloodbath*? It's not necessary that you update your résumé. Do you have any idea how difficult it was for me to leave my staff as VP? The last thing I want is to come storming into the White House like Genghis Khan. I want a harmonious transition. That's why I didn't make any personnel changes and kept key members of President Rodgers's staff. What happened in Kansas has nothing to do with Washington. Besides, Charles, if we're going to accomplish anything, you and I will have to double-team Walter Owens. That's not going to be easy. He's been in DC since the discovery of electricity."

Here lies a certain irony, she thought. As vice president, Kate had established herself as a credible politician in spite of the fact that no other Independent occupied a Congressional seat. Consequently, she had been as powerless as a gazelle among lions. But Walter Owens—veteran congressman for two decades— would use his leverage with the Republican-controlled Congress to amass a great deal of support. He would not play the role as a powerless VP. Her only hope to keep him from conspiring with his cohorts would be to make certain she kept him distracted with other activities.

"I didn't mean to be disrespectful," McDermott said. "I was merely *suggesting* that you not make waves just yet."

"Charles, this administration is going to make a lot of waves, and you're going to be paddling right beside me."

She was tempted to share Elizabeth's warning with him, curious what his reaction might be, but her instincts warned her to take a different approach.

"Hypothetically, Charles, let's presume that Weinberg's incorrect, that David didn't have a heart attack." She studied his face with concealed curiosity.

He sat forward. "What do you mean?"

She couldn't say the word without shuddering. "Suppose there are...questionable circumstances surrounding his death."

She could see the questions pooling in his saucer-like eyes. "Are you trying to tell me something, Madam President?"

"No, no, Charles. This is merely a what-if conversation."

He considered it, then shook his head. "One hell of a power struggle will begin."

"Explain."

"The justice department—more specifically, the FBI—will butt heads with the CIA. Both will want to control the investigation. The FBI will claim that this is a domestic issue, and the CIA will insist that it's international. Then Congress will get on the bandwagon. There are no specific laws outlining investigative procedures when a president dies in office under suspicious circumstances."

"The Warren Commission investigated President Kennedy's assassination, correct?" Kate asked.

"It was an executive order." He tapped his index finger against his temple. "Executive Order 11130. Lyndon Johnson's brainchild."

"So the Executive Office doesn't have to kowtow to Congress?"

"The commander in chief has complete authority to handle an investigation. Congress will bellyache, but legally, you've got the power."

The last thing Kate wanted was to engage in a power struggle with Congress, the FBI, or the CIA. But it was comforting to know that she wouldn't be forced into a submissive relationship with any branch of government if a thorough investigation were necessary.

"Why do I get the feeling that you know something you're not sharing with me?" McDermott said.

"Just speculating, Charles. It doesn't hurt to prepare for the unexpected."

He pondered for a moment. "What can I do to assist you?"

"Coordinate some meetings for me. Arrange a one-on-one conference with Walter Owens. Time to put on my diplomatic hat. Also, I'd like to meet with Cabinet members, the Joint Chiefs, the majority and minority leaders, the director and deputy director of central intelligence, the director of the FBI, and the director of the Secret Service. I'd also like to address the Senate and the House about two weeks after President Rodgers's funeral."

He scribbled hastily on his yellow pad. "Anything else?"

"Tell Bill Riley to be in my office at nine a.m. I want him to arrange a press conference so I can tell the media and the rest of the world about President Rodgers's death." She paused for a moment. "I guess I should also outline my future plans. Would you agree?"

"What *exactly* are your plans, Madam President?"

"Other than a thorough investigation of President Rodgers's death, you and I are going to have to figure out the rest."

***

On October 16, at ten a.m., an anxious, grieving country watched and listened as Kate Miles stood before Steven Cambridge, chief justice of the Supreme Court, and spoke these words:

"I, Katherine Anne Miles, do solemnly swear that I will faithfully execute the office of president of the United States and will, to the best of my ability, preserve, protect, and defend the Constitution of the United States."

She'd spoken these words before but not witnessed by over a billion people worldwide. The Blue Room was as quiet as a tomb.

Elizabeth Rodgers, former First Lady, grasped Kate's hand and embraced her. Kate squeezed her eyes shut, a current of emotions sweeping through her. She wrestled with fierce internal struggles, her sentiments teetering between anguish and cautious excitement. She'd fantasized about the presidency but never foresaw achieving this goal through such a dramatic turn of events.

Peter gave her a hug and a peck on the cheek. "Congratulations, Kate."

"Welcome to the White House, my dear," Elizabeth Rodgers said. Her eyes were red, and tears trickled down her cheeks.

Walter Owens firmly shook Kate's hand. "Congratulations, Madam President. I look forward to working with you." It always troubled Kate when a man's eyes betrayed his words.

Kate turned toward Charles McDermott, expecting a handshake, a hug, a congratulatory gesture. She caught a glimpse of his flushed face as he hustled toward the doorway as if he were late for an urgent meeting.

CHAPTER TWO

Olivia Carter, executive assistant to the chief of staff for policy, hesitated a moment before knocking on McDermott's door. Moisture dripped from her armpits, and she could feel the nervous sweat trickling down her sides. Often more intuitive than she wished to be, Olivia sensed that a major shake-up was in the works. She had no substantial evidence to support her premonition, but her gut welled with fear. President Rodgers had told her that she was his "shining star," that her strategies and insightful recommendations had helped him make several important decisions. But she suspected, rightfully so, that her past performance carried little weight with the new president. She tried to remain calm, forcing deep, quivering breaths. Walking into the chief of staff's office with terror in her eyes couldn't possibly strengthen her position. She remembered the desolate look she'd seen in her father's eyes the day his lifelong employer restructured upper management.

A new broom always sweeps clean.

He had told her this on the day he was forced into early retirement. It was the only time she'd ever seen Raymond Carter cry.

After going through her entire wardrobe, trying on business suits, dresses, mix-and-match outfits, Olivia decided to wear her cobalt-blue double-breasted Gucci. Her mother had given her this suit when Olivia graduated from San Diego State University and received an MBA. She'd never been superstitious, but she'd worn this suit to her successful interview with President Rodgers. If it had helped her get this job, she thought, perhaps its magic might assist her in keeping it.

Olivia was about to knock on McDermott's door when she noticed President Miles walking toward the Oval Office. The young woman could feel her toes curling in her shoes. The president had a vibrant energy that Olivia admired. Her stride was like that of a confident fashion model cruising down a run-way. Olivia felt an unexplainable connection to the president. Except that both were women, there was no logical reason for this connection. After all, Olivia didn't really know the former VP very well. But when in her life had logic ever controlled her emotions? If today wasn't the end of her political career, Olivia hoped that some of the president's charisma might rub off on her.

Their eyes met. The president smiled and waved. Olivia returned the gesture. She tried to read the president's body lan-guage, watching closely to see if she could sense negative vibes. The president hesitated before entering her office and gave Olivia a quick glance. Was she saying good-bye?

Olivia knocked on McDermott's door.

From behind the door, he yelled, "Come in, Olivia."

She opened the door and stepped inside. The office—at least three times bigger than Olivia's—was abundant with windows. It was a vast space of dark wood walls, neoclassic bookcases, and brass accents. A masculine domain. McDermott, sitting behind his bulky mahogany desk, looked like a dwarf. Tucked in the cor-ner was a sitting area with a chocolate-brown leather couch and two bone-colored wing chairs. Oriental rugs all but covered the gleaming parquet floors.

He glanced at his watch. "You're six minutes early."

Olivia thought reprimands were more appropriate for being late. "I can come back."

He pointed to the sitting area. "Make yourself comfortable."

She sat down, crossed her legs, and set her briefcase on the floor beside the chair. The office smelled like leather and stale cigarettes. A glass, half-full of a pale amber liquid, sat on the corner of the cocktail table. It looked like whiskey or apple juice diluted with melted ice cubes. She noticed water rings on the table—a dozen, maybe more. The COS apparently entertained associates who weren't considerate enough to use coasters under their glasses. Or perhaps McDermott himself was a thirsty man.

McDermott stood, removed his reading glasses, dropped them on the brown folder, and walked toward her. Expecting a handshake, she wiped her clammy hand on her skirt and offered it to the COS. Ignoring her gesture, he sat next to her, closer than she thought appropriate. His legs were spread wide, and his blue paisley tie hung down past his beltline. His knee pressed against hers.

She caught him glancing at her legs for an uncomfortable period of time. She'd been told that she had great legs but didn't appreciate McDermott's unwelcome confirmation.

"I thought you'd be happy to know that I convinced Miles not to clean house." He smiled. "So, congratulations, you're still employed."

She could hear the air drain from her lungs. "Thank God. Thought I was getting my pink slip today."

McDermott leaned forward and touched Olivia's knee. "God had nothing to do with it."

He left his hand on her knee long enough for Olivia to feel ill at ease. His hands were sweaty. Again, his eyes wandered to her legs. Longer this time. For an instant, Olivia thought about grabbing the glass on the corner of the cocktail table and whacking him in the side of the head. Maybe she could knock some sense into his perverted mind. She didn't figure that a moment's pleasure would be a fair exchange for her career, so she dismissed the wild notion. She uncrossed her legs and tucked her skirt securely under her lower thighs.

Men. The little head's always thinking for the big one.

"What do you think of President Miles?" McDermott asked.

If ever there was a loaded question, she thought, this was a doozy. At first, she envisioned a tape recorder hidden somewhere in McDermott's office. But that didn't make sense. What could he gain from setting her up?

Careful, Olivia, he's fishing for something.

"I don't know her well enough to have a strong opinion." She wanted to shut her mouth, but the words spilled from her tongue. "My instincts tell me she's gonna kick ass."

"Huh. I'm surprised to hear you say that."

"You getting a different vibe, Charles?"

"She seems…a bit tentative."

"Perhaps she needs some time to get her bearings. She didn't enter the White House under the most favorable conditions."

He touched her knee again. "Don't take this the wrong way, but America's not ready for this—a woman president, I mean."

She sensed a macho lecture forthcoming. "How could anybody know that? We've never had one."

"Men have kept the world progressing for centuries."

"They've also started every major war, invented the A-bomb, and a lot of them enjoy beating the crap out of their wives on a regular basis."

"That's feminist sensationalism, Olivia."

"Women haven't made contributions to the world?"

"Look, I didn't make the rules or author history books. Men control business and politics. Women are better at other things."

She eyed the glass for just an instant. "Like staying barefoot and pregnant?"

"Like staying out of the Oval Office."

"It sounds like you've given up on President Miles already."

"Just being realistic."

"With all due respect, your point of view seems rather medieval." She'd never been this outspoken, couldn't believe these words were coming so effortlessly. McDermott was her *boss*!

"I just don't believe she's going to make it."

Had she taken a moment to evaluate the volatile situation more carefully, she might have been able to stifle her roused emotions. But as a dedicated feminist, she could not control her fury.

"Are you going to lead the charge for her impeachment?"

McDermott's eyes burned through her.

She felt closer than ever to losing her job. "Shouldn't we give President Miles a chance to get her feet on the ground before we jump to any startling conclusions?"

He seemed to be heedfully weighing her words. "Perhaps you're right." McDermott fondled his tie and smiled. "I was merely testing the water, Olivia. You and I *are* on the same team, right?"

Another provocative question. "Of course."

Olivia's face felt feverish. Her body broke out in another cold sweat. If she wished to preserve her job, Olivia had to end this conversation. "Was there anything else, Charles? I have a full plate today."

"Bill Riley, Victor Ellenwood, and I are meeting for a cocktail tonight." His voice was edged with tension. "It would be a good idea for you to join us."

It was politically correct to accept. She knew that. To decline would make her a rebel rather than a team player. But even if she didn't suspect less-than-honorable motives, Olivia couldn't imagine what she had in common with any of these men. Charles, obviously, had other intentions. Riley was an egoistic ass. And...*Ellenwood*? To her, the director of central intelligence was a reptile. He had crocodile eyes. Always watching, waiting to pounce.

"Thanks for the invitation, but I've...already made plans." She wasn't pleased with his disappointed look. "Can I take a rain check?"

"Rubbing elbows after hours is an important part of politics," McDermott said. "It could help your career if you went with the flow a little more."

Sure, Chuck. Me and the boys'll break some bread, slam down a few Cuervos. Then back to your place, huh? Maybe do some lines? Dust off the video camera? A little gang-bang, perhaps?

"Can I call you later and let you know?"

His patronizing smile didn't fool her. "Yeah. Sure."

Olivia grabbed her briefcase and stood. She straightened her suit jacket and brushed the wrinkles out of her skirt. McDermott didn't get up. As she walked toward the door, self-conscious that McDermott was ogling her butt, she remembered something.

"Do you think President Miles can find thirty minutes for me?"

He gave her a peculiar look. "For what purpose?"

"I'd like to share some PR strategies with her."

McDermott's voice tightened. "I'll run it by her, but it might not be for several days."

She wasn't going to hold her breath waiting. "Thanks, Charles."

***

Peter Miles bent over to tie his shoes, and Kate feared the seam on his pants might tear. He'd recently had eight suits altered, and already, they were too tight. "Anything we need to do?" Peter asked.

"McDermott is handling everything," Kate said. "By Saturday evening, we'll be sleeping on Pennsylvania Avenue."

"Whoop-de-do." He whirled his index finger in the air in an apathetic manner. "What do you suppose my new title will be? First Man? First Gentleman? Or maybe they'll refer to me as the fat ass sleeping with the president."

"I know this isn't easy for you, Peter."

"You have *no* idea."

"Is there anything I can do?"

"Yeah. Run for governor of Kansas again."

"I understand what it's like to be on the sidelines."

"What the hell does that mean?"

"Do you have a problem being married to the president?"

"Did I have a *problem* being married to a governor?"

Kate stopped brushing her hair and stared at Peter intently. "I thought you were happy for me. You said you wouldn't mind taking a short break from your practice."

"That was before we moved to this godforsaken city."

Kate slipped on her navy-blue suit jacket and inspected her shoulders for stray hairs. She noticed Peter's slacks and didn't care for the way they looked.

Considering his sensitive mood of late, she was unsure how to diplomatically suggest that he change. "I'd love for you to wear your charcoal suit to the funeral."

Peter stood upright and let out a heavy breath of air. "Ben needs help with the Alexander trial." He glanced at his watch. "I have to catch a plane in about two hours."

Kate darted to the other side of the bedroom. She folded her arms across her chest. "You're *not* attending David's funeral?"

"Doesn't appear that way."

"Why didn't you tell me?"

"I just did."

Lately, they could feud about almost anything. "David's funeral services begin in an hour. Try to imagine how humiliated I'll feel if my *husband* isn't standing by my side."

"Let's not get all melodramatic, Kate." He fastened his belt. "Nobody's going to miss me. You're the president. I'm just an unemployed lawyer."

Again, he was wallowing. He'd had numerous opportunities to work in Washington. In fact, as the vice president's spouse, dozens of high-profile law firms had tried in vain to recruit Peter. But Peter had come up with one excuse after another why he turned down every job offer.

"If you have to fly to Topeka, I certainly understand. But can a day make a difference?"

"Every minute I spend in this city is like hanging by my thumbnails."

"Please, Peter, your timing couldn't possibly be worse. I would deeply appreciate it if you would reconsider. You can leave tomorrow or even later today."

He appeared to be considering her request. He put his hands on top of her shoulders and kissed her cheek. "I'm sorry. This trip is important to me. But I can postpone it for a day. Just do me one favor. I don't need any Secret Service agents protecting me from the boogeyman. The last thing I want is a couple of dark suits camping out in my back pocket while I'm in Topeka."

"I'll talk to Cranston."

***

On her way to the funeral, Katherine Miles was surrounded by a caravan of Secret Service vehicles. McDermott was on one side of her, his knee bouncing up and down, and Peter sat on the other side. Walter Owens sat across from her folding and unfolding his hands. Kate felt a strange detachment from the rest of the world, as if her life were a dream, one in which she was a spectator among participants. McDermott was talking about policies and protocol, outlining her agenda for the next few days, and Peter sat quietly, looking like he'd rather be anyplace else on Earth. Kate passively listened. In the forefront of her mind was the crisp memory of how this roller coaster ride to the White House had all begun.

***

"Kate Miles calling for David Rodgers."

"Mr. Rodgers is in a meeting." The secretary's voice was unfamiliar, saccharin sweet.

A meeting? Why do they always use the meeting excuse?

"This is quite urgent. Would you please interrupt him?"

"As I said, he's in—"

"Young lady, this is Governor Miles. Please tell David I'm on the line."

"I'm terribly sorry, Governor. I'll see what I can do."

Kate tucked the receiver between her ear and shoulder. Her fingers danced on the Toshiba laptop. Tonight, Kate would stand before the local chapter of the National Organization of Women and deliver a lecture on women in government. Kate frequently encouraged other women to enter politics. She wasn't always certain that her motives were as honorable as she wished them to be. She often believed that her support and positive approach repressed a hidden "misery loves company" agenda.

David Rodgers's voice broke her concentration. "Thought I'd be hearing from you soon. Hope you haven't been holding too long." His tone was bright and spirited.

"Great interview with Piers Morgan," she said. "It's not every day that a successful billionaire announces that he's running for president on the Independent ticket."

"Well, if the assholes in Congress knew how to run the country, I'd just sit in my cushy office and run Global Transportation. But I guess I'm more patriotic than I thought." He paused.

"Are you furious with me?"

"Beyond elucidation. A federal marshal should be knocking on your door any minute."

He huffed into the receiver. "I promised to give you another week, I know. But Piers pressed me. It was a golden opportunity, Kate. You *have* decided to accept…haven't you?"

"It's a conspiracy, right? Daddy and you put your conniving little heads together and figured you'd double-team me."

"Can I take the fifth on that?"

"I'm driving to the ranch for the weekend, David. You and I need to have a heart-to-heart."

Silence.

"David?"

"How about noon Saturday?"

"That's fine."

"Anything I should do to prepare?" Rodgers asked.

"Eat a big bowl of Wheaties. And bring your boxing gloves."

***

With the top down, the sun warming her face, the spring air blowing through her hair, Kate approached the White Stallion Ranch in her red Mustang convertible. The narrow road, lined with blossoming sugar maples and elm trees, colorfully announced spring's arrival. She passed harvested corn fields and acres of golden winter wheat. John Deere tractors worked tirelessly, plowing the earth, preparing the fertile soil for a bountiful summer.

She stopped in front of the main gate and pushed the floor shift lever into park. Thirty years ago, Kate had helped her father construct this front gate, digging holes with the post-hole digger, hand-mixing concrete for the four-by-four supports, nailing the crossbeams. She looked at the scar on her pinky and recalled how terrified she'd been when she cut her finger on the rusty nail. Kate had other scars, though. Deep scars etched into her heart. Time hadn't healed all her wounds.

Above the gate was the ranch logo. Two white stallions stood on their hind legs facing one another; above their heads in an oval circle were the letters *WSR*, painted black.

Familiar memories flooded her mind.

This was where she'd spent her childhood, where her appreciation of nature and love of animals began. It was a haven unmolested by the frenzy of big-city life. Free of politics and people in a hurry, there was no obsession with status here; people living in Linwood, Kansas, were just plain folks.

Of all the picturesque places on earth, the White Stallion Ranch was Kate's favorite.

She pulled up to the main house, a two-story log cabin her father had built. She parked the Mustang next to the broken-down tractor. When she got out of the car, she stretched toward the sky, trying to get the kink out of her upper back. She removed her luggage from the trunk and stood silent for a moment. Kate could hear a choir of birds, a dog howling, a rooster crowing. The sounds of midwestern America.

That her father was not on the front porch waiting to greet her did not surprise Kate. How many times had other priorities taken precedence over his only child? She carried her luggage up the steps and dropped it in front of the door. The hinges squeaked, and the front door swung open. Plump as ever, four-foot-eleven Maria Martinez greeted her with a warm smile. Her ebony-colored eyes glistened. Kate's father was lucky to have found such a nurturing housekeeper and cook who kept his domestic life in order. Kate stepped inside, and Maria embraced her.

"Miss Kate." Maria's Latino accent seemed more pronounced than Kate remembered. "Your father tell me you come today. I have missed you."

"You're looking well," Kate said. "Is Daddy still working you like a *burro*?"

"Oh, since your father retire, he no the same man. I do my business, and he stay out of way."

Kate could smell cilantro and garlic. "Are you preparing my favorite dish?"

"Burritos de pollo con salsa verde."

"Wonderful!"

Kate's eyes surveyed the expansive main living area. Her father always had a flair for southwestern decor. The room emulated authentic American Indian culture, complete with a life-size wooden sculpture of an Indian chief guarding the entrance to her father's private study.

"Where is Daddy?"

"He go to town. Promise to be back before you come." Maria lifted a shoulder, her face apologetic. "He always *el embajador*. I make coffee? Hazelnut?"

"You're a sweetheart."

After pouring herself a mug full of coffee, Kate went outside and stood on the front porch. In the distance, she could see her father's Chevy Blazer kicking up a cloud of dust as it raced toward the house. As his face came into clear view, Kate felt a knot twist into her stomach. He'd always made her nervous, expected so much of her. He'd talked her out of entering veterinary school, a childhood ambition, and convinced her to get a law degree from Cornell. He had said, "It will yield greater opportunities in the 'real world.'" Kate wasn't yet sure what the real world was. It seemed to be a place that continued to outdistance her.

Trevor Williams parked the Blazer next to Kate's Mustang. She'd intended to buy a BMW convertible, but her father, a die-hard domestic loyalist, had given her his classic lecture on the trade deficit and how foreign products have hurt our economy. Kate, ready to sign a contract, walked out of the BMW dealership and leased a Ford. At the age of forty-five, her decisions were still profoundly affected by him.

Hunched slightly forward, Trevor lumbered to the front porch and hobbled up the steps.

"My sweet Kate." He sounded wheezy, out of breath. "I've missed you." He gave her a bear hug.

"Is your back bothering you again?" she asked.

"A touch of sciatica. Nothing to worry about."

Her father was not as handsome as he'd been in years past. The blistering Kansas sun had left its signature on his weather-worn face. But his prominent jaw, spirited eyes, and trim physique made him appear to be ten years younger than sixty-nine. Once the president of Global Transportation, one of David Rodgers's most successful companies, he now spent most of his retirement mending fences and tending to his horses.

They sat together on the glider. Kate sipped her warm coffee. Trevor draped his arm around her shoulders. Kate gazed beyond the porch railing, her hungry eyes absorbing acres of rolling hills, horse stables, and barns, the stockade fence disappearing over the horizon. At this particular moment, she felt physically and spiritually close to her father, yet there was still a void in her heart since her mother died when she was so young. Time could never erase the years of loneliness she had felt as a child.

"I had an interesting conversation with David Rodgers," she said.

"How *is* David? Haven't seen much of him since I retired."

She knew he was lying. "So you sold me out, huh, Daddy?"

His reaction was a classic double take. He looked at her, and the muscles at the corners of his eyes twitched to a faint smile. "Just looking out for my little girl's future."

Her political career began when she was twenty-five. Running on the Democratic ticket, she'd been elected to the city council of Topeka, where she painfully learned that the sacred brotherhood of men possessed a ravenous appetite for women with idealistic political ambitions. After nearly fifteen years serving on the city council, winning every election by a huge margin, Kate Miles taught the male population a humbling lesson when she defied the odds and the polls, and became the first female governor of Kansas.

"This is a big step, Daddy. I'm not sure I'm ready for Washington politics."

Trevor Williams pulled her closer to him. "If you wait until you're ready, it'll never happen. This is the opportunity of a lifetime, honey. You have at your fingertips the ability to change the course of history."

"Do you actually believe David has a remote chance of winning the election?"

"With you as his running mate he does."

"You're giving me more credit than I deserve."

He turned toward her and gently squeezed her shoulder. "Kate, this country has been on the verge of a major revolution for decades. Discontented voters hunger for fresh leadership. American citizens have grown weary of the wimpy Democrats and greedy Republicans. David and you are at the right place at the right time. At no time in history has there been an opportunity for two Independents with fresh, innovative ideas and a new agenda to disrupt our two-party system. David's a leader. A persuasive, charismatic man. When he stands toe-to-toe with the other candidates and debates the issues, he's going to take their political track records and turn them into swiss cheese."

"How do I fit into this equation?"

"David and you enjoy a certain philosophical continuity. You both believe in major reform. Granted, you don't agree on every issue. Who does? But contrasting perspectives create an essential balance of power. Who would make a more powerful team than a dynamic businessman who can apply his proven methods of success to Washington and an honest, bright, idealistic young woman who still believes in Santa Claus?"

She kissed him on the cheek, her soft lips prickled by his leathery skin. "You could teach David Rodgers a thing or two about charisma."

They spent the next hour sitting quietly, enjoying their time together.

***

As promised, David Rodgers arrived at the White Stallion Ranch at eleven thirty a.m. He was wearing an olive-green suit and a "Save the Children" tie covered with smiling little faces. After perfunctory greetings, Maria served lunch. Afterward, Kate and Rodgers retired to the den. Out of respect, they asked Trevor if he'd like to partake in the meeting, but in spite of his sore back, he opted to saddle up Breezy, his favorite filly, for a ride around the fifty-acre ranch.

Kate felt like she was jumping out of her skin. It was as if all the oxygen had been sucked out of the room and drawing a breath was impossible. She wanted to believe that the uneasiness resulted from the pot of coffee she'd drunk, but she couldn't deny that Rodgers gave her the jitters. The den, of course, didn't help. The room exemplified her father's propensity for big-game hunting. There were stuffed trophies everywhere: a moose head over the doorway, two elks above the brick fireplace, a life-size grizzly baring his teeth.

To add to her discomfort, she'd forgotten to pack a business suit and was forced to wear jeans, cowboy boots, and a flannel shirt. Western wear had always been her favorite attire, but she felt out of place sitting across from a formally dressed presidential candidate looking like Annie Oakley's great-granddaughter.

Kate decided that the only way to approach Rodgers was head-on. "So, David, explain to me in detail why you've asked me to be your running mate."

He cleared his throat several times, and she sensed that the question caught him off guard. His green eyes were haunted by some inner anxiety. "You're the best choice, Kate."

"Come on, David, an orator like you can do better than that." She knew his primary motivation but hoped he'd be honest enough to admit it.

"When you were elected to the city council in Topeka, you went against the grain. Got things done. Spearheaded revolutionary legislation. People noticed. I knew it wouldn't be long before you were asked to run for governor. And you've done an extraordinary job in Kansas, but it's time for you to set your sights higher. Kate, I need a pragmatic running mate. Someone capable of being my right arm, yet independent enough to make things happen. A vice president who stands in the shadows and treads water isn't going to work for me. I want a partner with a backbone, with a roll-up-your-sleeves, get-the-job-done attitude. Doesn't that describe you, Kate?"

Her record had been well documented. Not only had Kate shocked the disbelievers by fulfilling all of her campaign promises, but she also instituted the Back-to-Work program, which granted private corporations substantial tax incentives for hiring and retraining displaced workers. As a result, several major corporations relocated to Kansas. In office for only two years, she had decreased Kansas unemployment from 11 percent to less than 6 percent, the third-lowest rate in the country, while increasing revenues 13 percent. Her face had adorned the covers of *Newsweek* and *Time*.

She knew she'd done a good job and appreciated that he recognized her accomplishments, but he was still cleverly avoiding the central issue. "OK, we both know that I'm a terrific governor. But I can think of at least ten people more qualified than I for the VP nomination. Why am I in front of the pack, David?"

He loosened his tie, unbuttoned the top button of his shirt, and sat forward in the chair. "It's a new century, Kate. Being a woman is a powerful attribute."

"So my *gender* is more important than my qualifications?"

"No, Kate, you're political qualifications *are* essential—"

"Admit it, David. If I were a man with the same track record, I wouldn't make the cut, would I?"

He smiled sheepishly. "OK, Kate. You wanna hear me say it? I can't win without the female vote. And Katherine Miles is the most influential female politician in the country."

"That's an arguable point, but thank you for being truthful."

"I hope you don't think I was trying to be dishonest."

She smiled. "A little wimpy, maybe, but not dishonest. As long as we're baring our souls, David, perhaps I should tell you what I expect. After you listen, you might come to your senses." She took a moment to compose her thoughts. "You said that I need to be your right arm. That has to be a promise, not lip service. I refuse to play the role as the token woman who rode your coattails to Washington. I want to be knee-deep in every aspect of the administration, and I expect to be included in all significant decisions."

"Look, Kate, I don't anticipate that Congress will receive two Independents with open arms. They're going to fight us tooth and nail on every issue. I want you to be a hands-on VP."

"That's great. But still, I have deep reservations abandoning the Democratic Party."

Rodgers laughed. "Kate, I can relate to your concerns. It isn't necessary that you abandon all your Democratic principles. But make no mistake about it, you owe the Democratic Party nothing."

Kate digested his words for several minutes. She surmised, considering not one Congressional seat was occupied by an Independent, that significant change would take decades.

"If we do win, David, how do you suppose we'll be able to accomplish anything? We have few allies in Washington."

"Neither the Democrats nor Republicans have complete continuity within their respective parties. You'd be hard-pressed finding two to agree on any issue. That's our advantage. Not having an allegiance to any particular party gives us the flexibility to reach across both aisles. This may be our most powerful tool. If you truly believe that big government has stripped Americans of the basic freedoms our forefathers died for and wish to give the power back to the voters, then fundamentally your goals are parallel to mine. And I believe we can muster enough support from both sides to pass some groundbreaking legislation.

"There's no way that the executive office can strong-arm Congress. But we *can* influence and educate voters. It's a long, tedious process. We must open their eyes to the failing system and show them a better way. Our goal is not to effect immediate change. That's a naive ambition. We must inspire Americans with new ideals. We're farmers, Kate. Plant a few seeds of ideas here and there, cultivate and water them, and eventually they'll blossom."

With great anticipation of one day entering Washington politics, for years Kate had been diligently working on a project she'd titled Healing of America. The concepts, many radical, consisted of innovative reform bills and amendments to the Constitution.

"Have you read my Healing of America bills?"

He reached into his briefcase and removed a folder as thick as a ream of paper. "I've made several notes throughout. It's brilliant, Kate."

"Does that mean you'll help me introduce it to Congress?"

Rodgers didn't reply immediately. Kate felt a slight pang at the base of her neck. This was the deal breaker. If he hadn't taken the time to review a project so vitally important to her, then perhaps her decision had already been made.

"I have two conditions. First, you must agree to some minor modifications—nothing too drastic. Mere technicalities. And second, I don't want to create false hopes, Kate. You need to know right up front that Congress is going to blow this out of the water."

Kate had no delusions that Congress would embrace her Healing of America bills with even a morsel of enthusiasm, but just to introduce them would be historic, the first important step toward achieving her long-term objectives and exposing Congress to a new philosophy.

This was the most consequential crossroad of her life. Reservations and fear engulfed her. If she accepted the offer and David and she were defeated, it could be a bitter end to a promising career. But Kate had always been a warrior. She hadn't climbed the political ladder without taking immense risks. Why should she change her aggressive posture now?

"OK, Mr. Rodgers, there are a few issues we obviously need to negotiate, but unless you confess that you're a communist or a serial killer, I think it's safe to assume that you've got yourself a running mate."

They both stood up as if on cue. David Rodgers firmly shook her hand. He pulled Kate close and embraced her. She gazed at the moose over the doorway. She thought she saw a reassuring wink.

**

Leonard LaPlant carefully studied the lab report. It wasn't very often that he was affected by death; he'd performed over three thousand autopsies. But moisture from his trembling fingers pressed damp spots into the paper. He swiveled in his chair, faced the cluttered credenza, and reached for the telephone. The medical examiner reviewed the lab report one more time just to be sure he had read it right.

Unknown toxin. Organic origin.

"Lord in heaven."

He dialed Charles McDermott's private number as instructed.

**

Kate waited by the curb on Pennsylvania Avenue, moments before the funeral procession began. Elizabeth Rodgers, sobbing uncontrollably, was by her side. Charles McDermott stood to her right, and Peter stood slightly behind her. Kate's jacket pockets were stuffed with damp Kleenex. She clutched her black handbag. The procession moved slowly. Kate struggled to inhale a breath of the thick, sultry air. Her chest felt compressed, as if her lungs were lined with concrete. She looked up at the billowing clouds, expecting a downpour any minute. Kate felt sure that this quiet tribute to a noble patriot would sweep the nation. David Rodgers's coffin, draped in Old Glory, proceeded ahead of them. From around the globe, sorrowful sobs echoed in the air; tears flowed from loyal supporters, friends, loved ones, and mournful citizens. In less than a year in office, he had captured the hearts of all Americans.

Like a sudden storm that emerges without warning, Kate felt the full impact of her loss. She could not deny that David and she'd had their political differences, but he had not merely been the president; he was a friend, a confidant, a mentor. He was a visionary who could have affected the course of history. The burden now rested on her shoulders, and she could feel the enormous weight buckling her knees.

For the first time in her adult life, the secure, confident farm girl from Kansas realized that she was standing in a pool of quicksand from which there was no escape.

***

It was a private meeting.

Only ethnocentric Germans could become members, not one drop of mongrel blood, only pure Aryan for three generations. Their vow was for life—a pledge to follow the doctrines unconditionally.

It was not a group that accepted resignations.

In a run-down, abandoned building in Oak Grove, Alabama, Jakob Hoffman stood before the Disciples of the Third Reich; his ice-blue eyes stared intensely at the chosen one. Soon, Hoffman's blood brother would achieve a great honor. He swept a calloused palm across his shaved head and wiped away the sweat. Hoffman clenched his fist and pounded it against his bare chest. "It's time to prove yourself, brother." He lifted the newspaper and pointed to President Miles. "Slaughter this swine like the pig she is."

Guenther Krause gaped at the picture, partially in shock, but intensely aroused.

"I'll bleed her like a fat hog." He removed the black bandana from his head and bowed toward Hoffman. "When do I gut the bitch?"

"As soon as we hear from Krieger in Washington."

CHAPTER THREE

Kate quickly discovered that the Oval Office was not a secure environment for one-on-one conferences, so she asked McDermott to meet her in her private office at seven a.m. She'd spent most of the night, between brief periods of disquieted sleep, studying background information on Cabinet secretaries and other staff members. She painstakingly examined their performance records and scrutinized their level of experience. In spite of her promise to McDermott not to "clean house," Kate still had to objectively evaluate her staff. As commander in chief, she was faced with the indelicate task of restructuring—if necessary. She found this impending onus to be particularly disconcerting.

Quite to her dismay, she had not been significantly involved with Cabinet members' appointments. David Rodgers had coddled this process with uncharacteristic selfishness. He had entertained Kate's recommendations with a ceremonial kindness, which in itself was a minor triumph, but Rodgers only selected Secretary of State Toni Mitchell directly based on Kate's suggestion. This quiet insinuation that Kate's selections did not warrant President Rodgers's utmost consideration had been the beginning of an enlightening realization. It was an event that fostered hard feelings and tense dialogue between devoted running mates and longtime friends.

Kate's thoughts were interrupted when she could smell McDermott's much-too-sweet cologne the moment he entered the room.

"Good morning, Madam President." McDermott strode across the room and fell ponderously into a chair opposite her.

"Coffee or juice, Charles?"

He shook his head. "No, thank you."

"Are all Cabinet members on board for the ten o'clock meeting?" she asked.

"Absolutely."

"Great. Let's go over the agenda, Charles."

McDermott's eyes took on a haunted look. "Madam President, I have a more pressing matter to discuss."

"What could be more important than my first Cabinet meeting?"

"President Rodgers did not die from natural causes."

Kate's back straightened, and she sat forward in the leather chair, her mind racing with wild thoughts. For an insane moment, she wanted to run out of the office, terrified to hear McDermott's announcement. She sucked in a heavy breath and looked over her reading glasses. "I'm listening."

"Leonard LaPlant called. The lab report verified a trace amount of an unknown toxin in President Rodgers's blood."

She gaped in stunned silence. Perhaps Elizabeth had not been delirious? "What exactly is an 'unknown toxin'?"

"Seems to be a mystery, Madam President. The lab has to run additional tests."

"And they're working on it?"

"As we speak."

"I want answers, Charles." She pinched her chin between index finger and thumb. "What else can you tell me?"

He pushed the hair away from his forehead. "The toxin is some type of venom produced by a living organism."

An invisible spider crawled up her back, and she quivered. "You mean like...*snake* venom?"

"That's unlikely. It was much more potent."

"What in God's creation is more poisonous than snake venom?"

"Don't know."

Kate was dumbstruck for a moment. "Was David on any medication?"

"He took daily medication for his blood pressure. But as far as I know, he was as healthy as an ox."

She thought about how fastidiously the Secret Service monitored everything she consumed. "I want the names of the agents on call that night."

"I'll talk to Cranston."

She folded her hands on her lap and sat back, her mind searching for rational thoughts. As the word slipped off her tongue, her arms blossomed with goose bumps. "Suicide?"

He vigorously shook his head. "Not a chance."

She wanted to ask how he could possibly know this but instead stored his answer in her memory. "Who else knows about this?"

"No one."

"This information is to remain classified until we meet with Cabinet members." She twisted her pearl necklace. "Tell Bill Riley to clear his calendar. I need him at the ten o'clock meeting. And ask Ellenwood, Kramer, and Cranston to join us."

"Anything else?" McDermott asked.

"Is Elizabeth Rodgers still in Washington?"

"I believe so."

"Get her here ASAP."

McDermott stood. "I've taken the liberty of increasing security measures. With all due respect, I ask that you limit your activities to the White House, Madam President. For the time being."

At first, it seemed like a prudent recommendation. But McDermott was forgetting the obvious. "Remaining in the White House proved to be quite unhealthy for President Rodgers."

"A valid point. But I don't want you to take unnecessary risks. I promise you'll be safer here than anywhere else."

"I guess I'll have to take your word for it, Charles."

***

When Kate walked out of her private office, Emily Hutchins, her personal aide, reminded her that she had a nine o'clock appointment. Kate told Emily to cancel it. On her way to her private quarters, no fewer than twenty people respectfully smiled and waved at the president as she trudged down the main corridor, but she was dimly aware of their greetings. Her legs felt like Jell-O, and a strong, primitive impulse urged Kate to run away. But where? The Secret Service agent posted beside her front door snapped to attention as she approached the entrance.

"Can I be of service to you, Madam President?"

She forced a smile. "No, thank you, James."

She stepped into the apartment and made a beeline for her bedroom. Kate closed the door and sat on the bed. She'd only been president for thirty-six hours and already felt like she was riding on a runaway train. What she needed was a warm bath, something to soothe her body and mind, something to ease the tension in her shoulders before a day of marathon meetings. She removed her clothes, walked into the bathroom, and turned on the water to fill the soaking tub. She wanted to light a candle and pour herself a crisp glass of Chardonnay, even at this early hour. But if someone got a whiff of alcohol on her breath, the next thing you know, some Photoshop whiz would do his magic, and she'd see her photo on the front page of the *National Enquirer* chugging wine from a paper bag. No, drinking alcohol just before a Cabinet meeting would be unwise.

About to step in the tub, Kate glimpsed at her reflection in the full-length mirror. As always, her eyes were drawn to her breasts. She remembered her sixteenth birthday, one of the few birthdays she actually spent with her father. It was a day she'd never forget.

***

Kate was sitting in front of the vanity mirror with her white terry cloth robe hanging off her shoulders. Over the last year, she had tortured herself with alarming frequency. But it was not something she consciously chose to do. Her uncontrollable curiosity was an addiction. Most teenage girls were infatuated with their flowering bodies, enthralled with an era of discovery. For Kate, however, it was an exploration of disappointment and utter terror. Today, as she studied her breasts with withering optimism, she painfully realized that her left breast would never fill a C-cup like her right one, that she'd spend the rest of her life stuffing tissue in her bra, fearful that someone would notice. She had believed, in some romantic way, that nature might have been merciful, that one morning she'd wake up and all would be well. But now it appeared that her fantasy was a hopeless wish. One breast would always be noticeably smaller than the other. When and if she ever fell in love, how could she know with certainty that her lover wouldn't think of her as damaged goods?

There was a soft knock at her bedroom door.

"Honey, can I come in?"

She wrapped the robe around her shoulders, tied it in front, and swiveled around in the vanity chair. She wiped her eyes on her sleeve.

"Come in, Daddy." She knew he'd take one look at her and recognize she'd been crying. Fathers always knew. She smiled her most convincing smile.

"What's the matter, honey?"

She wanted to tell him. Perhaps in his vast wisdom he'd find a way to comfort her. But how could a teenage girl talk to her father about her *breasts*?

He sat on her bed and patted the mattress. "Come sit beside me." He was wearing the blue flannel shirt Kate's mother had given him years ago. The collar and cuffs were severely frayed. The left pocket displayed an ink stain the size of a quarter. In spite of its raggedy appearance, Kate was certain he'd never throw it away.

She ambled over and sat next to him.

He slid his arm around her shoulders and fiddled with her hair. "There's a story I've never told you about your mother. I wanted you to remember her as a perfect woman, but it's time you hear the truth."

Kate was three when her mother had died. Her only remembrances of Victoria Williams were through the colorful stories her father had painted throughout her childhood. She could see the urgency in his eyes, so she quietly listened.

"Your mom, lovely as she was, had her share of misfortune. Her left leg was almost two inches shorter than her right. She'd hobble around with the strangest limp. I told her it was quite sexy. Your mom said I was nuts." He pulled her closer. "You'd think that her bad leg would be enough for any one person to deal with, but no...God had not been kind. Your mom was stone deaf in her left ear." He grasped Kate's hand and pressed it to his lips. "Nobody's perfect, sweetheart."

A gust of anxiety gripped her. Was he referring to her breasts?

"Kate, you're a remarkable young woman. God has blessed you with a lovely face, a keen intellect, and the figure a fashion model would die for. But Mother Nature doesn't always play fair."

He paused for a moment, and she watched his eyes well with tears.

"A piece of your mother lives in you, Kate. When you're feeling insecure about your body, think about your mother and her physical problems. Through her, you can find comfort and strength."

Kate thought there was more to the story, but he left her with a delicate kiss. She walked to the vanity and sat in front of the mirror once again, reflecting on her father's compelling words, trying to envision the hobble she couldn't remember. Like sitting beneath a heat lamp, a rush of warmth filled her face. Her body tingled as if a tiny charge of electricity flowed through her veins. In her mind's eye, she could clearly see her mother's face. That gentle smile. Those adoring eyes. She couldn't explain it, but from this day forward, Kate felt certain her mother's spirit would be with her whenever she needed her.

***

Although the hot bath had helped to relax Kate's muscles, her senses were still numb from McDermott's shocking announcement. Before entering the Cabinet Room, she paused for a moment and evoked every ounce of strength to maintain her composure. She opened the door, and a chorus filled the air: "Good morning, Madam President."

She stood before the Cabinet members and sucked in a deep breath. Also in the room were Vice President Walter Owens, Press Secretary William Riley, Executive Assistant to the Chief of Staff Olivia Carter, Director of Central Intelligence Victor Ellenwood, Deputy Director of Central Intelligence Carl Kramer, and Director of Secret Service Albert Cranston. Unconsciously, Kate wiped her sweaty palms on her suit jacket. She could tell by their troubled looks that the group suspected this meeting would not be business as usual. Rarely had any president assembled such a wide spectrum of staff members without significant purpose. Kate didn't want to begin her first administrative meeting with a morbid announcement, but President Rodgers's apparent assassination took precedence over everything.

"Good morning, ladies and gentlemen," she said. "I'm afraid that I am the bearer of ghastly news." She pointed to Charles McDermott. He sunk in his chair as if she were pointing a cocked pistol at him. "Mr. McDermott has just informed me that President Rodgers did not die of natural causes."

The room was as quiet as a mortuary.

"It appears that President Rodgers was somehow poisoned," Kate added.

Like they'd seen the head of Medusa, the esteemed group turned to stone. This momentary condition was quickly replaced with restless anxiety. It was almost a minute before Secretary of State Toni Mitchell broke the silence. "How could he have been poisoned in his private quarters?"

"Details are sketchy at this point, Toni," Kate said.

"How are we going to handle the media?" Press Secretary Riley asked.

McDermott said, "They're going to be like a pack of wolves. I can see the headlines now." He gave Cranston a quick glance. "The Secret Service is going to be crucified."

Kate pointed her pen at the press secretary. "I want an honest statement, Mr. Riley, but let's not encourage widespread panic or unnecessary speculation."

"I understand, Madam President."

Albert Cranston pressed his palms on the table and stood. "There are implications here that trouble me. In fact, they challenge the credibility of my department."

"Mr. Cranston," the president said, "nobody is pointing fingers."

Cranston said, "To assume that President Rodgers was poisoned in his private quarters is a direct reflection on the Secret Service."

McDermott sat forward and leaned an elbow on the table. "Whether or not President Rodgers was poisoned in his private quarters is an arguable point. The more compelling issue is this: On the day he died, he did not leave the premises. So somewhere within the White House, deadly poison was introduced into his bloodstream. Somebody—or some*bodies*—on staff had to be involved."

A lull fell upon the room.

Olivia Carter said, "Don't forget, Charles, that several hundred people tour the White House every day."

"But their access to much of the structure is restricted," McDermott shot back.

"At this juncture," Cranston said, "we cannot discount any theory." There was an obvious air of relief in his voice.

"My department is ready to move immediately," Director of Central Intelligence Victor Ellenwood said. Years ago, Ellenwood had been nicknamed the "Silver Fox." Silver because of his full head of silver hair, and fox because few people were as cagey as he.

Kate, recalling McDermott's warning about a power struggle between the FBI and CIA, was glad the FBI director was in Hong Kong. She knew her hands were full dealing with Ellenwood.

"I've considered this situation at great length," Kate said, "and have decided to form a special commission."

Ellenwood glared at Kate with a striking boldness. "What do you mean?"

"I want to appoint two Cabinet members, two senior senators, and members of both the CIA and FBI to investigate President Rodgers's death. I would like each of you to carefully consider this and give me your written recommendations by noon today."

"Madam President," Ellenwood said, "why would you appoint a commission when the CIA is readily at your disposal?"

"The situation is much too explosive to be handled by one agency," Kate said. "A cooperative effort makes more sense."

"Not to me, Madam President." Ellenwood's voice tensed. "My department is quite capable of handling this exclusively."

"I do not dispute that, Victor. However, this is an enormous undertaking, and a well-chosen commission would produce greater results."

"Do you question the competency of my department?" Ellenwood almost shouted.

"I am neither attacking the CIA's integrity nor trivializing their role in government. I am merely stating that a carefully selected commission will be more effective."

"Like the Warren Commission was?" Ellenwood said.

"I'm not going to spar with you, Victor."

Secretary of State Mitchell stood. "Surely we can come to a mutually agreeable compromise."

"There *can't* be a compromise," Ellenwood insisted. "Either the CIA handles the investigation exclusively or they don't."

"I agree with you, Madam President," Olivia Carter said. "The controversy surrounding President Kennedy's death consumed the Johnson administration. Why do you think he chose not to run for reelection? To this day, no one has an accurate account of how and why Kennedy was assassinated. If we do not employ every resource available to apprehend the assassin in a timely manner, public opinion will grow unfavorable. And this administration cannot afford to jeopardize its credibility."

Kate was impressed with the young strategist's incandescent zeal.

Victor Ellenwood hammered a fist on the table. "Ms. Carter, the last thing we need in Washington is another snotty-nose kid trying to get an A on her Government 101 exam."

"Victor," Kate said, "I have zero tolerance for comments like that. Let's keep this meeting productive."

Walter Owens raised his hand as if he were in grade school. "I must concur with Victor, Madam President. An assassination requires an international investigation. For such a formidable task, who is better equipped than the CIA?"

David Rodgers, on several occasions, had spoken highly of Carl Kramer, Ellenwood's deputy director. In fact, Rodgers had hinted that he wished to convince Ellenwood to retire early and appoint the less rigid Kramer as DCI. Perhaps by selecting Kramer to head the investigation, Kate thought, she could placate Ellenwood and at the same time recruit a competent leader for the commission.

"Mr. Kramer, how would you feel about heading this investigation?"

The muscular deputy director slid his palm across his crewcut hair and looked at his boss. For an instant, there was an esoteric communication between the two men. Ellenwood eyed Kate, his cold stare like Arctic ice. Kramer's look shifted to the president. Kate had not intended to place Kramer in a compromising situation with Ellenwood.

"Perhaps you need some time to think about it, Mr. Kramer?" Kate offered.

"Madam President, my only hesitation is that I am overwhelmed you have enough confidence in me to head the investigation. I would be honored to accept this responsibility."

Neither Ellenwood nor Owens was pleased. This was obvious to Kate. She understood Ellenwood's viewpoint, but why was Owens against appointing a special commission? She could hear their faint grumbles of disapproval. Her role as president was not to win the Miss Congeniality award. She had a job to do. None of the other attending members appeared to have further comments. Or they had determined that Kate's position was so rigid that it would be futile to offer any further suggestions.

"Does anyone have anything more to add?" Kate said.

No one said a word.

"In light of the situation, I'd like to adjourn. Let's reschedule another meeting later this week. And remember, recommendations on my desk by noon. I want this commission to begin its investigation in forty-eight hours."

Traces of conversation lingered as they filed out of the room. For the first time since entering the Cabinet Room, Kate sat down in the blue leather armchair with the presidential seal embossed on the upper part of the seat back. Sitting where President Rodgers had sat several days ago gave her an eerie feeling. Reminders of him clamored in her head like crashing cymbals. Kate remained at the head of the table studying her notes. McDermott approached her.

"Madam President, as your senior advisor, may I speak freely?"

She gazed up at him and felt a kink in her neck. "I'd be disappointed if you didn't."

"Watch out for Ellenwood. Been around Washington a long time. Has a lot of clout with influential people. The less you lock horns with him, the better."

"Thanks, Charles. I'll keep that in mind." There was more than a warning reflected in his eyes. "Do you disagree with my decision?"

"My opinion's immaterial."

"Didn't you just remind me that you're my senior advisor?"

He nodded.

"Then advise. Did I act inappropriately?"

He chewed on his lip. "You did fine, Madam President."

"I can live without undeserved accolades, Charles. I need your objective opinions."

"I'm aware of that."

Kate wasn't so sure.

***

In spite of the former president's death, Katherine Miles still had to deal with the business of running the country. Her day ended at ten thirty p.m.

She was sitting in the Oval Room, sipping a cup of herbal tea, munching a garlic bagel with salmon cream cheese, reflecting on a day of revelations and self-recrimination. She was troubled by the undertone of the meeting, disturbed by the lack of participation from Cabinet members. Perhaps she had been *too* rigid? She'd always had a difficult time distinguishing between assertiveness and arrogance. She had not endeared herself to her constituents. Their silence spoke volumes.

The luxury of her private quarters was conspicuous to the point of interrupting her deep concentration. She could not focus her eyes anywhere without viewing priceless antiques, original oil paintings, or sculptures. As president, she expected certain luxuries, but her political platform, the foundation of her value system, was based on a philosophy condemning big government and senseless spending. How, then, could she reside in such a lavish environment without feeling like a hypocrite?

The Oval Room served as the main living room. Adjacent was a magnificent dining room and a gourmet kitchen that would please the most discriminating chef. There were four spacious bedroom suites, each with private dressing rooms and lavish baths. And of course, the pride of White House accommodations were the historic Lincoln Room, a suite for distinguished guests, and the Queen's Bedroom, a unique sanctuary designed especially for royal visitors. All this room and comfort and her husband hadn't spent one night with her.

She extended her legs on the yellow couch and sipped her tea, recalling what McDermott had told her. As president of the United States, she was entitled to refurnish her living quarters and the executive offices in the West Wing. The silverware, china, lamps, rugs, furniture, bedding—virtually everything could be replaced at her whim. To preserve the integrity of the White House, however, she had to select the finest American and French furnishings associated with the heritage of past presidents, a tradition initiated by Jackie Kennedy. When she'd asked McDermott what would happen to the current furnishings, he'd said, "Who cares?"

She cared. And Kate wasn't going to spend one hard-earned tax dollar senselessly.

With teacup in hand, Kate explored her elegant quarters. She walked through suites, inspected closets, wandered in and out of rooms she'd never been in. Finally, with excitement and apprehension, she accepted that the White House would be her residence for the next three years—if the Grim Reaper did not pay her an untimely visit, which now appeared to be a startling reality. She collapsed on her lonely bed at one twenty-three a.m. McDermott and Olivia Carter were meeting her in the Oval Office at seven forty-five so they could all watch William Riley's press conference.

***

McDermott grabbed the remote, turned on the television, and sat next to Olivia on the striped couch. She moved a few inches away from him. Still yawning from another sleepless night, Kate sat at her desk, intently watching Press Secretary Riley on the Sony TV. He stood before a crowded room of journalists who Kate believed had no idea what the press conference was about. When he made the jolting announcement, Kate watched the anxious group turn into a pool of hungry piranhas. Cameras flashed, cellular phones lit up, and frenzied reporters waved their arms frantically, all asking pointed questions.

At eight twenty a.m., McDermott clicked off the Sony LED.

Kate could barely suppress her seething anger. "Who approved that announcement, Charles?"

"I did."

"And you're comfortable with what he said?"

"He tossed enough crumbs to keep the vultures at bay."

"The only point he conveyed with clarity was that President Rodgers didn't die of heart failure. Shouldn't he have been more specific?"

"Too much honesty and the press would turn his words into a soap opera. I think Riley's announcement was politically favorable."

"What are your thoughts, Olivia?" Kate asked. She noticed a strange gleam in Olivia's eyes, like an understudy who'd just been offered the lead role in a Broadway play.

"By now, everybody in the White House knows President Rodgers was poisoned. Why postpone telling the public something they're going to find out anyway? If an overzealous reporter finds out before we make an official announcement, we're going to have a cover-up scandal hanging over our heads."

"I agree with you, Olivia," Kate said. "We've placed ourselves in a vulnerable position, Charles."

"Madam President, in another week, when we have more definitive information, we'll give the press what they want."

"In another week, my face is going to be plastered on the covers of every seedy tabloid in the country. Tell Riley to schedule another press conference. I have no intention of concealing information the public has a right to know."

McDermott's face filled with blood. "Whatever you say, Madam President."

***

The thought of telling Elizabeth Rodgers that her husband had indeed been assassinated filled Kate with dread. She sat adjacent to the former First Lady, trying to compose a speech with gentle diplomacy. She remembered what Elizabeth had whispered in her ear: *Be careful. Things are not as they seem.* Elizabeth had known something about David's death, and Kate was convinced it was more than conjecture or intuition.

Kate had never been preoccupied with death, not until she'd entered the Oval Office and the possibility of assassination became so real. And of course, there were the nightmares during restless moments of sleep. Vivid images—a mannequin-like man pointing a gun at her, a grotesque hand sprinkling cyanide on her food, a pillow covering her face—flashed through her dreams like frames of a horror film spliced into the wrong movie. Kate now bitterly understood that if someone wanted her dead, and possessed enough ambition, there was virtually no place for her to hide.

As far as Kate knew, David Rodgers had been poisoned in the security of his private quarters, surrounded by Secret Service agents. What could she possibly do to protect herself from a determined assassin? Confine herself to a cage? Live her life in a solitary environment with armed guards?

As she studied Elizabeth's tense face, it was obvious that the former First Lady was more than grief stricken; she was devastated. She suspected that Elizabeth knew she hadn't been invited to the Oval Office for tea and crumpets.

"What is it, my dear?" Elizabeth's intuitive question caught Kate by surprise.

"I have something to tell you about David."

"If it's dirty laundry, I don't care to know. Let him rest in peace. And let me embrace my sweet memories."

With little forethought—long before she had a chance to examine her words—Kate blurted, "I'm sorry, Elizabeth, but in all probability, David was assassinated."

Seemingly undaunted by the harsh announcement, Elizabeth looked as if Kate had just told her that a button was missing on her sweater.

"Did you hear what I said?" Kate's voice was a few decibels too loud.

"Quite clearly."

Kate and Elizabeth stared at each other in silence.

After studying her fingernails in great detail, Elizabeth leaned forward. "Kate, I didn't discourage David from entering the presidential campaign. He was much too enthusiastic. From the moment he took the oath, I silently feared for his life. It was like being married to a policeman or fireman. Each morning, I wondered if today would be the last day we'd share. His idealistic platform won the hearts of Americans. But it alienated many people—too many, perhaps. One man, no matter how determined, cannot take on the most powerful people in the world and not expect consequences. David laughed when I suggested he not try to save the world single-handedly. He used to say, 'One day, my face is going to be carved into Mount Rushmore, right next to Teddy Roosevelt.'"

Elizabeth paused for a moment. Kate watched her eyes fill with tears. But suddenly, like some kind of Frankenstein monster being charged with electricity, Elizabeth came to life in a fit of rage. Her face contorted, she clenched her fists, and pounded one on Kate's desk. "I want the bastards to *die*, Madam President! Life in prison is *much* too humane. *Find them*! *Execute them*!"

Aghast at such a dramatic transformation, Kate sat back in the chair as if Elizabeth were going to strike her. She waited for the wave of emotions to pass. Kate told Elizabeth about the intensive investigation, that she'd appointed a special commission. Kate swore that there would be no mercy; whoever was responsible would pay dearly, that her husband's death had not been in vain. But Kate couldn't tell her who, how, or why. Only that an unknown toxin killed him.

"How did you know, Elizabeth? What I'm telling you cannot be a total surprise."

Elizabeth stared at Kate intently. "Some things, Kate, you just know."

They parted with a firm embrace. Elizabeth warned President Miles not to trust anyone. Kate promised to be careful. How she'd keep her promise was yet to be determined.

CHAPTER FOUR

Kate quickly learned that the Oval Office could operate more efficiently with a revolving door at the entrance. Nonstop traffic zoomed in and out all day long and often into the evening hours. It served as the nerve center for the Executive Branch. It was an arena where battles were fought, policies argued, a place where relationships were made and careers were ended. Information was integrated into its most concise form and funneled into this throbbing office. It was a pulsating hub of strategy and social commerce.

Every morning at seven a.m., Kate met with McDermott and Olivia Carter. A staff of twenty-five watched the world with a discriminating eye. They examined seventeen major newspapers, eight magazines, twenty-two political blogs, and several TV news programs with an emphasis on FOX News, MSNBC, and CNN. Their only task was to gather information. Every worthy event was evaluated, validated, and then compacted into synopsis form so that the president could get a broad, yet brief, overview of consequential news, anything that affected the United States or its allies.

This was merely the starting gate.

Throughout the day, Cabinet secretaries, members of the Joint Chiefs, the CIA, the FBI, marched in and out of the Oval Office nonstop. Each with their own agenda, they conferred with Kate and tried to convince her to endorse whatever partisan issue was at the top of the heap. More often than not, conflicts of great proportions erupted. Harmony was not the order of business. Kate generally felt like a solitary matador trying to fight a herd of charging bulls.

On this particular day, Kate was enjoying an uncommonly quiet morning. McDermott stormed into the Oval Office without knocking and slammed the door behind him.

"Sorry to bother you, Madam President, but we need to talk."

Kate leaned back and watched McDermott approach her. His cheeks were flushed. He wasn't wearing a suit jacket, which was unusual, and it looked like he'd either slept in his cotton shirt or taken it out of the hamper. His hair was disheveled too. Recognizing the importance of the situation, Kate led McDermott through the door to her private office. No one dared invade this sanctuary without an invitation.

She sat in the Victorian armchair adjacent to the window overlooking the rose garden. McDermott sat opposite her in the damask-upholstered Queen Anne chair. She watched him incessantly blinking and wondered why he was so frazzled. His hands were trembling.

"You look like you need a Valium."

He hesitated a moment and let out a heavy sigh. "The venom that killed President Rodgers was from a sea animal known as a box jellyfish." He removed a piece of paper from his shirt pocket. "Cubomedusa is its scientific name."

"So the mysterious poison is from a *fish*? That's, by far, the most absurd thing I've ever heard."

"It gets worse. Crazy as it sounds, this particular jellyfish is found only off the coast of northern Australia and in waters near the Philippines."

"I'm supposed to believe that someone extracted jellyfish poison from halfway around the world, flew it to Washington, and got it into President Rodgers's bloodstream—*without* it being detected by the Secret Service?"

"Maybe you should speak to LaPlant yourself." His voice was edged with impatience.

She got up, turned her back on the COS, and gazed out the window. "OK, let's assume that someone figured out a way to bypass the Secret Service. How could President Rodgers have consumed enough jellyfish poison for it to be lethal?"

"The box jellyfish produces the most toxic venom in the world. LaPlant said an ounce or two could stop a healthy heart in a very short time."

Katherine Miles pivoted on the balls of her feet. Her eyes locked on McDermott. "I'd like someone to research this box jellyfish and give me a detailed report."

McDermott pointed to a brown folder. "I've already done my homework, Madam President. There are few substances in the universe as deadly as Cubomedusa venom. One jellyfish has enough venom to kill sixty people." McDermott swallowed hard and looked at his notes. "The venom attacks the central nervous system, the heart, and the skin, and the victim feels an intense burning throughout his or her body."

Kate could feel her throat knot up. It was like sitting in front of a dentist, trying to force that last swallow just before she had to open wide. A strained whisper was the best she could do. "How badly did he suffer?"

Stress lines formed on McDermott's brow. "When someone is actually stung by a box jellyfish, death comes quickly—in as little as three minutes." He hesitated and stared at the folder. "But in this situation, President Rodgers didn't drink enough to kill him quickly. It was likely a long, painful process."

McDermott loosened his tie and licked his lips. "It wasn't pleasant, Madam President."

Kate curled her fingers into fists and could feel her nails digging into her flesh. She envisioned David Rodgers doubled over in excruciating agony.

"Damn! Damn! Damn! When we find these bastards, I want to personally flip the switch and watch them roast!" She sat on the window seat and could feel her pulse throbbing in her temples. "I'd like some privacy, Charles. Tell Emily not to disturb me unless it's urgent."

After McDermott left, Kate stared out the window at the few remaining roses. Soon they'd surrender to autumn's frosty nights. It was the cycle of life. She wanted to speak with Leonard LaPlant, to find out more about the poison. But she was afraid to learn the truth. She didn't want to hear the morbid details of how horrible his death might have been. Then something occurred to her. If David's final moments had been agonizing, why hadn't he called out to Elizabeth? Elizabeth had told Kate that David went to sleep and never awakened. How could anyone have suffered as much as he had and not yell for help?

She went to her desk and pushed the intercom button.

"Emily, I need to speak with Leonard LaPlant, the medical examiner."

***

Less than twenty-four hours after McDermott had told her how David Rodgers died—barely enough time for her to catch her breath—President Miles faced an anxious group of journalists. McDermott had urged her to let William Riley make the announcement, but after his first ambiguous press conference, she decided to take control before things got out of hand.

Her state of the union address to Congress was only days away, and she hadn't yet drafted an outline. What would she say to 535 constituents, most of whom would rather tar and feather her than give her the time of day? One thing was certain: somehow she'd have to find a way to dazzle them, to convert at least some of her adversaries into supporters.

Kate gripped both sides of the podium so tightly her knuckles turned white. She saw familiar faces: Ed Applegate from the *Post*, Kimberly Butler from the *Times*. Some were supporters, others harsh critics, but all could affect her credibility with the power of their words. She awaited her cue, watching for the red light just above camera number one. Her charcoal business suit accentuated her honey-blonde hair. An audience of 120 journalists and seventy million Americans intently listened.

She reached for her reading glasses.

"Good morning, my fellow Americans." She'd argued with Riley, but he insisted that she start her speech this way. "A terrible tragedy, an injustice of gross proportions, has befallen the White House and the entire country."

Befallen? Was Riley kidding?

Kate disliked these words more now than she had when she'd read them earlier. Who the hell did Riley think she was, Lyndon Johnson?

"I am unable to give you specific details at this time, but David Rodgers was assassinated."

The crowd, of course, reacted to this stunning announcement with a wave of chatter.

Out of the corner of her eye, Kate could see Riley shaking his head, his look one of disapproval. "He didn't have to run for president. He could have spent the rest of his life traveling the world with his beloved wife, enjoying the fruits of his labor, rewarding himself with his vast financial resources. But as a concerned patriot, he answered a calling. His country beckoned him, and he did not turn his back. Instead, he sacrificed his life for the America he loved. He was not only the president of the United States; he was my dear friend."

She pounded her fist on the podium and ended by saying, "I stand before the world and make two promises: First, I will utilize every resource available and aggressively pursue President Rodgers's assassins. When apprehended, they will be prosecuted to the fullest extent of the law, swiftly and without mercy. Second, David Rodgers's dream of a once-again united America will not fall by the wayside. I make this pledge: with your continued support, we will return this great country to peace, prosperity, and equal opportunity for all. Thank you."

For an agonizing moment, silence enveloped the room. Kate held her breath. If her speech had any impact, why was she staring at expressionless faces? Sweat trickled between her breasts, and a stab of anxiety twisted into her gut. Then the reporters stood and applauded thunderously.

She waited for the room to quiet. "I'll do my best to answer some questions."

A hundred journalists yelled, "Madam President!" Questions shot out like bullets from an assault weapon.

"Are there any suspects in the president's murder?"

"Do you believe there is a conspiracy?"

"Wasn't his food tested by the Secret Service?"

"How does it feel being the first female president?"

"Do you think you're in danger?"

"How many staff members will you replace?"

"How do you propose to gain the support of Congress?"

She fielded the questions well, answering some directly, waltzing around others.

But overall, Kate felt as though the press conference had gone well. Better than she'd anticipated. Though, until she watched CNN and examined the morning edition of the *Washington Post*, her instincts meant very little.

***

Retirement is a time when most people do those leisurely things they've always wished they could do. For Trevor Williams, retirement was a prison, an era of solitude that allowed him too much time to think. He couldn't believe that the home he'd built—with bloody knuckles, lungs full of sawdust, and a sprained knee—was now an oversized structure of lifeless furnishings. And for what? So he could die like a hermit? He glanced at the *Topeka Examiner* for the third time, feeling less surprised than the rest of the country. He, perhaps more than anyone, knew for certain that his daughter was indeed in danger. What could he do about it? He had talked Kate into accepting David Rodgers's offer in the first place. Once again, he'd made a decision concerning Kate that wasn't in her best interest. He wondered how many other parents lived vicariously through their children.

Trevor's jaw tightened, and he gritted his teeth. He stood slowly and could feel a dagger twisting in his lower back, a hot flame running down the back of his thigh. His herniated disc announced further deterioration. Trevor limped over to the oak desk and thumbed through the Rolodex. He never cared much for computers. He picked up the telephone and dialed Kate's private number. He didn't expect her to answer. Presidents didn't actually answer their own telephones, did they? Maybe a busy president could find time for the father who'd never found time for her.

***

"I'm sorry, Charles," Kate said, "but I refuse to remain a prisoner in the White House any longer."

"But, Madam President, all I'm asking is that you postpone your engagements for another week. Riley will draft a credible story for the press and explain why you're temporarily out of the limelight. Before you know it, things will be back to normal."

She hesitated for a moment, inordinately annoyed with his persistence. For some unknown reason, she felt he had a hidden agenda. Kate breathed deeply and tried to calm herself. "As long as I reside on Pennsylvania Avenue, nothing will ever be normal for me, Charles. What could possibly develop in the next week to make my situation less ominous?"

He began pacing the floor. "Over thirty CIA and FBI agents are working around the clock. Not to mention that Carl Kramer has shifted the special commission into high gear."

"Do they have any leads?"

He shook his head.

She placed her palms on her desk and stood. She walked over to the COS and rested her right hand on his shoulder. Kate gripped it tighter than she'd intended, and he winced beneath her grasp. She eased her grip and looked over her reading glasses.

"Charles, I do appreciate your concern, but I can no longer be held hostage by some imaginary threat."

He stuffed his hands into his pockets.

"David was murdered right here in the White House. How do you expect me to feel secure?"

His eyes studied the floor. "I'd like to go on record as opposing your decision."

"It will be so noted, Charles."

"In writing, please, Madam President."

"*What?*"

"If you're going to ignore my advice on an issue as important as your safety, I want my warning officially noted."

The corners of her mouth curled up. "They taught you a lot more than law at Harvard, hey, Mr. McDermott?"

"Just crossing the t's and dotting the i's."

"What you want is to cover your ass in case I'm mingling with the taxpayers and one of them decides to put a bullet in my head."

"Call it whatever you will."

She could smell alcohol on his breath. If it were after lunch, Kate might not have given it a second thought. Although frowned upon, three-martini lunches were not uncommon. But it was ten forty-five. "That's the name of the game in Washington, isn't it, Charles? Cover your ass. It's as much a part of politics as corruption."

McDermott looked like a whipped puppy. "I didn't mean to insult you, Madam—"

"Write a memo and I'll sign it, Charles."

She walked back to her desk and opened her daily planner. "I need to speak with Carl Kramer ASAP." She thought for a moment. "And set up a meeting with Albert Cranston. If I'm going to be out in the world rubbing elbows with assassins, I'd like to know how the Secret Service plans to protect me."

***

Peter Miles waited patiently at Ben's Café. He thought he'd left DC to get away from politics for a while, but he'd quickly learned that Washington was like dog shit. Once you stepped in it, the smell stuck to your heels. Late last night, he had received the call from Charles McDermott. He had told Peter that a man named

Jack Miller, CIA Special Agent, needed to meet him. And it was urgent. He sipped a brandy and looked at his Movado watch for the fifth time in the last ten minutes. Why had they contacted him? Peter Miles was a litigator, not a politician. He knew that it had something to do with Kate. What else could it be? Maybe she'd ruffled some feathers? Could it be that Kate wanted him back in DC and had sent one of her minions to twist his arm? It didn't seem like Kate's MO. Then again, she'd never been president of the United States.

Easing his way toward Peter, a short, stocky man in a dark-brown suit approached Peter's table. The man stopped several feet in front of Peter. He discretely looked to his left, then to his right.

"Mr. Miles?" he whispered.

Peter stood. The man's cheeks were pink and slick, like the butt end of a cured ham. He had spooky eyes. Peter reluctantly extended his hand. The man shook it loosely, and Peter felt like he was grasping a dead fish.

The man flashed his identification. "Jack Miller. Sorry to have kept you waiting." The man sat across from Peter. "I'm with the CIA, and we have a situation in Washington that requires your assistance."

Barely able to hear his whisper, Peter leaned toward him. "What kind of situation?"

"As you and the rest of the world now know, President Rodgers was assassinated. We're deeply concerned that your wife may also be a target."

Peter Miles lifted the snifter and gulped the rest of his brandy. He studied the man's cratered face. Peter didn't like his squinty eyes.

"She's in serious jeopardy, Mr. Miles."

"If the CIA and Secret Service can't control the situation, what the fuck do you expect a midwestern attorney to do? Stand in front of her wearing a bulletproof vest?"

"The president of the United States was assassinated, Mr. Miles. We have reliable information suggesting that your wife is in grave danger. Are you prepared to take responsibility?"

Almost yelling, Peter's voice raised an octave. "What the *hell* do you expect *me* to do?"

"Talk to her. You're a persuasive man."

"And what should I persuade her to do?"

"She's not safe in Washington."

Peter clasped his hands together and turned them inside out. His knuckles cracked. "Are you suggesting that I ask her to *resign*?"

"It's in her best interests."

Peter laughed. "You apparently don't know Kate very well, do you? You talk to her. Or better yet, tell McDermott to have a chat with her. I'd pay to see that performance."

"This is not a game, Mr. Miles. If you don't help us…Your wife's demise will rest on your conscience."

"Why hasn't someone in Washington approached Kate directly?"

"We feel that you will have greater influence."

"You guys really didn't do your homework, did you? What makes you think she will listen to me?"

"All I can say is that we have our reasons."

"I'll bet you do." Peter gulped the rest of his brandy. "OK, let me get this straight. I fly to DC, convince my wife to resign, and then what? Isn't her successor going to be in danger as well?"

Miller shook his head. "David Rodgers and your wife are Independents, Mr. Miles. We believe that some very powerful and influential people stand to lose a great deal if your wife proceeds with their radical agenda."

Peter Miles sat back in his chair and motioned for a cocktail waitress. "I'll fly back to Washington in the morning. But it's a waste of time."

Jack Miller reached inside his jacket, pulled out an envelope, and laid it on the table. "There's a nine o'clock flight tonight. Be on it."

Shaking his head, Peter picked up the envelope. "You guys are right out of a Tom Clancy novel, aren't you?"

Miller stood up and pushed in his chair. "There's one more thing, Mr. Miles. This conversation never took place."

CHAPTER FIVE

Cranky and light-headed, totally pissed off that Kate hadn't honored his request to be free from Secret Service agents, Peter Miles arrived at Dulles Airport just before midnight. After retrieving two pieces of luggage from the baggage claim, the agents walking in his shadow, Peter decided that he really needed a cup of coffee, but the airport restaurants were closed.

"You guys mind if I have a smoke outside while we wait for the limo?" Peter said to the agents.

"The limo is already waiting, sir," the taller agent said.

"Well, let it fucking wait."

He stepped outside, the agents close behind, and like a junkie needing a quick fix, he frisked his pockets, frantically trying to locate his Camels. He might survive without caffeine, but nicotine was as vital as oxygen. He yanked the pack from his inside pocket. Only two left. Using the Zippo with the Marines insignia, he fought the wind to light the cigarette. He inhaled deeply and filled his lungs with the calming smoke.

Why did Miller want *him* to talk to Kate? What did he expect *him* to say? Miller had been vague. Peter did not believe that Kate's welfare concerned them. Something didn't feel right. They were purposefully trying to wedge him in the middle of a danger-ous power play.

Then Peter finally understood that he, too, could be in danger.

The black limo with the presidential seal.

Peter glanced to his left, then to his right. He took a deep hit on his cigarette. The area was dotted with people. An over-weight black woman was hailing a cab. A pretty redhead pushed an elderly man in a wheelchair. Two men were talking, looking his way, one staring at Peter longer than a stranger should. Maybe sizing him up?

If Kate's life was in danger—the mere thought of it terri-fied him—then so was his. Every time he sat next to her in the presidential limo, every time he stood by her side, every time he boarded Air Force One, he could potentially be at the wrong place at the wrong time.

Maybe her resigning wasn't such a bad idea, after all.

***

Kate was sitting in the Oval Room, sipping a glass of lemony spring water, futilely attempting to read, when Peter opened the door. Prior to his arrival, Kate had been contacted by the Secret Service to ensure that she wouldn't be startled when Peter walked in at one a.m.

She was draped in a satiny navy-blue robe, her bare feet tucked beneath her, hair pulled back into a stubby ponytail. She heard him drop the luggage on the foyer floor but didn't look his way. He came over to her, leaned forward, and gave her a chaste kiss on her left cheek. She rubbed her face where his sandpaper-like stubble prickled her sensitive skin.

She focused on the book and didn't utter a sound.

Peter sat next to her, bent forward, unlaced his shoes, and slipped them off. "Sorry if I woke you." He was out of breath.

A big fan of the classics, Kate was reading *The Old Man and the Sea* and didn't lift her eyes from the text. "No reason to apologize. You know me. Always a night owl." She dropped the Hemingway classic on the sofa. "So, what brings you back to Washington?"

He exhaled heavily. "Kate, I know you're pissed off, and you have every reason to be."

"It's nice to know that there are still a few issues upon which we agree."

His narrow eyes scoured her face. "I am *not* looking for a fight, Kate."

"Why haven't you called?"

"I thought about it, but I was too busy."

"Too busy to telephone your wife?"

"I've been a bit self-absorbed."

"I never would have guessed."

Out of the corner of her eye, she could see him shaking his head.

"My trip to Topeka wasn't just to help Ben with the Alexander trial. I needed some time to think."

Her eyes met his for the first time. "Is there someone else, Peter?"

"God no, Kate, it's nothing like that."

It never is, she thought. "Are you going to explain or torture me further?"

"It's late, and we're both irritable. Why don't we talk in the morning?"

"It *is* morning, Peter."

He combed his fingers through his thinning hair. "I've been doing a lot of soul-searching, Kate. Neither you nor I have any business being in the White House."

"There are about fifty-three million voters who might disagree."

"We had a good life in Topeka. I hate DC, and I don't believe you like it, either."

"I don't. As a matter of fact, I find it overrun with whiny adolescents representing themselves as responsible adults. But I *am* the president of the United States, and unfortunately, the White House was built in Washington."

"Why don't we leave Washington?"

At first, she couldn't imagine that he was serious, but then she looked into his eyes. "Have you lost all sense of reason? How do you propose I do that?"

He nibbled on his lower lip. "Kate, people will understand. David's assassination changed everything."

His words struck a raw chord in her. "Are you asking me to... *resign?*"

"Do it for us, Kate. For our marriage. If anything ever happened to you—"

She sprang up quickly and perched her hands on her hips. "I haven't even had time to plant my feet on the ground, and you want to yank the rug out from underneath me? I don't understand any of this. Who are you, Peter?" She sat on the sofa and gulped a mouthful of water. "I will not, under any circumstances, resign."

"I don't want to see you end up in a body bag, Kate."

Kate's preoccupation with death was not a topic she needed to be reminded of. "I cannot fathom your motivation, Peter. What in the world—"

"Kate…I'm flying back to Topeka in the morning." He looked up at her, his eyes watery. "With or without you."

***

Kate lay beside Peter, listening to him snore, unable to believe he could sleep so peacefully. Didn't he *care* about saving their marriage? About her presidency? That she could even lie next to him, in the same bed, seemed unimaginable. She felt utterly betrayed.

After wrestling with her pillow for an agonizing hour, replaying their conversation in her mind, Kate could no longer remain within the oppressive walls of the Presidential Suite. She had no idea where she'd go—the president couldn't just stroll out the front door of the White House and meander merrily down the street—but she had to get away from Peter. She threw on her navy-blue Champion sweats and Reebok tennis sneakers and dragged a brush through her unruly hair. When she stepped into the hallway, Michael, the graveyard-shift Secret Service agent stationed outside her door, jumped to attention.

He glanced at his watch; his tactful eyes gave her out-of-character ensemble a quick once-over. "Anything wrong, Madam President?"

Got a couple of hours, Mike? "No, Michael, just stretching my legs. Insomnia, I guess."

"You're not leaving the building, are you, ma'am?"

"If I do, you'll be the first to know."

She thumped down the stairway to the first-level entrance hall and walked into the Blue Room, an oval room used for formal receptions. Kate stood in front of Thomas Jefferson's life-study portrait and looked up at him as if he were alive. She focused on the minute details of his face.

"How about a little advice, Tom?" His lips seemed to move, but Kate realized her eyes were tearing. She tried to imagine what historians might write about her, wondered if a noted artist like Rembrandt Peale would ever feel compelled to paint *her*, if a successor might one day admire *her* portrait. Kate was overcome by a more realistic prophecy—morose visions of a malignant presidency. Perhaps her administration would be like a dark cloud hanging over the country, an era of discontent and turmoil. She tore her eyes away from the portrait and tried to disarm the time bomb ticking in her conscience.

Kate examined one of the original Bellangé chairs positioned beneath the portrait. She was tempted to sit in the chair but felt it would be sacrilegious in some strange way. Much of the furniture in the White House was like artifacts in a museum, meant only to visually appreciate but never touch. She moseyed into the Red Room, a sitting room decorated with French and American mahogany furniture. She eased her weary bones onto the red Empire sofa. Awestruck by the historic memorabilia surrounding her, she imagined how many former presidents, diplomats, and members of royalty had sat where she rested right now. She laid her head back, her eyelids heavy as concrete. How had her marriage gotten to such a hopeless state? She glanced at her wedding ring and thought about the day Peter had proposed.

***

It was a typical Sunday afternoon. Kate had invited Peter to the White Stallion Ranch to celebrate the first anniversary of their meeting. Their relationship had stagnated; it had become routine and boring. Kate, in her infinite optimism, was hoping that a romantic dinner and a heartfelt talk might jump-start the failing relationship. She had an eerie feeling about today; something extraordinary was going to happen.

They'd just finished dinner. Maria had the weekend off, and Kate's father was in Chicago. After piling the dishes in the sink,

Kate cuddled up next to Peter on the sofa in front of the fireplace. Peter exhaled an I-ate-too-much sigh and discreetly loosened his belt buckle. Kate grasped his hand.

"I can't believe it's been a year," she said.

"Time sure flies when you're having fun."

"Is that what we're doing, Peter?"

He slid his hand between her legs and squeezed her inner thigh. "What's the matter?"

She wanted to tell him that she needed more, that the relationship was in limbo. But didn't he know? Couldn't he *feel* the void? She didn't want to pressure him, but...

"There's something missing, Peter. We need to find a balance between independence and permanency. I'm just not sure what that is." "Kate, I'm in love with you. If I haven't made that clear, I'm sorry." He eased off the sofa as if he'd just had back surgery. He grabbed the fireplace poker and rearranged the crackling logs. When he sat down, he slid his arm around her shoulders.

"You have no interest in children, Kate. Told me repeatedly that kids are the only reason to marry. Has that changed?"

"I'm not sure, Peter. At this point in my life, I don't know what the hell I want. But I can tell you this, being a mother wouldn't be the worst thing in the world."

He moved his head toward her and kissed her cheek. "Want to make love?"

Don't ask! Sweep me away, Peter. Carry me into the bedroom. Take me!

She nodded yes, but her heart told her no.

He stood and extended his arm; Kate could see a fever of excitement stirring in his wide-open eyes. Like an obedient child, she grasped his hand. A lingering scent of charred apple wood followed them into the bedroom. She'd seen this play before. It was a script from which he never improvised. She stood facing him and watched him undress. She searched her senses, quietly desperate to be filled with desire. Kate wanted to be aroused; she ached to have her gut explode with passion. But she felt no fire in her belly. Physically, she believed that Peter did his best to satisfy her. Emotionally, however, he fell short.

With his boxer shorts still on, he pulled down the comforter and hopped into bed. He rolled to his side, dug his elbow into the pillow, and propped his head up with his right hand. "Care to join me?"

It wasn't quite a Don Juan invitation. She'd given up on the Gothic-novel lovers who naive little girls dream about, the blood-pumping, heart-pounding, sweaty palms kind of romance.

With each piece of clothing peeled from her body, Kate could feel his penetrating stare. She'd never felt comfortable with any man seeing her naked. As her bra fell to the floor, she turned away and strategically shielded her breasts with her forearms. The troublesome left breast was always there to taunt her. Even though it never seemed to bother Peter—not once did he ever mention it—she still felt overwhelmingly self-conscious. With a fluid motion, she slid under the covers.

He didn't kiss her, stroke her hair, or make love to her with words. Peter didn't understand enticement or foreplay. Nor did he comprehend the magic of eye contact. After a one-year relationship, Kate grudgingly accepted the fact that Peter would never comprehend that a kiss—long, hot, breathless—was the fuel that ignited all lovemaking, every nerve ending inflamed by the simple pleasure of a kiss. How many times had she given him a guided tour of her body? How many times had she stressed the importance of foreplay? How many times had she told him that she wanted a partner who understood the difference between a sprinter and a long-distance runner? He just didn't get it.

He slipped off his boxers and gently moved his body on top of her. That was the one thing she'd always loved about Peter. He always seemed conscious of her comfort and was never overly aggressive. Kate closed her eyes. It was a union for which her body was not quite ready. She kept her eyes shut, and her mouth searched for his, hoping he'd at least kiss her. His only interest was orgasm.

Another world record.

When he finished, he kissed her forehead. "How did I do?" he asked.

This was always his after-sex question. She wanted to be totally truthful, but when she had tried this approach in the past, it only served to frustrate her and make him feel inadequate. He did manage to give her some physical pleasure, but it was little more than a teaser. "You did great, honey."

He rolled off her and smiled broadly, obviously satisfied that he was a great lover.

The aftermath was always the same. She lay motionless, trying to focus on a spot in the center of the colorless ceiling, trying to make sense of their relationship. She could hear his rhythmic gasps. Soon he'd be snoring.

At times like this, secret thoughts were jarred loose from the private caverns in her mind. Babies. Skin soft as a lambskin glove. Talcum powder. Johnson's shampoo. Ivory soap. The clock was ticking, hammering. But her battery was almost dead.

"Will you marry me?" he whispered, his words crashing through the silence of night. "I know that I don't always show my true feelings, Kate. Maybe all men are built this way. But you are the love of my life, and I want to wake up next to you every morning and see that beautiful smile."

She could not have been more shocked if she stuck her finger into a live light socket. It was a question that carried with it a series of complicated thoughts. A fading vision of a white knight, a distant fantasy of motherhood, flashed in her mind. If she believed for one minute that, somewhere in the world, a mysterious stranger was waiting to sweep her off her feet, she might have turned down his proposal.

Maybe marriage will solidify our relationship. Maybe things will change. Maybe it will help advance my political career.

Logic overcame her instincts. Like so many unfulfilled women, Kate settled for the consolation prize before there were no prizes to be had, before Mother Nature and gravity did what they did best to middle-aged women.

"Yes, Peter. I *will* marry you." As the words reluctantly slipped off her tongue, a feeling of anxiety overwhelmed her.

He kissed her on the lips for the first time that evening, and like in the past, her heart did not feel what she desperately wanted it to feel.

***

Kate sat forward and shook her head. She looked around the Red Room, feeling disoriented. The muscles along her shoulders tightened, reminding her why she sat alone at five thirty a.m. From the beginning, Kate thought, their marriage had been an arrangement, a merger, two mismatched people hoping to beat the odds and make something out of nothing. It had been an unsteady foundation upon which a secure relationship could not be built.

Maybe that's why things are crumbling.

She stood and stretched, reaching for the fifteen-foot ceiling. When her mind was more alert, she walked into the West Wing, her body feeling as if she were trudging through mud. She wanted to check her calendar to prepare for another turbulent day. As

Kate reached for the doorknob, a voice echoed from down the hall. McDermott's door was ajar. She stood in front of his office and listened.

"...he arrived a few hours ago. Yes. I wouldn't worry about it. It's just a matter of time. I'll keep you posted."

Who was he talking to? What did it all mean? Kate wasn't yet sure if McDermott was totally on her team. Under the circumstances, an unexpected visit might answer a lot of questions. She wanted to rush inside, catch him off guard, examine his eyes. The eyes never lie. But what would it accomplish? Right now, she needed a long shower and a pot of coffee.

As she walked up the stairs, his words echoed in her mind: *It's just a matter of time*. Was he implying that it was just a matter of time before she resigned? What else could it mean?

She remembered that her dad would arrive on Saturday. His timing couldn't be better.

CHAPTER SIX

Hoping to rouse her senses, Kate struggled through the coldest shower she could endure. But after ten minutes, she realized that nearly freezing her body wasn't the remedy she'd sought. She towel-dried her hair, wrapped a terry robe around her shivering body, and shuffled barefoot toward the kitchen. Walking down the long hallway, she could smell hazelnut coffee. Oh, how she needed coffee! Because Kate rarely ate breakfast, the service staff didn't begin their day until eight a.m. But it was standard procedure for Adelina Menendez, the housekeeper and a vivacious Brazilian redhead, to make an early visit just to brew Kate fresh coffee. She grabbed the Krups carafe, poured herself a mugful, and drank it black. Unlike most mornings, when one cup got her going, today she guzzled a second, and third, cup of strong coffee.

While sitting at the table, mulling over her agenda for the day, Kate could feel the coffee launch an unfamiliar assault against her stomach. It wasn't indigestion or heartburn, more like a sharp cramp focused around her navel. It couldn't be her period, she thought, it was more than two weeks away. It had to be the black coffee. She tried to get up, but a fierce pain folded her in half.

Slowly, with great care not to stand upright, Kate eased off the chair. Slightly bent forward, she gripped her stomach with both hands and struggled toward the nearest bathroom. In the medicine cabinet, she fumbled for antacids. By chewing four Tums, twice the recommended dose, Kate hoped to counteract the hostile caffeine. A shade of relief came quickly, but the cramp would not subside. Suddenly, she could feel a welling current of vomit churning in the back of her throat.

The pain deepened further.

David Rodgers. The jellyfish poison. The symptoms.

Fraught with panic and utter misery, she fell to the floor. Her first frenzied thought was to yell for help. But when Kate opened her mouth, all she could elicit was a guttural moan.

What Kate needed was a doctor. Or maybe a priest.

***

When Adelina Menendez tiptoed into Charles McDermott's office, he was pacing the floor, sucking on a Lucky Strike. She locked the door.

"I've been waiting for you," he said. "Did anybody see you come in?"

"I do not think so."

"What do you mean, you don't *think* so?"

"No one saw me."

"Are you *sure*?"

"Yes. Yes. I am positive."

Charles assumed a familiar position on the leather sofa. He didn't have to say a word.

Her generous lips curled to a smile. She unbuttoned the front of her light-blue dress, slipped it off her shoulders, and let it slide down her bronze body. It caught on her hips so she wiggled it to the floor.

Adelina's full breasts heaved out of the black lace bra. McDermott fixed his eyes on her skimpy thong panties. He adored garter belts and stockings. She stepped out of her shoes and ambled over to him. With a naughty smile, she knelt on the floor in front of him. She grasped his knees, spread his legs apart, and licked her ruby-painted lips.

McDermott unbuckled his belt, pulled down his zipper, and rested his head against the back of the sofa. He clutched a handful of her curly red hair and closed his eyes.

Adelina Menendez took him to that special place.

***

By the time Dr. Weinberg arrived, Kate had vomited three times, and the pain had been reduced to a dull ache. Had it not been for the housekeeping staff, Kate might still be lying on the bathroom floor in agony. Albert Cranston and six Secret Service agents fastidiously searched drawers, inspected cupboards, and tried to find anything out of the ordinary. They confiscated the remaining brewed coffee and sent it to the lab.

Kate lay on the yellow sofa with a wet washcloth pressed against her forehead. With her other hand, she rubbed her stomach. Dr. Weinberg and Cranston stood over her.

"How do you know it wasn't poison?" Kate asked.

Dr. Weinberg handed her samples of Tagamet from the supply in his black bag. "If it were, Madam President, I'd be calling Leonard LaPlant's office."

"Suppose it wasn't as potent as the poison that killed President Rodgers?" Kate said.

"The coffee's being tested, Madam President," Cranston said, "but I assure you, you were not poisoned."

She sat up, and her head began to spin. "Who's testing it, the same agents who tested David's last meal?"

Cranston groaned. "I understand your concern, Madam—"

"I don't think you understand anything." She threw the washcloth on the cocktail table. "Why don't you and your agents finish what you're doing and give me some privacy?"

Cranston gathered his agents and left immediately.

Dr. Weinberg picked up his black bag. "It'd be a good idea for you to have a complete health appraisal, Madam President. I can arrange it at your earliest convenience."

"Maybe next week doctor. My plate is a little full right now."

The doctor set his bag on the carpet and adjusted his glasses. "I've seen four presidents come and go. Not one of them found time to take care of themselves. Things will keep. Your health may not."

"I'll buzz you in a day or so."

"Your elevated blood pressure concerns me. I'd like to do an upper and lower GI to find out what's going on with your digestive system as well."

"It's nerves, Doctor. I always puke and get excruciating stomach pain when I think I've been poisoned."

The doctor shrugged his shoulders. "Have a good day."

***

From the cedar walk-in closet, Kate grabbed her blue business suit and laid it on the bed next to Peter. She could not fathom that he'd slept through her entire ordeal. The sun peeked through the partially opened drapes. When Kate glanced at Peter's slightly illuminated face, she could see he was sound asleep.

How could she ever look at him again with respect? She considered waking him, but at this particular moment, she despised him. He'd spoken his piece, and to embroil him into another exasperating conversation was not something her stomach could tolerate.

Kate wondered if the president could call in sick. Wasn't there a law that entitled her to personal and sick days like the rest of the working world? She quickly dismissed the notion and forced herself back to reality. She quietly dressed, slipped on her shoes, checked herself in the full-length mirror, then headed for the West Wing. Her first appointment was not until eight a.m. She glanced at her watch. Good. She had plenty of time to clear her mind and shift her focus to the business of the day.

As she walked through the crowded corridors, she shared good-mornings with those she passed. She took the stairway to the first floor and crossed the hallway toward the executive offices. As she approached the Oval Office, she remembered her early morning adventure. Who had McDermott been talking to at such an early hour?

It's just a matter of time.

Kate tiptoed down the hall and knocked on his door. Perhaps she'd blindside him, put him on the spot before he could gather his thoughts.

No answer. Again, she knocked and twisted the doorknob. Locked.

She opened her office door, took one step inside, and stopped dead. Her stomach, still churning and tumbling, warned her to remain calm.

He was standing over her desk. His head snapped up.

"*Charles?*"

McDermott walked around the desk and glanced at his watch. "You're here bright and early this morning, Madam President." His voice seemed mellow, more relaxed than usual.

"What are you doing?"

She watched his Adam's apple rise as he swallowed hard.

"Olivia wants to see you. I penciled her in at four."

"Do you know why?"

"Something about PR strategies."

"What time did you get in?"

"Four thirty. Amazing what you can accomplish before the floodgates open."

She pondered for a moment. Peter's quick departure would raise a lot of imposing questions, and if the media sniffed marital problems, they'd turn it into a soap opera. She didn't wish to see her picture on the front page of the *National Enquirer*. She had to speak with *someone*.

"Can I confide in you, Charles?"

***

As president, Kate relished the sumptuous dinners prepared especially for her. It was a presidential benefit she most enjoyed. But she rarely had time to eat a normal midday meal. She had just finished a turkey sandwich; the tang of Grey Poupon hung in the back of her throat. Her stomach had settled down, finally, and it was the first solid food she'd eaten in eighteen hours. She was relieved when the lab results confirmed that the coffee she had drunk prior to her stomach pain hadn't been tainted in any way. It was pure Columbian hazelnut. On her list of things to do, this was one less issue for her to worry about. At least for now.

Having been in the White House only ten days, Kate observed that the endless meetings with everyone from Cabinet members to senators to generals, solving problems, brainstorming, and strategizing were rudimentary functions of the presidency. Everything revolved around conferences.

Emily knocked. "Madam President, Vice President Owens is here."

"He's early." She could think of few things as unsavory as facing Owens.

"He's a *very* impatient man."

"I'll be with him in a couple of minutes."

Kate had felt uneasy with it, but confided in McDermott. She asked the COS how to handle Peter's departure. He had said, "Sit tight until we have an opportunity to evaluate our options." She couldn't afford to let fate take control. She dialed Peter's cellular number.

"Miles here."

"It's me."

"I missed you this morning," Peter said. "Wanted to say good-bye."

"My office is a five-minute walk."

"Had I known you were there—"

"Where are you?"

"On my way to the airport."

"Are you alone?"

"I'm in one of your limos."

Agents, of course, would accompany him.

"I want you to keep our separation confidential. Nobody needs to know our business. You *are* going to continue helping Ben, correct?"

"More than likely."

"Then make that the reason we're apart."

"In a week or so, a lot of people are going to ask questions," he said.

"Let them."

"What happens when the Alexander trial is over?"

She didn't answer.

"Kate?"

"I'll cross that bridge then."

"Consider it done."

There was a long pause. "Thank you," she said. Her voice was unsteady.

"You all right?"

"Fucking terrific, Peter."

She didn't let him say good-bye. For a moment, she sat silently, bits and pieces of their relationship dangled in her mind like a collage. Kate forced the memories out of her thoughts. She opened her center drawer, removed a small mirror, and checked her eyeliner. It really was waterproof. When she regained her composure, she buzzed Emily.

The vice president, former Speaker of the House, entered her office with a harrowing flourish. His overbearing posture was immediately visible. He extended his hand as he shuffled his portly body toward the president. Kate stood and reached across her desk.

How had he ever been elected to Congress?

He grasped her hand with a viselike grip. "Good afternoon, Madam *President.*"

The pretense hidden in his distinct annunciation set Kate's nerve endings ablaze. Along with a sleepless night, the recently acquired title of estranged spouse, and a gut turned inside out, Owens's smug attitude removed any possibility of an amiable conversation. Walter Owens was a champion of the double entendre, an Olympian in the sport of subtle one-liners. Kate was not mentally prepared for this battle. She was still brooding over her disorderly life. Even Gandhi could antagonize her today.

Owens sat in the wing chair and craned his neck, gazing around the office like he'd never been here before. "The presidency certainly affords you enviable luxuries, doesn't it?"

She tried to smile, but her lips narrowed to a thin line. Owens was pushing her.

He adjusted himself in the chair, his wide hips barely fitting between the armrests. Kate noticed blood filling his cheeks. He folded his fat little fingers together as if he were going to pray. She couldn't imagine the god to whom Owens prayed.

"Madam President, I'll not waste time with pleasantries. There's an uneasiness in Congress. My colleagues presume that I have a privileged link to the White House or some magical influence over you, so many come to me with their concerns."

"Considering that you're the VP, I can understand why."

He fixed his stare on her and leaned forward. "My constituents ask me a lot of sensitive questions."

"What goes on in the White House is common knowledge. Tell them to read the *Post*."

"There is deep concern with the Healing of America platform. Do you intend to follow through and introduce these radical bills to Congress?"

She wasn't quite sure what his angle was just yet but knew better than to respond yes or no. "That's a difficult question. I'll reserve the answer until I've had the opportunity to confer with my advisors."

"But as I understand it, *you* drafted these bills."

"That is correct, Walter."

"Then why would you require consultation from your advisors?"

"It's lateral thinking. Perspectives from a different angle are quite illuminating."

"Madam President, your State of the Union address is in three days. Surely you must know whether or not you will discuss your bills."

"I'm going to postpone the State of the Union address." It was a decision she hadn't made until this moment.

He sat upright in the chair. "May I speak candidly?"

"Isn't that what you're doing?"

"It is not my intention to undermine you, Madam President, but you have not been in Washington long enough to fully understand the dynamics."

Kate was nearly over the edge. "Why don't you give me a crash course, Walter?"

Her comment seemed to excite him. He struggled to cross his legs. "Politicians are really gymnasts. We are forced to juggle voters while balancing on a very narrow platform. If we lean too far right, we alienate the liberals. And if we lean to the left, the conservatives are up in arms."

"Sometimes it's good to fall on your ass. It puts things in proper perspective." She could see Owens's face flushing. "Instead of waltzing around the issue, Mr. Vice President, why don't you save both of us a lot of time and tell me what's on your mind."

His forehead was dripping wet. He blinked several times and folded his hands. "Introducing the Healing of America bills is a huge mistake. There is a vast difference between ideology and reality. Initiating drastic policy changes is a tricky business. Legislation is a slow, tedious process. One cannot approach delicate and sensitive issues so recklessly. Your Healing of America bill tries to tackle tax and welfare reform, a Medicare and Social Security overhaul, and reducing the national deficit, all at the same time. That's a tall order, Madam President, and it places lawmakers in a precarious situation. Voters get their dander up."

"If my bills are good for the country, why shouldn't I move forward in a timely manner?"

"Because journalists and naive voters do not understand the complexities of running a country. Not everything is black and white. They see what they want to see and hear what they want to hear. They don't bother to examine a bill line by line. They blindly endorse any proposal having to do with tax reform, the environment, or health care, whether it's practical or insane. It's all about voter perception."

She pondered his speech for a moment, desperately wanting to give him a tongue-lashing. But her father had taught her to count to ten. "You make some good points, Walter. But is this what government is all about, treading water for four years? Is getting reelected more important than doing what's best for the country?"

"Madam President, getting reelected is *everything*. If you believe differently, you're in for a rude awakening."

Counting to ten didn't always work, especially when she was dealing with a pretentious clod. "When the time is right I have every intention of introducing these bills, Walter, and I don't care how much resistance I get from Congress."

His hands tightened around the armrests. She could see his knuckles turning white. With an unsteady voice, he said, "I have been asked to advise you, Madam President. If you introduce the Healing of America bills to Congress…They're going to be dead on arrival." Owens's face looked like it was going to explode.

"So you and the boys on Capitol Hill want to play hardball?"

"I'm merely giving you a reality check, Madam President."

"Are you familiar with these bills, Walter?"

"Not in great detail."

"Has *anyone* in Congress bothered to examine the bills thoroughly?"

He blinked nervously. "That's unlikely."

Her eyes narrowed with contempt. "So what you're saying is that even if these bills have tremendous merit and could effect necessary changes in government that would be beneficial to all American citizens, Congress isn't interested?"

"It's not that cut-and-dried, Madam President."

Kate was seething with anger.

He sighed deeply. "What shall I say to my constituents?"

"Tell them to load their six-shooters, Walter, because there's a new sheriff in town and she doesn't take prisoners."

He didn't look flustered. There was a hint of joy in his brown eyes. It seemed to Kate that he'd wanted her to stand her ground.

"Thank you for seeing me on such short notice," he said, his voice affable. He didn't offer his hand.

"It was my pleasure, Walter."

He turned, walked toward the door, then stopped. "Madam President, there is one more thing." The level of his baritone voice dropped to a whisper. "How well do you know Charles McDermott?"

He seemed determined to jab her one more time.

"As well as I could know anyone I've worked with for ten months. Why do you ask?"

"You might want to be careful when taking him into your confidence."

She bit her tongue.

Kate waited long enough for him to leave the West Wing. She pushed her intercom button. "Emily, find McDermott for me. *Immediately.*"

***

Along with other luxuries of flying first class, American Airlines made available an unlimited assortment of alcoholic beverages the minute the plane left the gate. Although Peter Miles was always searching for a reason to overindulge, he rarely drank while flying. Today, however, was different. He was deeply troubled, unsettled about his decision to leave Kate. How do you walk away from a marriage with complete peace of mind?

He looked over his shoulder at the two Secret Service agents cramped side by side a few rows back, seated in the terribly uncomfortable economy section. He chuckled to himself.

You got what you deserved, assholes.

Peter wanted to sit alone. But a young man jogged down the gangway, stepped onto the plane only minutes before they secured the door, and plopped down next to him, out of breath. Peter ordered his third Bloody Mary.

The young man's name was Tony Martino. He was on his way to LA, worked for IBM, just got transferred, born and raised in Maryland, never been to the West Coast. He was a hyperactive, nonstop talker who couldn't relax if he overdosed on Valium. After his autobiography ended, the grand inquisition began.

"Where you from? Where you headed? Married? Children? What do you do for a living?"

Peter had always been suspicious of over-friendly strangers. In fact, now that he thought about it, he didn't really trust anybody. Two decades as a litigator could taint even Mother Teresa. But alcohol had a tendency to loosen Peter's tongue, regardless of his cynicism.

"My wife works in Washington," Peter said. He wasn't drunk enough to tell Martino who she was. "Things have been a little shaky lately, so I'm taking a hiatus from the marriage. Going back to my hometown. Topeka." He was surprised the young man didn't recognize him. Then again, wearing a Kansas City Chiefs baseball cap and tinted glasses might have had something to do with preserving his anonymity.

Martino excused himself, said he'd had too much coffee. Peter took advantage of the peace and quiet, rested his head against the seat, and closed his eyes.

***

President Miles sat alone in her private office waiting for Carl Kramer, deputy director of central intelligence. She rescheduled her meeting with Olivia Carter for tomorrow morning. Olivia hadn't sounded pleased, but a conference with Kramer, head of the assassination commission, was her top priority.

The day had sailed by. Ten hours had never passed so quickly. Reflecting back on her conversation with Vice President Owens, Kate presumed that McDermott's observation had been correct. Owens *had* tried her on for size. But for what purpose?

She hadn't told McDermott that Owens had maligned him, but thought it wise to observe her chief of staff more closely. He had been acting a bit peculiar of late.

Kate swiveled her chair and faced the window. Leaves of russet and pale yellow tumbled across the lawn. A beady-eyed black crow sat pompously on the white birch tree, staring at Kate. His head was cocked to one side, critically studying her. She remembered the Poe tale "The Raven." It seemed that this crow knew something. She could see a foreboding message in his black eyes.

They were close. She could feel it. Evil was on its way.

***

Jakob Hoffman placed his hands on top of his blood brother's shoulders and kissed him on both cheeks. "We got the call. You fly to Washington tomorrow."

"Trust me," Guenther Krause promised, "the bitch is as good as dead."

CHAPTER SEVEN

The melatonin was not working its magic. Weary and restless, Kate again glanced at the clock radio. Three thirteen a.m. The last three hours had felt like a decade. Her skin ached the way it did when she had the flu. Without Peter lying beside her, the king-size bed was cold and lonely. She sat up and punched the center of the pillow, digging her fist deep into the down feathers. Her stomach was beginning its insidious acrobatics act again. Terrified that the unexplainable cramp would return, she shook a Tagamet out of the box laying on the nightstand and popped one in her mouth. A glass of lukewarm water sat next to her lucky 1898 silver dollar. She gulped a mouthful and washed down the medication. She lay back down and buried her head in the pillow.

How could the president of the United States feel so completely detached from the world? Droves of people surrounded her every day, yet their presence seemed alien, as if the rest of the world occupied a different plane of existence than she. This was not the first time she'd felt dislocated. Did she need a psychiatrist? A straitjacket? Or perhaps Peter had been right. Maybe she didn't belong in Washington.

Lying in bed alone, plagued with uncertainties, strangely missing Peter's snore, evoked unsettling memories. Her father's lengthy and frequent business trips had forced Kate to become intimate companions with loneliness long before she could spell her name. She'd learned that loneliness wasn't merely a three-syllable word or a fearful emotion. Loneliness was a living, flesh-eating beast. For most of her childhood, the beast sucked the life out of Kate, savored every drop of her.

Kate reached for her lucky silver dollar. She rubbed its smooth texture between her thumb and index finger. For her fifth birthday, her father had pressed this lucky coin to his heart before giving it to her. He'd promised that whenever she needed him, all she had to do was hold the lucky coin to her heart, and he'd come to her in spirit. She'd decided right then that she'd forever treasure it.

***

Carl Kramer's boss hadn't said much to him lately. But Kramer expected he'd get an earful today. Ellenwood had been simmering for a while. Kramer'd witnessed his infantile behavior for almost eight years. He knew why Ellenwood was fuming. President Miles had stepped over the DCI's authority. When she'd appointed Kramer head of the assassination investigation—Kramer couldn't help but chuckle at this—it was like rubbing Ellenwood's face in dog shit. He'd been humiliated in front of his peers, stripped of his authority. Kramer understood Ellenwood's attitude, but he didn't want to stare at his sulky puss at seven a.m. and listen to him whine. Maybe that's why Kramer's nerve endings were aflame. To pacify the old coot, Kramer had agreed to this early meeting without protest. As long as the DCI didn't interfere with Kramer's primary agenda, he'd respect Ellenwood's authority.

Kramer had a more serious concern than his boss. Yesterday, he'd been forced to postpone his afternoon meeting with the president. A conference of paramount importance. Carl Kramer had placed himself in an embarrassing predicament with the last person in the world he wished to alienate. He couldn't afford to anger the new president, but Ellenwood had insisted he cancel the meeting. The deputy director was beginning to understand the twisted irony of politics.

Kramer sat opposite Ellenwood, crossing and uncrossing his legs, fidgeting. Why wasn't the air-conditioning working? Then he remembered it was October.

"When are you meeting with the president?" Ellenwood asked.

"In about an hour."

"What're you going to tell her?"

"Not a great deal more than she already knows."

Victor folded his arms across his chest and leaned back in the chair. "How long have you been working for me, Carl?"

"Eight years next month."

"Like your job?"

At first, he thought it was a rhetorical question, but Ellenwood's eyes demanded an answer. "I love it."

The DCI sat forward. "I've been considering early retirement, Carl. With my recommendation, you'd be a natural to step into this office. As long as you continue playing by the rules. You're not feeling those patriotic oats, are you, Mr. Kramer?"

Carl shook his head. "I don't follow, sir."

"The CIA enjoys a unique privilege. An exemption from conventional rules. That's why the department works so effectively. But I don't have to remind you of that, do I, Mr. Kramer? You know that confidentiality within the agency is gospel. I'd like to remind you of your priorities. You have a responsibility to the president, and I'd never ask you to compromise yourself. But your first loyalty is to the agency. Sometimes you have to make choices, Carl. Difficult choices."

Carl could feel perspiration trickling down his breast bone.

Ellenwood continued. "Before you advise the president of any new findings, be certain that I'm informed first."

"Sir, I'd never jeopardize the integrity of this office."

"Then we understand each other, Mr. Deputy Director?"

"Clearly, sir."

***

Kate sipped a cup of tea while waiting for Carl Kramer. She didn't know the DDCI well, but his first report card was looking grim. Yesterday, Kate'd postponed her meeting with Olivia Carter to meet with Kramer. But fifteen minutes before it was scheduled, Kramer canceled. Not the conduct she expected. Perhaps he didn't feel accountable to her? In the past, she'd witnessed the omnipotent arrogance of the CIA. If he dazzled her today, she'd give him the benefit of the doubt.

Emily knocked. "Carl Kramer is here."

The stocky DDCI entered the Oval Office and stood by the door at attention. The erectness of his body led Kate to believe that he'd been in the Marines before joining the CIA.

She stood and walked around her desk. "Good morning, Carl." She pointed to the chair.

Kramer had an awkward gait, more like an ape than a man. "Good morning, Madam President." He sat in front of her desk and maintained his rigid posture. She noticed his outdated suit and too-wide tie.

"I've been anticipating this meeting with great anxiety," Kate said. "Enlighten me, Carl." She sat behind her desk.

Kramer began to reiterate points she already knew: President Rodgers's blood pressure problem, his medication, the jellyfish poison, and facts that were merely public knowledge. She wanted to interrupt him but waited patiently. As he chattered on, Kate compulsively tidied her desk. Crooked lampshade. Stapler askew. Paper clips scattered about. She passively listened, noticing dots of perspiration beading on his forehead. Kramer talked so expressively with his hands he looked like a traffic cop at the Washington Monument.

He paused to take a breath.

"It's old news, Carl. I want to know *how* David Rodgers was poisoned and *who* did it."

The DDCI shook his head. "It wasn't from his food."

"How can you be sure?"

"When President Rodgers and Elizabeth sat down to dinner, the First Lady's steak was larger than the president's. So they *traded* dinner plates."

Her eyes widened. "So if the food had been poisoned, Elizabeth would have died?"

"Exactly."

"Then how, Carl?"

"Mrs. Rodgers doesn't drink, but the president had a glass of wine with dinner."

"I'm sure the wine was tested by the Secret Service," Kate said.

"It was an unopened bottle from his private stock."

"He had a private stock?"

Kramer nodded. "He had a thirty-five-bottle wine cooler with a selection of vintage wines he personally selected. The cooler was locked at all times, and only President Rodgers had a key."

Kate stood and walked around the desk. She folded her arms and sat on the corner. "Am I missing something? How did the assassin get into the locked cooler?"

"The cooler stores wine at about fifty-five degrees. This is to preserve the integrity of the wine. But red wines—like the one President Rodgers selected—should be drunk at room temperature."

"What does this all mean?" Kate asked.

"President Rodgers removed the wine from the cooler about two hours before dinner so it would be room temperature by the time Elizabeth and he sat down to dinner."

"So, anyone who had access to Rodgers's quarters could have tampered with the wine?"

"Exactly."

Kate thought about that for a minute. "That still doesn't explain how jellyfish poison got into an unopened bottle of wine."

"That puzzled me at first. Until I did some research. Most fine wines use foil to cover the cork, and the foil has two tiny pinholes. Three different vineyards verified that. They puncture the seal so the top of the cork can breathe. Otherwise, mold can grow."

"How could anyone tamper with a vineyard-sealed bottle of wine?"

"With a hypodermic needle. One puncture hole to remove some wine, another to inject the same amount of poison. No one would ever know that the wine was tampered with."

President Miles chewed on her cracked fingernail; her eyes darted around the room. "You said President Rodgers had one glass of wine?"

He nodded.

"What happened to the rest of it?"

"That's a mystery, Madam President. After President Rodgers's death, the FBI combed every inch of his private quarters. Every grain of sugar and salt, every drop of ketchup and mustard, anything edible from M&M's to balsamic vinegar was tested and retested for poison. Everything was clean."

"Everything except the missing bottle of wine." She analyzed his words for a moment. "Did you ask Elizabeth Rodgers about the wine?"

"After the president went to bed, she put the wine in the refrigerator."

"Then what the hell happened to it?"

"I wish I knew."

She recalled what McDermott had told her about the venom. What was Elizabeth doing while David died in agony?

"Did Elizabeth tell you what she was doing prior to discovering President Rodgers?"

"After he went to bed, she listened to Mozart on her iPod."

That *could* explain why she hadn't heard his cry for help. "What have you concluded, Mr. Kramer?"

"It was someone on the inside. Someone very close to the president."

"Any suspects, Carl?"

"Not at this time, Madam President. Members of the FBI and Secret Service thoroughly interviewed over fifty staff members, including ten people who had access to President Rodgers's private quarters. Each has been screened thoroughly, their integrity unquestionable."

"Evidently not, Mr. Kramer." The same ten people who served President Rodgers now served Kate. And one of them could, in fact, be the killer. She shuddered at the thought of an assassin wandering through her quarters with carefree privileges. But if each had survived the scrutiny of the FBI and Secret Service, what could she do, fire all of them? "How do you propose we proceed?"

"I don't want to spook you, Madam President, but the White House employs nearly five hundred staff members, and it's likely that one of them, at the least, knows something about the assassination. Our interviews are ongoing, but it's going to take a while to interview every one of them. In the meantime, the best we can do is to make certain you're not in harm's way."

They talked for a few more minutes. She asked if there was anything he needed. He thanked her and promised he'd solve the assassination mystery within the week. Just as he reached for the doorknob, she called his name.

"Where did the president get that bottle of wine?"

He didn't look at her. "It was a gift," he whispered. "A rare bottle of Penfolds Shiraz." He paused for a moment.

Kate could see stress lines on his forehead.

"Victor Ellenwood brought it back from his trip to Sydney."

Questions flooded her mind. She almost called him as he walked out the door but decided to give the DDCI a little slack. At least for now.

Kate sat at her desk for a few minutes, reflecting on Kramer's words. Victor Ellenwood wouldn't be stupid enough to give the former president a bottle of poisoned wine. Not without covering his tracks. But why would *Ellenwood* want to assassinate David in the first place? How could he benefit from President Rodgers's death? McDermott had told her that the jellyfish were found only in waters near the Philippines and off the coast of Australia. Ellenwood had recently vacationed in Australia. A coincidence? Could Ellenwood be more scheming than she'd thought? He wasn't nicknamed the Silver Fox for nothing. Not a jury in the country would deliver a murder conviction based on circumstantial evidence. The DCI gave the president a bottle of wine. So what? Who could prove it was poisoned? Without the bottle, it was merely speculation. Even if the bottle *were* recovered, how could it implicate *anybody*?

Kate Miles's brain felt like a maxed-out computer. One more byte of menacing information and her hard drive would surely crash.

Emily burst through the door.

She had never charged into the Oval Office without first knocking. She dashed toward the president as if she were power walking. Under her left arm, Emily carried what appeared to be a newspaper. She laid it across Kate's desk. Kate slipped on her reading glasses and glanced at the headlines.

Marital Trouble in the White House?

Kate looked up at Emily's chalk-white cheeks. "Please hold my calls for a few minutes."

Kate's face burned. Her hard drive had just crashed.

‑◄ ★ ►‑

CHAPTER EIGHT

To avoid postponing another meeting with Olivia Carter, Kate met with McDermott and Press Secretary Riley at seven a.m. She craved coffee this morning; her pounding temples warned her of an imminent migraine if she didn't feed her caffeine addiction soon.

As if the young woman could read Kate's mind, Emily knocked gently and peeked in the Oval Office. She walked in with a cup of coffee.

"You look like you could use a pick-me-up this morning." She set the cup on the corner of Kate's desk, resting it on the coaster. "Mr. McDermott and Mr. Riley are waiting to see you, Madam President."

McDermott and Riley entered and exchanged greetings with the president. They sat opposite her. McDermott laid his briefcase across his legs, flipped it open, and removed a manila folder. Riley crossed his legs and adjusted his tie.

In spite of her stomach's rampage, Kate sipped the piping-hot coffee, careful not to slurp. *Hazelnut. Thanks, Emily.*

The newspaper still sat on her desk. She pointed to the meddlesome headlines and fixed her stare on McDermott.

"Seen the paper?"

Riley said, "I've prepared a statement. Brief and to the point. It's imperative that you contest this rumor immediately."

McDermott opened the folder, removed a piece of paper, and handed it to the president. Kate laid it on top of the newspaper without looking at it.

"You both feel that I should refute a rumor that's true? What does that say about my credibility?"

McDermott said, "If it had been a trashy tabloid, I'd advise you to ignore it. But people believe the *Post.*"

She picked up the one-page statement and scanned it. "Trying to win the Pulitzer Prize for fiction, Mr. Riley?" She crumpled it in a ball and tossed it in the pail beside her desk.

McDermott sat forward. "You haven't done anything formal. Why not gloss it over? The public doesn't need to know every time Peter and you have a little quarrel."

"They don't need to be lied to, either," Kate insisted. "If Peter and I officially separate, I'll make a statement. But I refuse to stand in front of two hundred and fifty million people and recite a bald-faced lie." She *had* urged Peter to keep their separation confidential, and in a broad sense, Kate felt that she'd withheld the truth from the public. But to consciously lie to the world was quite another story. She didn't have time or the patience to debate an issue on which her position was immutable.

"Unless there's something else, Mr. Riley, you may be excused."

Riley couldn't leave the office quickly enough.

Kate stood and folded her arms across her chest. "How do you suppose the *Washington Post* got this information?"

McDermott's ears turned scarlet red. "I have no idea, Madam President."

"Only Peter and you had knowledge of this."

"I can't speak for your husband, but I did *not* breathe a word of this to anyone. I would never, under any circumstances, betray your confidence."

"I'm sorry if my query sounds like an accusation."

"As a matter of fact, it does."

"Don't get all indignant with me, Charles. I merely asked a straightforward question."

McDermott looked like a rabid dog. "If you doubt my loyalty, Madam President, perhaps I should…" He blinked nervously.

"Resign?" Her eyes studied him critically. "That's a bit extreme, Charles. Are you going to overreact every time we have a little spat? What the hell happened to the Charles McDermott with the titanium backbone?"

"I'm afraid he's a little stressed out."

"What's troubling you?"

"Frankly, Madam President, when I try to advise you, you either disregard my recommendations or bite my head off."

For several days, Kate had not been a pillar of patience and was more aware of this than McDermott realized.

"If I've been a bit too ferocious lately, try to be tolerant of me, Charles. Can you possibly imagine what my life is like? David Rodgers has been murdered, Peter left, and Walter Owens is not making my transition easy. To top it off, I'm living on Excedrin and Tagamet." Her throat knotted up, and she took a deep breath. "I'm not attacking *you*, Charles. I'm venting my frustrations, and you're usually the closest target."

"I'll try to keep that in mind." His eyes were still burning a hole through her.

"Have I created ill feelings? We can't have bad blood between us," Kate said.

"Maybe I've been a touch sensitive myself lately."

"If I didn't trust you implicitly, you wouldn't be my chief of staff."

"I'll accept that as a compliment."

She shook his hand and noticed that he had difficulty looking in her eyes. "Are we OK, Charles?"

"We're fine, Madam President."

***

Under the name William Thompson, twenty-two-year-old Guenther Krause used his phony driver's license and Visa card to rent a car at the airport. As instructed, he checked in at the Ambassador Hotel two miles from Georgetown University. To his delight, many students were sporting radical hairdos—some heads completely shaved—making Guenther's buzz cut less conspicuous. He preferred wearing military attire—mid-calf black boots, fatigues, camouflage shirt—but he was dressed in baggy jeans and an oversized sweatshirt to blend in with other students.

After hours of pacing the floor of the cramped hotel room, Guenther sat on the bed. He could feel his body sink into the worn mattress. If it sagged any lower, he thought, his ass would touch the floor. Of all the fancy hotels in DC, why had his brothers put him up in such a second-rate joint? He glared at the telephone. Why hadn't his Washington brothers called him with further instructions? He hated waiting. The Whopper he'd bought at the airport Burger King was cold, but he bit into it anyway to quiet his gurgling stomach. He wiped his sleeve across his mouth. Having nothing to do but think, Guenther tried to envision what the capitalist-pig journalists might write about him. At first, he anticipated mass hysteria. They would call him a monster, a lunatic, proclaim him to be a crazed terrorist. But eventually they'd understand. Guenther Erich Krause would galvanize his name in history books as a great liberator of the chosen race, a man courageous enough to sacrifice his life for his beliefs. Guenther was young and idealistic, but not naive. He knew in his heart that this was a suicide mission. But life on Earth was insignificant.

That his brothers had chosen him for this divine vocation would dignify him with the highest reward: sainthood beside his Aryan god. None of his blood brothers, not even Jakob Hoffman, would die for their beliefs. They *talked* about loyalty, honor, commitment, but Guenther would prove his patriotism in the most profound way. He'd never see his brothers again. But when they cheered his name, knelt before his photograph, praised and venerated him, Guenther Krause, exalted nationalist, would enjoy the celebration from another world. His fate had taken a higher path.

Guenther set the half-eaten burger on the bed. He looked at the picture hanging on the wall above the dresser. A white farmhouse with black shutters. A windmill. Horses grazing. A serene country setting. Familiar. His father had decided to leave Frankfurt, Germany, when Guenther was barely a toddler. Why his father had chosen to move to a backwoods town in the Alabama countryside, Guenther would never understand. But then again, when had his father ever made a decision that made sense?

His index finger traced along his belly, gently outlining the circular scars. The edges were still coarse and bumpy. When he closed his eyes, he could see the broken-down farm, the dilapidated furniture, his father's crazed look. Guenther could almost hear his pathetic childhood screams, smell his father's burning cigar. There was something peculiar about sizzling flesh. It didn't smell like grilled burgers or pork chops. Human flesh had a sickening-sweet stench. It was an odor that had heaved vomit into Guenther's throat many times. Guenther Krause was well acquainted with the vile smell of burning skin. He remembered the last time his father had played the game.

***

Guenther had just gotten home from school. He sat in the living room next to his younger brother watching Animal Planet. He'd always been fascinated with whales and dolphins. Today, he watched a special on orcas. Guenther was about to grab the last Oreo cookie and pop it in his mouth, but he could see the disappointed look on his brother's face. Oreos were Derrick's favorite. Guenther pointed to the plastic dish.

"Want the last one?"

The ten-year-old boy nodded vigorously, stuffed the cookie in his mouth, and gulped the last mouthful of milk.

About to run to the kitchen and see what else he could snack on, Guenther heard a car pull in the driveway, a door slam. He glanced at the wall clock above the TV. Three fifteen. Too early for either of his parents to be home from work. He peeked out the window and saw his father, obviously drunk, stumbling toward the front porch. Guenther knew exactly what his early arrival meant. In a panic, he placed his hands on top of Derrick's shoulders.

"Listen to me," Guenther ordered. "Get your ass up to your room and hide in the closet until I come get you."

"Why?"

"Dad's home, and he's drunk."

Familiar with his father's behavior when he overindulged, Derrick complied and disappeared up the stairway.

Jurgen Krause walked in the front door and slammed it hard. He staggered toward Guenther and plopped on the couch next to his son, grasped his knee with a viselike grip, and dug his fingernails into the boy's skin. Guenther fiercely chewed his lip but knew better than to make a sound.

"Where's Derrick?"

Guenther knew all too well why he wanted his brother. It was Derrick's turn to play Jurgen's twisted game. Guenther couldn't let that happen.

"I'm guessing he's still at school."

"I don't believe you."

"I ain't lyin'. He had to make up some kinda test."

Jurgen wiped his nose on his shirtsleeve. "Then I guess you'll have to take his place. Or you can tell me where he really is and spare yourself a whole lot of pain."

Guenther sat silently. He guessed that, under the circumstances, his father would have an extra-special treat for him today. But he had to protect his brother.

Jurgen weaved his way to the kitchen, steadying his wobbly body with outstretched arms. He filled the plastic pitcher to the top. Two quarts of warm water. As he negotiated his way back to the living room, he held the container close to his body as if he were carrying a priceless vase. He handed the pitcher to Guenther without saying a word. Twelve-year-old Guenther knew the routine. He had to drink it all. Without leaving a drop.

He gulped more than half the pitcher quickly; the last pint was always the toughest. After two minutes, Guenther slurped the last of the water, and his stomach felt like he'd swallowed a beach ball. Jurgen snatched the pitcher away from Guenther, turned it upside down, and shook it. Three or four drops dribbled out of the opening and dripped on the carpeting.

Jurgen's face twisted into a monster mask. "I teach you to be a man." He grasped a handful of Guenther's hair and violently yanked him off the couch. "When your *vater* says drink it all, he *means* drink it all!"

The first punch hammered Guenther's left kidney, the second walloped his right. Guenther's lungs drained of air, but he didn't utter a sound. Jurgen snapped Guenther's head from side to side and repeatedly pummeled his son's kidneys. With each punch, Guenther could feel urine squirt in his underwear. He released Guenther's hair, and the boy collapsed to the floor.

Jurgen pointed to the wall. "Get up, *huhn!*" His father always called Guenther a chicken.

He had pounded Guenther's kidneys before, but today, as Guenther staggered to the corner, he felt light-headed and nauseous, terrified he'd pass out. He tried not to think about what his enraged father might do if he lost consciousness. As instructed, Guenther stood in the corner of the living room, next to the black-and-white console TV. He tried to stand upright, but his lower back felt as if it were broken.

The one time Guenther miraculously managed to hold his pee for the full hour, Jurgen had hugged him and praised his son as a great *soldat*. But not today. Something was terribly wrong; his kidneys were on fire. For the first fifteen minutes, it was barely tolerable. Guenther pressed his inner thighs together and held his penis. But then the dance began. The boy's efficient kidneys processed the excess liquid his body couldn't absorb, and his small bladder overfilled. He doubled over in excruciating pain.

Jurgen stomped over to Guenther. He poked his index finger in Guenther's chest.

"Maybe now you will tell me where your brother is."

Guenther could barely speak. "At school," he whispered.

His answer infuriated Jurgen. "You hold your pee until I tell you!"

For eight minutes, Guenther was folded in half in fierce agony. It felt like someone had shoved a garden hose inside him and turned it on full blast. When Guenther had failed in the past, his father would grab a fistful of his hair and slap Guenther's face bloody.

He'd yell at him with violent rage, his eyes bulging monstrously, and call Guenther a *huhn*. Then that maniacal smile would cross Jurgen's face. He'd light his Dutch Master's cigar and puff clouds of blue smoke until the tip was as red as a brake light. He'd make Guenther lie on the couch. With one hand, Jurgen would grasp Guenther's wrists and hold them securely. He'd puff his cigar red hot and twist the burning end into Guenther's stomach and back. Guttural screams echoed from Guenther. But Jurgen hadn't ended the game quickly. He'd relight the cigar again and again, until he was satisfied his son had learned a lesson about discipline. Guenther couldn't even imagine what was coming today.

As he stood in the corner, Guenther's bladder let loose. He could feel the urine soaking his pants and hear it puddling on the wooden floor. But something unusual happened. Jurgen looked at him with a gaping stare, but he didn't charge toward him as he'd done a dozen times before. No bloody face. No cigar twisting in his belly. Instead, his father dashed out the front door as if the house were on fire. Guenther guessed that his father was on his way to school, looking for Derrick. But then Guenther looked at the puddle forming around his sneakers. His urine was as red as beet juice.

That was the day Guenther Krause decided to kill his father. Before Jurgen Krause killed him—and his younger brother.

***

Kate heard a gentle knock on the Oval Office door, and Olivia Carter peeked inside. The svelte young woman, trim yet shapely, almost flowed into the office. Olivia was always a smart dresser, and Kate admired her perfectly tailored business suit.

"Hope you haven't been waiting too long," Kate said. "It's been like Georgetown Plaza on Christmas Eve around here. Sorry I had to cancel yesterday."

Olivia sat down and adjusted her glasses. "It's not necessary to apologize, Madam President. I know how terribly busy you are."

For an instant, Kate forgot why Olivia was here. Then she remembered that the young woman wanted to discuss PR strategies, which at this particular time, and all things considered, seemed appropriate. "Tell me something that will lift my spirits, Olivia. I feel as though I've spent the last few days with the Prince of Darkness."

The young woman glanced past Kate and peered out the window. It looked like she was organizing her thoughts, but her eyes were distant. "I'm quite uncomfortable with what I have to say."

"Don't worry. The Oval Office hasn't been bugged since the Nixon years."

Olivia's shoulders rolled forward, and she folded her hands on her lap. "I hear a lot of scuttlebutt, Madam President." Her voice tightened. "Most of it I take with a grain of salt." She pushed her hair behind her ears. "Sometimes...I don't."

Kate gave her a long, searching look.

"Can I ask you a direct question?" Olivia said.

Kate didn't have time to answer.

"Are you going to resign?"

It felt like a punch in the solar plexus. Kate recalled her dream. "Why would you ask such a question?"

Olivia wiggled in the chair. Her voice dropped to a whisper. "Victor Ellenwood was talking to one of his agents the other day. I picked up bits and pieces of the conversation. I heard your name and the word *resignation*."

Kate could barely suppress her anger. "And who was Victor talking to?"

"Agent Jack Miller."

She didn't know him, but there were dozens of agents she'd never met. "The higher you climb the political ladder, Olivia, the greater the speculation."

"Is it a rumor, Madam President?"

Kate's recent conversation with Peter replayed in her mind. It now seemed obvious that Peter wasn't the only one who wanted her out of the White House. "Do you think I'd let another *man* into the Oval Office without a fight? This is the beginning of an era."

The sparkle returned to Olivia's voice. "I can't tell you how relieved I am to hear that. I believe in you, Madam President. I'm on your team one hundred and ten percent."

Kate did not doubt Olivia's loyalty, but at this particular moment, the young woman's commendation was overshadowed by Kate's fierce anger. She wanted to politely excuse herself, march into Ellenwood's office, and wring his neck. But now was not the time.

"I've given your objectives careful consideration," Olivia said, her face still beaming. "I'd like to share some strategies with you."

"I'd love to hear them, but first, let me run something by you." Kate paused for a long moment. "You've seen the headlines in the *Post*?"

Olivia nodded.

"Both Charles McDermott and William Riley have advised me to make a rebuttal statement. Any thoughts on that, Olivia?"

"The article was pure speculation, Madam President. They did not identify one credible source. My advice, let it run its course. In a few days, another sensational rumor will capture the spotlight."

"Unfortunately, it's not a rumor."

Olivia didn't look as surprised as Kate had anticipated. "Pardon my intrusion, but may I ask if you are pursuing a legal separation?"

"It's more of an unofficial parting. Peter needs a little space, and Topeka's where he thinks he'll find it."

"Then I advise you to ignore it. It's not unusual for a president to be separated from a spouse from time to time. Eleanor Roosevelt, Mamie Eisenhower, Betty Ford—to name a few—had very active calendars. They were often separated from their husbands for extended periods. And it barely raised an eyebrow."

Kate liked this spunky young woman. "I appreciate your honest feedback, Olivia." Kate pondered for a few moments. "Now, tell me about your strategies."

Olivia opened her briefcase, shuffled her notes, and nervously adjusted her glasses.

"Many of your roadblocks are much the same as they were for President Rodgers. But your gender, unfortunately, adds a little twist. Congress is the central problem. As an Independent, you do not have the clout or the political leverage to achieve nonpartisan support. Your most powerful tool is virtually useless. If you veto a bill, Madam President, it will probably sail through Congress anyway. Those you introduce are going to be killed."

This was not a revelation to Kate, of course, but she hoped that Olivia had discovered an innovative way around conventional politics. "You're painting a grim picture, Olivia."

"It gets worse. You probably weren't aware of this, but President Rodgers postponed introducing your Healing of America bills with good reason. He was terrified he'd be publicly humiliated. He'd been forewarned that the bills would die in record time."

Kate recalled Walter Owens's arrogant warning. "I wasn't aware of that." Why hadn't David been honest with her?

"President Rodgers didn't want to tell you because he hoped he'd find a way to influence Congress through the back door. Unfortunately, fate got in the way."

"Is there an upside?" Kate asked.

Olivia's eyes looked like a child's on Christmas morning. "If it weren't for your popularity with women voters, David Rodgers never would have been elected president. *You* won the election." Olivia searched her notes. "Recent polls indicate that you have an amazing sixty-seven percent approval rating among women and thirty-nine percent with men. These voters represent the back door you're looking for, Madam President."

"I don't think I follow you."

"How do you feel voters would react to the Healing of America bills?"

"Any with a grain of common sense would recognize the overall benefits to the country."

"Perhaps it's time for you to do what FDR did. Directly appeal to the people who elected you. Expose their oppressors. Tell your voters that a stubborn, myopic Congress refuses to consider legislation that can dramatically affect the social and economic posture of the country and improve their quality of life. Encourage them to write to their representatives. There's strength in numbers, and your strength can come from the voters."

"What you're saying makes sense from an idealistic perspective, but wouldn't I alienate Congress even more?"

"Take off the gloves, Madam President. Go a few rounds with bare knuckles. Show these pompous asses what you're made of."

Kate reflected on her suggestion for a long time. Was the young strategist correct? Perhaps so, but there remained an unspoken roadblock. Was Kate persuasive and evocative enough to arouse and activate apathetic Americans? Could she stand toe-to-toe with Congress and win over voters?

Kate glanced at her watch. Her hurried schedule forced her to cut their meeting short. "I really hate to rush you off, but I've got another meeting in five minutes. Albert Cranston's going to detail the security plan for my Georgetown lecture next week."

"Georgetown *University*?" Olivia almost shouted.

"You sound surprised."

"It's one of the most conservative universities on the East Coast." Olivia smiled. "But I guess when you're the president—regardless of your agenda—speaking engagements are abundant."

"At first, I turned them down. But Vice President Owens is an alumnus, so I figured it wouldn't be the worst thing in the world to keep my VP happy."

***

Charles McDermott found a rare few minutes of quiet time, so he loosened his tie and sprawled out on the leather sofa in his office. He couldn't stop thinking about the historic events over the last few weeks and the first time he'd met David Rodgers.

McDermott had been amazed when David Rodgers had announced his candidacy for president as an Independent. But he wasn't shocked when Rodgers contacted him. Harvard had never produced a political strategist like McDermott. A long list of successful politicians could attest to his credentials. He remembered the evening David Rodgers had won the presidency.

It was November 5, at ten forty-eight p.m., eastern standard time, when ABC News projected that David Joel Rodgers would be the next president of the United States. The penthouse apartment on the sixteenth floor of the Ritz-Carlton rocked with celebration. Champagne corks popped as if it were midnight on

New Year's Eve. David Rodgers embraced and kissed his wife, Elizabeth, then he congratulated Kate and Peter Miles. McDermott was standing by the window, melancholy, absorbed with private thoughts. There was a drawback to winning an election, especially when the odds were beyond computation. For Charles McDermott, the high was like a phenomenal orgasm. When it was over, though, a haunting fear that he'd never again achieve such an intense fulfillment haunted his thoughts. Winning the presidential election as an Independent—a benchmark in history—eclipsed any hope of greater euphoria. What the hell would McDermott do now to one-up this event?

Rodgers grasped McDermott's hand and pumped his arm vigorously. "Well, Charles, we did it. You are a fucking genius! So what's next for you?"

"It'll take a month for me to unwind. Thinking about the South Pacific. Then I guess I'll sign up for unemployment."

Rodgers reached inside his jacket, removed an envelope, and handed it to McDermott.

McDermott tore the end and looked at the cashier's check. A spurt of adrenaline coursed through his veins. "We agreed on a million."

"Consider it an advance."

McDermott examined the check again to be sure the number hadn't changed. "Am I missing something?"

"You'd make a hell of a chief of staff. Why don't you join me in Washington?"

***

Guenther drove the rented Chevy Malibu to the Georgetown campus. As he'd been told, a parklike area with wooden benches and manicured grounds bordered the front of the library. He parked in the visitor's lot and sat in the car for a few minutes, observing herds of students scurrying in every direction.

He made his way to the center bench facing the library and adjusted his Redskins cap. A light mist hung in the air. Gusty wind whirled multicolored leaves across the grass. The sun winked through the gray sky.

He waited.

A man sat next to him. Guenther fixed his eyes on the maple tree across the sidewalk. The man smelled like a damp basement.

The man said, "Nice day for a white wedding."

"Yes it is," Guenther responded.

The man pushed a small brown package against Guenther's thigh. He picked it up and set it on his lap. He turned to look at the mysterious person and watched as he scuffed away.

Guenther rushed back to the hotel room. When he tore open the box and saw the chrome Colt .45, it was like staring into bright sunlight. His eyes burned with memories.

He had killed his father with a similar Colt .45. Shot the bastard six times. Twice in the face and two times in each kidney. Without feeling an ounce of remorse, not a hint of self-reproach, Guenther had watched his father's bleeding body twitch and convulse, and the thrill was so intense that he wished he could kill him again.

The juvenile courts ordered a thorough psychological evaluation. Dr. Wagner determined that he was a deeply disturbed young man. An abused child. Big surprise.

Guenther wondered why they needed a shrink to figure out he was fucked up. He was confined to the Maplewood Institution for criminal teenage boys. The abuse didn't stop. Older inmates had their way with him more than once. But it was better than having his belly branded with Dutch Master's cigars. Better than a two-hundred-pound dickhead pummeling his piss-filled kidneys. Most important, he had spared his brother, Derrick, from further physical and emotional abuse.

Guenther met his first true friend at Maplewood. Wilbert Altbusser explained the ways of the twisted world to Guenther. White America had become infested with blood-sucking, welfare-stealing, lazy bums. But an elite group of Aryan whites, descendants of Adolf Hitler, saviors of the master race, would terminate the epidemic of inferior ones.

When Guenther Krause completed his five-year incarceration at Maplewood, Altbusser sponsored his membership into the Disciples of the Third Reich.

As his fingers caressed the handle of the Colt .45, Guenther Krause smiled for the first time since leaving New York. He pressed the release button and the ammunition clip fell out of the handle and bounced on the bed. He picked it up, flicked out a bullet, held the hollow point between his thumb and index finger, and examined it adoringly. He kissed the end of it and felt inexplicably aroused. A feeling almost as intense as when he'd killed his father.

CHAPTER NINE

Kate's emotions teetered between joy and vexation. It was the same feeling she'd experienced dozens of times as a child while anxiously awaiting her father's return from a business trip. It had always been a bittersweet reunion. Part of her loved him unconditionally and cherished every moment they shared. But she could not suppress the anger or resentment she felt for all the lonely nights she had cried herself to sleep.

Since taking the oath of office more than two weeks ago, she'd spoken with her father on the telephone several times but hadn't seen him. Hoping to spend as much time with him as her hectic schedule allowed, Kate had made arrangements for her father to stay in one of the guest suites on the third floor. Except for her urgent early morning breakfast meeting, Emily had cleared Kate's calendar for the day. She could barely imagine an entire day without endless meetings on everything from policy to protocol.

While sitting in the formal dining room casually eating breakfast, Charles McDermott, Secretary of State Toni Mitchell, and Secretary of Defense Richard Alderson briefed Kate on the latest developments in the Middle East.

"Our deepest fear may be coming to fruition, Madam President," Alderson said.

"Iran is up to no good. President Ahmadinejad deployed a massive platoon—our sources estimate ten thousand—and an arsenal of artillery into Jordan. They're assembled about twenty miles from the Israeli border. Given the fact that the Iranian president has stated more than once that Israel should be wiped off the face of the Earth, I think there's good reason for us to be alarmed."

Kate dropped the rye toast on her plate. "Is there conflict with Jordan?"

"No, Madam President," Alderson said. He looked at McDermott with his deep-set eyes.

McDermott set down his fork and swiped the linen napkin across his mouth. "The Israeli ambassador has informed us— quite candidly, I might add—that further movement toward their border will be interpreted as a hostile act."

Kate gripped the armrests and leaned forward. "What exactly does that mean, Charles?"

"The Israeli Air Force is standing by on full alert."

It was the last thing Kate wanted to hear this morning. She filled her mouth with Mint Medley herbal tea; her stomach was in no mood for coffee. "Why would King Abdullah allow Iranian troops into Jordan?"

"We've tried to contact the Jordanian ambassador to ask him that very question," Alderson said, "but he can't be reached."

McDermott rested his elbows on the table and folded his hands. "It would be appropriate to call an emergency meeting of the Joint Chiefs."

Kate glanced at Alderson. "Do you agree, Richard?"

The fifty-five-year-old retired Army colonel nodded. "The situation is volatile, Madam President. We need to take immediate action. Historically, Jordan has remained neutral during conflicts between Israel and other Middle Eastern countries. But since King Hussein's death in '99, his son, Abdullah, has not demonstrated the same peace-keeping qualities as his father."

Kate looked at her toast and decided she wasn't hungry. "How quickly can we convene the Joint Chiefs?"

"By the end of the day," Alderson said.

"We should contact King Abdullah," Toni Mitchell said. "Maybe send a representative to Jordan?"

"Richard," Kate said, "make arrangements to fly to Jordan. Track down King Abdullah. Find out what the hell's going on. In the meantime, Charles, alert the Joint Chiefs. Schedule a meeting for first thing tomorrow morning. And, Toni, try to reach Prime Minister Netanyahu. We don't need the Israeli Air Force dropping bombs on their neighbors." She thought for a moment. "What's the Iranian ambassador's name?"

"Ahmad Habib," McDermott said. "A real seedy character."

"Has anyone been in contact with him?" Kate asked.

Alderson shook his head. "No, Madam President."

"Ask him to fly to Washington." Kate said.

McDermott and Alderson eyed each other.

Alderson said, "No Iranian has set foot on Washington soil for over a decade."

"I want to change that policy," Kate said. "Invite him to the White House."

"It's a waste of time," Alderson said.

Kate glared at him.

Toni Mitchell sat forward and cleared her throat. "Madam President, Middle Eastern culture defines a woman's role in society as completely subservient. Ambassador Habib will regard your invitation as an insult."

Kate didn't need a history lesson in Middle Eastern culture. Did the secretary of state think she was *that* naive? "Perhaps it's not a coincidence that this offensive began shortly after I became president."

Alderson said, "It's possible that Ahmadinejad wishes to test your resolve, Madam President."

McDermott nodded. "I agree."

"Contact Ambassador Habib, Toni. Ask him in the most emphatic terms to come to Washington. Don't take no for an answer."

"I'll give it my best," Mitchell said.

"Give it more than your best." Kate's face hardened. "Tell Mr. Habib that the future of his country may be in jeopardy."

Alderson and Mitchell left the room, but McDermott remained.

"What's on your mind, Charles?"

"If Habib does come to Washington, are you personally going to meet with him?"

"That's my plan."

"With all due respect, Madam President, you should not be directly involved in any negotiations at this level. Alderson and Mitchell should handle it."

"So when do you suggest I get involved, when Iran and Israel are engaged in an all-out war?"

"All I'm saying is that you have a well-qualified staff and they—"

"I appreciate and respect your advice, Charles. But maybe the reason we're in this situation is because, historically, past presidents weren't involved in a crisis soon enough. I intend to change that." Her eyes met his, and she could see a wounded look. Once again, she ignored his advice. Maybe it was time for her to reconsider her resolve. What benefit did she gain from her advisors if she never followed their advice?

***

Escorted by two Secret Service agents, Trevor Williams walked in the front door of the Presidential Suite. Kate was standing in the foyer waiting. Cordially nodding their heads to the president, the agents left with Trevor's luggage. Kate's father greeted her with a firm embrace. He rubbed her back and pressed his lips to her cheek. His burlap-like skin was rough against her face, but she didn't care. Kate hadn't been held like this for an eternity. She closed her eyes and enjoyed the closeness. For a moment, she thought of Peter. The familiar smell of Old Spice awakened her memories. Trevor stood back and grasped Kate's upper arms with both hands, appraising her thoroughly, like a critic examining fine art.

"Let me look at you," he said. He studied her face. "You're not sleeping well, are you?"

His uncanny perception never ceased to amaze her. "There are lots of things to toss and turn about, Daddy."

They went into the study, a small room off the Oval Parlor, and sat next to each other on the Victorian sofa. He held her hand loosely. There were many things she wanted to discuss with him but could not disclose anything that would compromise the confidentiality of the presidency. It was an unsettling feeling, as if her silence betrayed him, insulted his integrity. The words hung in the back of Kate's throat. She'd always been free to share everything with him. She'd shared her most intimate secrets, yet she couldn't talk about the Middle East or President Rodgers's assassination or anything that might breech her oath of office.

"Where's Peter?" he asked.

The question caught Kate completely off guard. "He had some important business back in Kansas." That's all Kate wanted him to know at this time and hoped he'd let it go.

"How are you adjusting to the White House?" he asked.

"When my term is completed, I'll be a qualified firefighter. As soon as I extinguish one blaze, two more ignite."

"Maybe you could use a good hook-and-ladder man."

It sounded like a riddle.

"How would you feel about me getting an apartment close to DC? Maybe Virginia or Maryland."

"Are you talking about selling the *ranch*?"

"Heavens no, my dear. This would be a place for me to hang my hat once or twice a month with hopes that a lonely father might get to see his daughter now and then." He grinned. "I know that you have more important priorities, so I won't set my expectations too high. Ten minutes here, twenty minutes there. Maybe dinner once in a while. Just as long as I can see you when it's convenient."

There was nothing he could have said that would have blind-sided her more. She teetered between disbelief and excitement. "But what about the ranch? Who will tend to the horses and stay on top of the maintenance?"

"Well, I'm sure that Maria will find ways to keep busy. And I know at least a dozen people who would be willing to take care of the horses."

"Are you sure this is something you really want to do?"

"Only if you're on board one hundred percent. If you think it's a bad idea, just say so. It won't hurt my feelings. Honest."

Kate's only hesitation was knowing that her insane schedule might make their visits few and far between. "I'd love for you to be closer to DC occasionally, but—"

"You don't even have to say it, Kate. I know that I'll be on the bottom of a long list of priorities. I won't be offended if running the country takes precedence over spending time with me."

Kate realized that a backlash resulting from this decision was inevitable. All her critics, no doubt, would make the case that she was so insecure she needed her daddy close by. Well, maybe that was the case. But had she ever made a decision that wasn't heavily scrutinized—even how she styled her hair? There was no way for the president to please everyone. It was an occupational hazard.

"How soon would you want to make this happen?"

"I can start looking for an apartment right away."

Kate smiled. "I'm looking forward to having you close by, Daddy."

***

Kate spent the day with her father. She tried to insulate herself from politics, but distractions were everywhere. It wasn't like visiting him at the White Stallion Ranch. She couldn't fill her lungs with the fresh country air or purge her mind of worldly tasks. Her eyes couldn't marvel at the acres of virgin soil. And she wasn't able to saddle up Breezy and ride to her heart's content. No sugar maples swaying gently to autumn breezes or picturesque landscapes or choirs of starlings. Only buildings and monuments and carbon monoxide and assassins.

As she guided him on a private tour of the White House, she could feel the walls closing in, every square inch a sobering reminder of her supreme responsibilities—none of which she could share with him.

Kate and Trevor were standing in the China Room in front of the enclosed curio, admiring the china used by Franklin Roosevelt.

"Would you like to go out to dinner, Daddy?"

"Can you do that sort of thing?"

"I'm the president. I can do almost anything."

She contacted Director of Secret Service Albert Cranston and asked him to make arrangements for them to dine at Café La Fleur. Cranston, pointing out that her request to dine out was highly unusual, tried to talk her out of it, but in spite of his noble efforts, she exercised her executive authority and vetoed his appeal.

***

Two limos pulled up to the main door of the White House—one for Kate and her father, the other for Secret Service agents. As she waited for an agent to open the limo door, the see-your-breath air nipped Kate's cheeks. She bent into the limo, curiously aware of the wiper blades slapping across the windshield. That was one of the peculiar things about Washington's weather, she thought. At times, the humidity was so thick it required that you turn on the windshield wipers even though it wasn't raining. Tonight, the air was heavy with moisture. She knew this was not destined to be the intimate evening she'd hoped for, but at least her father and she could spend some time away from her prison.

They drove east on Constitution Avenue, past the National Museum of American History, the IRS building, the Department of Justice, the Federal Trade Commission. The limo turned onto Seventh Street and drove through the greenery of the Mall, an area once decaying with railroad yards and warehouses in disrepair. Now the Mall was gleaming with congressional office buildings and the magnificent Union Station. Kate glanced out the smoked-glass window. It was still early enough for tourists to be wandering the streets and gathering around historic buildings, memorials, and monuments. She watched joggers and cyclists, even a few brave Rollerbladers who seemed impervious to the damp air.

The ride was hauntingly quiet.

When they reached Café La Fleur, Kate and Trevor remained in their limo while the agents in the other vehicle piled out and went into the restaurant. After several minutes, the driver opened the rear door, and two agents escorted them in. Kate and Trevor were led to a private dining room in the back of Café La Fleur and were seated at an elegantly set table big enough for eight people. There were fresh flowers everywhere. The table was set with exquisite crystal, purple linen napkins with gold bands, and a white lace tablecloth.

While they dined, Kate was careful not to speak too loudly. The Secret Service agents hovered like vultures, most within earshot. The last thing she needed was more speculation about her personal life.

"I don't think I've ever seen you so uptight." Her father cut his steak and placed a generous piece in his mouth.

"That's because I've never been the president of the United States." She'd wanted to lecture him about cholesterol when he'd ordered the beef, but Kansas ranchers were rather set in their ways.

The Secret Service had checked the wine, but still Kate was not sure she could enjoy it without thinking about David Rodgers. She filled her mouth with the '85 Mondavi Reserve, allowing it to awaken her taste buds. The magnificent Cabernet was bold and full-bodied. Wild berries and currant exploded in her mouth. Kate hadn't forgotten Carl Kramer's supposition, but for how long could she deprive herself of life's simple pleasures? She swallowed the wine with less difficulty than she'd anticipated. The long finish was opulent with flavor.

Trevor set his knife and fork on the table. "I've spent the entire day with you, yet I feel as though we haven't been together. Anything you want to talk about?"

You have no idea, she thought. "Peter doesn't think I belong in Washington."

Trevor had never approved of Peter, and Kate knew that her comment would create more ill feelings. But why should she protect her estranged husband?

"Is that Peter's observation or yours?"

The question struck a sensitive chord. A week ago, the answer would have come without a conscious thought, but today, Kate was plagued with doubts. "I'm having a difficult time distinguishing the good guys from the bad. It seems there are only a handful of people I can trust."

"Congratulations. I wish I'd had just one supporter when I was running Global Transportation for David. When you're the top dog, everybody's trying to get a piece of you. Ambitious people have little regard for loyalty, especially if they can profit from your downfall. Be warned: if the reward is substantial, even your most trusted confidant can be seduced by ambition. Don't drive yourself crazy trying to figure it out. Loyalty comes from strength. Strength comes from wise decisions."

"I find myself overanalyzing situations to the point of confusion. I even ignore the advice of my top advisors."

"Let your sixth sense guide you, honey. You've always had keen insights. Listen to your advisors. But ultimately, you must go with your gut instincts." He reached across the table and laid his hand on top of hers. "When you were governor, you fostered bold legislation. You went against the grain and fought for what you believed in. Because of your determination, Kansas is now a more prosperous state. You have the ability to make sound decisions. You've proven that. You've done it in the past, and you need to do it here in Washington. Don't ignore your intuition, Kate. It's your most powerful ally."

She glanced at the adjacent table. Two Secret Service agents were staring at them as if trying to read their lips. She lowered her voice. "I got into the Oval Office by default, Daddy."

"David didn't win the election alone. You were instrumental in that victory. Don't you think that most voters considered what would happen if the president couldn't complete his term? They elected *you* just as much as him. Stop second-guessing yourself, and take the bull by the horns." He leaned toward her, almost whispering in her ear. "Show these city slickers that a Kansas farm girl is someone to be reckoned with."

***

Hoping to soothe her knotted lower back and minimize her restlessness, Kate decided to take a bath before going to bed. As much as she loved seeing her father, spending the day with him brought back harsh memories of her childhood. She removed her clothes, gathered her hair on top of her head and secured it with a hair clip. Before submerging her body, Kate stood naked in front of the full-length mirror. She turned from side to side, appraising her figure. Except for her left breast, Kate was quite pleased with her reflection. Even without a husband or swarms of men fluttering about like bees over flowers, she still felt attractive. But for how long could she defy the aging process?

Kate eased her body into the hot, steamy water and rested her head against the back of the tub. Soaking a washcloth, she squeezed out the excess water and covered her face with it. In spite of having her father here in Washington and spending hours and hours with staff members and colleagues, the beast from her childhood had found her again. Would she ever elude this demon of loneliness? She now understood what Peter'd meant when he'd talked about Topeka, their friends, the kind of life they'd enjoyed. An eerie emptiness enveloped her. She felt like a fragile ceramic figurine—polished exterior, but hollow inside. One careless jolt and she'd break into a million jagged pieces. It was time for her to reevaluate her political career and her marriage. For once, maybe she'd listen to her common sense instead of her heart. Now was not the right time to think about such issues. She had more pressing business to deal with. She left her quarters and headed for the Situation Room.

***

The National Security Council consisted of four members: the president, vice president, secretary of state, and secretary of defense. Their advisors—the Joint Chiefs of Staff—were six members of the armed forces: four generals and two admirals. All members were present in the Situation Room. Kate sat silently as Secretary of Defense Alderson briefed the esteemed group on the recent developments in the Middle East. She studied their eyes, searching for any hint of what they might be thinking. With the exception of Walter Owens, who incessantly shook his head, raised his eyebrows, and mumbled oohs and aahs, the members remained as deadpan as professional gamblers.

"As you can see, the situation is volatile," Alderson said. "King Abdullah has every right to invite Iranian troops into Jordan. On the other hand, Israel is entirely justified in feeling threatened. Ahmadinejad's track record speaks for itself. We either have to remain in a wait-and-see mode or take action. Either way, we're dealing with a very delicate situation."

General Cumberland's husky voice bellowed. "Have we spoken with King Abdullah or the Jordanian ambassador?"

"I'm leaving for Jordan this afternoon," Alderson said. "This isn't the kind of thing you discuss over the telephone."

General Wolfe steepled his fingers. His eyes narrowed with suspicion. "You're wasting your time with King Abdullah. His father was in cahoots with Saddam long before the Middle East war. And Abdullah is even more conniving. Think it's a coincidence Saddam and the former king have the same last name?"

"How about the Iranian ambassador?" Admiral McCormick asked.

Toni Mitchell stood. "I've invited him to Washington."

"You *must* be joking," General Wolfe said. "Habib will *never* come to America."

Mitchell said, "I reminded him that we still have a half dozen Stealth bombers in Saudi Arabia."

"That won't rattle him," Wolfe said. "Those goddamn people have a death wish. Can't wait to meet Mohammed or Allah or whoever the hell they worship. We should take aggressive action immediately. Before things get out of hand. What the hell do you think they're doing in Jordan, taking ballet lessons?"

Kate's eyes shot daggers. "What should we do, General, level Tehran and kill a million innocent people?"

"Innocent?" Wolfe yelled. "Have we all forgotten what those animals did to the Kuwaitis? Have we dismissed the September eleventh slaughter of over three thousand Americans? And how about the endless conflict in Iraq and Afghanistan? Little Arabs grow up to be big Arabs. And all of them have the potential to be terrorists."

Kate knew that the Air Force general was a hawk but didn't realize his claws were this sharp. "Before we even *think* about military action, we need to explore every diplomatic remedy. We must give both King Abdullah and Ambassador Habib the opportunity to respond." Kate looked at General Cumberland. "Excluding Iraq, how many American troops are in the Middle East?"

"Since September eleventh, Kuwait, Saudi Arabia, and Turkey have been more receptive to our military presence. Between those three nations, we've got approximately fifty thousand troops. Ready to go."

"Admiral McCormick, how about the Navy?" Kate asked.

"Our battleships are situated ideally in the Mediterranean, and we've got two carriers in the Arabian Sea, equipped with F-18s. They're a long way from Iran, but I can redirect the carriers to the Persian Gulf."

"If we do, will it be construed as an aggressive act?"

"No more offensive than Iranian troops polishing their weapons on the Israeli border," McCormick said.

"Do it," the president ordered. "Contact our sources in the Middle East. If there's any change in the status of those Iranian troops, if they even *glance* at Israel or do anything remotely warlike, I want to be informed at once." She asked one more question, not directing it to anyone in particular. "How accurately can we pinpoint an air strike?"

This was Wolfe territory, and he couldn't wait to answer. "Madam President, we can thread a needle."

Square-jawed Marine General Frank Wallace spoke for the first time. "I'd like to remind everyone that back in two thousand two, Iraq did not respond to anything but military force, nor did the Taliban in Afghanistan. There's no reason to believe that the defiant Arab extremists have changed their attitudes. We should give them an ultimatum, Madam President. Either they get their butts out of Jordan immediately, or we blow them to kingdom come."

Toni Mitchell shook her head violently. "General Wallace, are you suggesting an air strike on *Jordanian* soil?"

"If necessary," he answered.

"But that will erase years of goodwill between our countries. We should do everything possible to preserve this relationship. And besides, don't you think we should consult members of the United Nations before we act?"

"My dear Secretary of State," General Wolfe said, "were you aware that when we went into Kuwait to clean up the carnage after Desert Storm ended, much of the military equipment left behind in Iraq's hasty departure was Jordanian? Excuse my candor, but Abdullah has been in bed with Ahmadinejad for a long time, and so was his father. Any delusions you might have about a favorable relationship with Jordan is merely a wet dream. If President Bush had waited for the United Nations to get off their asses, Iraq would still be ruled by a dictator."

Kate was glad neither General Wolfe nor General Wallace could get their itchy little fingers anywhere near red launch buttons. "Before we consider a military offensive, I'm going to give Ambassador Habib the opportunity to respond."

General Wolfe looked at her with penetrating eyes. "And if he doesn't?"

Kate met his stare. "Then I'll consider aggressive measures."

They talked for several minutes more. When the meeting ended, Kate waited for the room to clear and asked Walter Owens to remain.

"Contact Dean Whitney and send my apologies. Tell him I have to postpone my lecture—indefinitely."

"That's not going to endear you to him," Owens said. "I had to turn the thumbscrews to give you this chance."

"We're in the middle of a major international crisis. I can't even think about a lecture right now."

"It's not as if you're going to be out of touch, Madam President. Georgetown is just a stone's throw away."

She considered it for a moment. "OK, Walter. But tell the dean that I may have to cancel at the last minute if an emergency arises."

"Very well, Madam President."

Kate remained in the room for several minutes and reflected on the meeting. As Owens walked out the door, he glanced over his shoulder, and she noticed a peculiar sparkle in his eyes.

★

CHAPTER TEN

Kate was sitting in the Oval Office conferring with McDermott and Olivia Carter. They'd just finished discussing the details of her meeting with the Joint Chiefs.

"You were right, Olivia. The events in the Middle East have captured front-page headlines. No one seems to care about my separation from Peter."

Olivia had been gloating somewhat, and McDermott's annoyance was obvious. The COS didn't like being outmaneuvered by his understudy.

"Oh, they care, Madam President," McDermott said. "It's far from being over."

"I wouldn't be concerned," Olivia said. "It's old news."

McDermott's lips tightened to a thin line.

The intercom rang.

"Madam President," Emily Hutchins said, "a Wendy *Marshall* has called the White House several times. She said she's a personal friend and it's urgent she speak with you."

Wendy's name brought back fond memories of a life less complicated. "Did she leave her number?"

Emily recited it slowly.

Kate scribbled the number on her yellow pad.

"That's strange," Kate said to McDermott and Olivia. "An old friend from my college days is trying to reach me. I haven't seen her in over twenty years."

When she finished with McDermott and Olivia, Kate hurried into her private office and asked Emily not to disturb her. She glared at the telephone for several minutes and remembered the fun times she had shared with Wendy. When they graduated, Kate and Wendy vowed to stay in touch, but like many people, the details of their busy lives got in the way.

Kate glanced at the yellow piece of paper and pressed the numbers with her fingertip. She recognized Wendy's soft voice immediately.

"Wendy...This is Kate Miles."

"*President* Miles? I was afraid my message wouldn't get to you. Congratulations, by the way. I knew someday you'd make center stage."

"How's everything with you?"

"Living in Long Beach, south of LA. I publish a local newspaper—the *Long Beach News*. Heard of it?"

She hadn't, but thought she'd be polite. "As a matter of fact, I have."

"I'm flattered. Never gonna get rich, you know, but I live near the ocean and keep the wolves away. Been married for almost twenty years."

"Kids?"

"Two. Josh is eighteen, and Liz will be thirteen next month. Not looking forward to having a teenage daughter. Remember all the trouble I used to get into?"

Kate sure did. "So what can I do for you?"

"Don't want to sound melodramatic, but your telephone isn't tapped or anything, is it?"

"This is a secure line, Wendy."

Wendy's voice hushed to a whisper. "A really creepy character from the CIA contacted me several days ago. He about scared the daylights out of me. At first, I thought it had something to do with my newspaper. One of our columnists loves to slam politicians. No disrespect intended. Anyway, he asked me a whole bunch of questions—about *you*. Wanted to know *everything* I could remember. Said it was standard procedure. A matter of national security. Said that thoroughly investigating a president's background prepared them for potential scandals."

Kate's heart fluttered in her upper chest. "What was the agent's name?"

"Miller. Jack Miller. He told me it was my patriotic duty to keep our conversation confidential. I hope I did the right thing by calling you."

"You did. And I thank you." Kate had to find out more about Jack Miller. But not from Wendy. "If anyone *ever* contacts you again, call me immediately."

"Sure, Madam President."

"And, Wendy, please don't breathe a word of this to anyone."

"You have my word on that."

Kate could only hope that Wendy would keep her promise

"If you ever get to the West Coast, look me up. I'd love to see you again."

"I'm glad you called."

Kate slammed the receiver into its cradle harder than she'd intended. Her first impulse was to barge into Victor Ellenwood's office, grab his skinny little chicken neck, and wring it until his eyes bulged. But what would she accomplish? Ellenwood would claim that he was doing his job, trying to protect her. Kate had to approach Ellenwood less directly. Jack Miller, she recalled, was the agent who'd discussed her supposed resignation with Ellenwood. What else had the little snake been up to? Or was it *snakes*? Kate wasn't quite sure how to handle the situation yet, but whatever the plan, her attack had to be strategic and stealthy.

Be patient, Kate. Patience is a virtue.

A virtue she hoped she possessed.

CHAPTER ELEVEN

Carl Kramer sat across from President Miles and coughed into his clenched fist. "Select members of the special commission and I have interrogated each staff member who had access to President Rodgers's private suite, and we haven't uncovered even a remote lead, Madam President."

"That's not what I want to hear, Mr. Kramer." She drummed her fingers on the desk. "I selected you to head the investigation because I expected timely results."

"I've been working day and night."

"Are members of the commission assisting you?"

He nodded. "Not only is the commission assisting me with the investigation, but I have the full support of the CIA and FBI."

"Then why haven't we made any progress?"

"The assassination was well planned, Madam President. Whoever is responsible covered their trail impeccably."

Kate locked her eyes on the jittery DDCI. "You've got a week, Carl. If something doesn't break by then…well…I'll be forced to reevaluate."

The color drained from his face. "I won't let you down."

She shook a breath mint out of its container and popped one in her mouth. "Why do you suppose Joseph Vitelli resigned so suddenly?"

"I'm not sure," Kramer said. "It's hard for a chef to find a more prestigious job than cooking for the president."

"Seems like a curious coincidence that he resigned a few days after David Rodgers was assassinated. Have you checked him out thoroughly?"

"Never even gotten a parking ticket."

"He told me he was moving to the Netherlands," Kate said, "that he'd be working for a five-star restaurant in Amsterdam."

"We're already checking on that, Madam President."

Kate knew that this was not the best timing, but after her conversation with Wendy Marshall, she couldn't wait any longer. "How well do you know Jack Miller?"

Kramer shook his head. "I don't know a Jack Miller."

Kate leaned forward. "He works for *your* department, Mr. Kramer."

"Maybe he's a new hire and I haven't met him yet."

"You're the deputy director and you don't know all the agents?"

"With all due respect, Madam President, the CIA has hundreds of agents all over the world—"

"I'm well aware of that, but from what I gather, Jack Miller works out of the Washington office. So I assumed that you knew him."

"Is there a problem with him?" Kramer asked.

"Mr. Miller's too inquisitive for his own good."

"What do you mean?"

She didn't want to get specific. "He's sticking his nose where it doesn't belong."

"Want me to find out who he is and slap him down?"

"I don't want to spook him. I'd rather catch him off guard."

"If he's acting inappropriately, Madam President, why don't we confront Victor Ellenwood?"

"Carl, let's keep this confidential. Find out whatever you can about Miller—where he came from, what he's been involved with since joining the CIA. Report that information directly to me."

He scratched the back of his head and gave her a pitiful look of appeal. "Madam President, I'm ethically obligated to inform Victor of any issue involving the CIA."

"Trust my judgment, Mr. Kramer. Victor doesn't need to know."

He turned his folded hands inside out and cracked his knuckles. "You're placing me in an awkward situation, Madam President."

"Welcome to the club."

He stroked his mustache with his index finger. "I guess it wouldn't be my first covert investigation."

"And it won't be your last."

Kramer stood and shook Kate's hand. "There is one other issue, Madam President. I've uncovered an interesting tidbit about Mr. McDermott's extracurricular activities."

***

Only moments after Kramer and Kate parted company, Charles McDermott and Toni Mitchell stormed into the Oval Office without knocking. The chief of staff was panting like a marathon runner. The secretary of state stood behind him, pale faced and unanimated. "We've just been informed that three Iranian long-range missiles have hit Tel Aviv," McDermott said. "Thirty-seven Israelis are confirmed dead."

Kate shook her head violently and slammed her palms on the desk. "I knew it! I *fucking* knew it!" She sprang up like a jack-in-the-box and planted her hands on her hips. "Where did you get this information?"

"Alderson," McDermott said. "He couldn't locate King Abdullah, so as per your instructions, he flew to Israel and met with Benjamin Netanyahu. Alderson was trying to assure the Israeli Prime Minister that the situation was under control. The missiles exploded several blocks from the Prime Minister's home. Alderson said they could see burning buildings from Netanyahu's living room."

"That should boost Israel's confidence in our peacekeeping abilities," Kate said. She pointed her pen at Toni Mitchell. "Contact Prime Minister Netanyahu. Express our deepest sympathy. Charles, contact the Joint Chiefs. I want to meet with them in two hours."

McDermott said, "Mr. Netanyahu asked Alderson to relay a message to you, Madam President." Toni Mitchell clutched McDermott's shoulder. "If the United States does not respond within twenty-four hours, the Israeli Air Force will begin air strikes against Jordan and Iran."

"Toni, I'd better have a word with Prime Minister Netanyahu. Get him on the telephone." The secretary of state hustled out of the office. "We can't let this happen, Charles."

"Netanyahu has always been militarily aggressive," McDermott said. "He began his career in the infantry at the age of fourteen, led the 101 Special Commando unit in 1983, and eventually became an infantry brigade commander. He cut his teeth on the battlefields and isn't afraid to get his knuckles bloody. If he deploys the air force, it's going to be a bloodbath."

"We need to alert the United Nations."

"No time, Madam President. We have to act swiftly."

Smiling through grim eyes, Kate said, "I guess Ambassador Habib has declined my invitation to Washington."

***

With the exception of Admiral Michael McCormick, all members of the Joint Chiefs of Staff met with the National Security Council in the Situation Room.

General Wolfe chewed on the end of an unlit cigar and adjusted his tie. "Hate to be a know-it-all, Madam President, but I tried to warn you. Those two-legged sand lizards can't be trusted."

Kate wanted to smack him in the side of the head and wipe that cocky smirk off his face.

General Wallace said, "If we'd sent a dozen sorties into Jordan and blown them to kingdom come, we wouldn't be facing this debacle."

"No, General," Kate said. "But we might be facing an all-out war." She glanced across the table at Toni Mitchell.

The secretary of state just shook her head.

Kate said, "Why don't we let the historians argue what could have or should have been done, and expend our energy on a judicious solution to the current crisis?" Kate opened her day planner and looked at notes from the last meeting. "General Cumberland, how are we situated in the Middle East?"

"Our battleships and carriers are in favorable positions in both the Persian Gulf and Arabian Sea. We're locked and loaded and ready to strike Iran. And we have clearance to use Saudi airspace to bomb Jordan."

"Jordan!" Toni Mitchell shouted. "Madam President, you *cannot* be thinking about an offensive against Jordan. The missiles were Iranian, not Jordanian."

General Wolfe let out a bellowing howl. "And from where do you suppose they were launched, Ms. Mitchell?"

"We already know that Iran has long-range missiles capable of reaching Israel. Military action against Jordan would be insane. Madam President, I urge you not to do anything hasty."

General Wallace said, "The Jordanian ambassador has vanished, and Secretary Alderson could not reach King Abdullah. Do we need more evidence of Jordan's complicity, Madam President? My vote is to launch aggressive air strikes against both countries."

General William Cumberland, Chairman of the Joint Chiefs, stood up. Kate admired the medals decorating the front of his crisply pressed jacket. "Ms. Mitchell is correct. We cannot, under any circumstances, order military action against Jordan unless we have irrefutable evidence that they are directly responsible for the attack on Israel. Their posture toward Iran may be sympathetic, even supportive, but that does not give us authority to launch an offensive. Ahmadinejad is the culprit. We should employ every resource to rid the world of him and his entourage."

"Whatever we choose to do," Kate said, "it must happen quickly. I personally spoke to Prime Minister Netanyahu, and he's prepared to initiate a massive offensive against Tehran and Amman. I convinced him to sit tight, but frankly, I don't know how long I can keep him on ice."

"You're to be commended, Madam President," General Cumberland said. "Mr. Netanyahu is very independent. And terribly arrogant."

"He tried to grandstand," Kate said, "but when I told him I'd cut his foreign aid faster than he could say four billion dollars, I captured his attention."

General Wolfe said, "The time has come, Madam President, for us to coordinate strategic air strikes."

General Charles Kelley spoke for the first time. "We can pinpoint Iran's communication center, major air force base, arms-producing facilities, and artillery factories. We are capable of destroying them with the precision of a surgeon."

"Do Iranian civilians occupy these targets?" Kate asked.

"Minimally," General Kelley said. "But it's impossible to launch such an offensive without some collateral damage."

"How long will it take to organize an attack?" Kate asked.

General Wolfe said, "Twelve hours."

Not in her wildest dreams had Katherine Anne Miles foreseen a day in which a simple nod would give her the power of God. One affirmative word and she could end the lives of hundreds of people. She realized that her decision was the lesser of two evils; there was no clear-cut right or wrong. But by employing conservative military measures, perhaps she could minimize casualties and circumvent a major war.

After several minutes of concentrated thought, Kate said, "I do not see a diplomatic solution. We must respond militarily." Kate watched Toni Mitchell's face turn white. "Here are the ground rules. First, no air strikes against Jordan. If a new development changes their role in this ordeal, we'll reevaluate. Second, I will not consider Iranian facilities that employ nonmilitary citizens or those that are in a close proximity to populated neighborhoods. I want facts and figures on my desk within the hour. Prove to me that civilian casualties will be minimized. Third, I refuse to order an American pilot to risk his life for another country. Israel is our most valued ally, but I'm not going to order American pilots to launch such an attack. Admiral Canfield, can we recruit enough volunteers to initiate this offensive?"

"Absolutely. Navy pilots are a special breed. Dedicated patriots, Madam President. Manning this mission on a voluntary basis will not be a problem."

"We have an agenda, then," Kate said. "Let's reconvene at six p.m. At that time, we'll jointly decide which facilities will be targeted."

They randomly filed out of the Situation Room. Kate sat at the center of the long table and reviewed her notes. She thought it strange that Walter Owens hadn't uttered a word. Perhaps he wished to speak with her privately as he'd done after the last meeting. Concentrating on her heavy thoughts, Kate did not notice that Toni Mitchell was still seated at the end of the conference table. The secretary of state stood, and Kate jumped.

"Sorry, Madam President, I didn't mean to startle you."

"It doesn't take much these days."

Toni Mitchell walked around to the center of the table and sat opposite Kate. She looked over her reading glasses at Mitchell's sympathetic face.

"You don't have a choice, Madam President."

"I wish I could believe that." Kate removed her glasses and dropped them on the table. She massaged her throbbing temples with her fingertips.

"Anything I can do for you?" Mitchell asked.

"Just continue to support me."

Mitchell smiled.

Kate remembered the dispirited look on Mitchell's face when she'd outlined the guidelines of an air strike. "You don't approve, do you?"

Mitchell shrugged. "It's not a black-and-white issue. You're doing what you have to."

"You didn't answer my question."

"I'd be lying if I said I agreed completely. But if I were in your shoes, I'd be inclined to do the same thing. It's easy being a judge and jury when someone else's neck is over the chopping block." Mitchell reached across the table and laid her hand on top of Kate's. "You have my unreserved support."

Kate wasn't convinced that the secretary of state was a willing advocate, but at this juncture, she'd cling to any glimmer of support.

***

President Miles left the Situation Room and went directly to the West Wing. Emily was sitting at her desk just outside the Oval office.

"Urgent messages?"

"Emily shook her head. "None, Madam President."

Kate stepped into the Oval Office and sat behind her desk. In less than two hours, she'd be faced with the most consequential decision of her life. Was there another way out of this dilemma? She buzzed Emily.

"Yes, Madam President."

"Please ask Mr. McDermott to contact Richard Alderson at the American Consulate in Tel Aviv. I need to speak with him as soon as possible."

"Right away."

***

Lieutenant Kyle Stevers sat among eleven fellow shipmates wondering why he'd been awakened at four a.m. In the claustrophobic briefing room, the twenty-five-year-old fighter pilot passively listened to Lt. Commander Andrew Bradley growl. Bradley, as gracious and cordial as ever, stood before the group of yawning pilots and pointed to a map of Iran. Less interested in Bradley's geography lesson than a lecture in quantum physics, Stevers's thoughts drifted to the impending reunion with his wife, Debra, and his two-year-old son, Todd. He hadn't seen his family in over six months and anxiously waited for his tour of duty to end.

True to character, the Navy had made a seductive offer: a ten-thousand-dollar signing bonus for four more years. But no amount of money could induce Stevers to reenlist. Just twenty more days and he'd bid the USS *Ronald Reagan* farewell for the last time. No more cots as hard as a rock or substandard meals cleverly camouflaged with greasy gravy. No more wackin' the weenie at two a.m. And no more Commander "Rip-Me-a-New-Ass" Bradley making his life a living hell.

To the rest of the world, the USS *Ronald Reagan* was the most sophisticated carrier the Navy had ever built. But to Lieutenant Stevers, it was one hundred thousand tons of floating aggravation in the middle of the Persian Gulf.

Joining the Navy had been the biggest mistake of his life. Since being seduced by the glitz and glitter of *Top Gun* when he was just a child, he'd decided to become a pilot. But once his dream became a reality, he soon discovered that a pilot's life was not nearly as glamorous as Tom Cruise's. In fact, it was only slightly better than any seaman recruit's. What infuriated Stevers most was that, other than routine drills and mock dogfights, he'd not seen one *minute* of combat. He hadn't joined the Navy to fly F-18 fighters on Sunday-afternoon cruises.

"Lieutenant Stevers!" Commander Bradley shouted. "Would you be interested in joining the rest of us? Or should I mail you a fucking invitation?"

This was *exactly* the sort of bullshit that made Stevers loathe the Navy. Stevers lifted his head. His ice-blue eyes locked on the fifty-two-year-old commander storming toward him. The veins in Bradley's neck were standing out on livid edges.

"Sorry, sir." Stevers smiled, sprouting dimples on both of his cheeks.

Bradley stood over Stevers, glaring at him, his bulldog face snarling. "You're not out of this man's Navy yet, hotshot. I still own your ass till the end of the month."

Bite me, you big blowhard.

"Since you'd rather play with your putter than listen to me, why don't you set an example for the rest of us and be the first volunteer?"

"Volunteer for what, sir?"

"We're organizing a little going-away bash for President Ahmadinejad. A BYOB party. Are you in?"

Lieutenant Wes Travis, Stevers's best friend and navigator, elbowed him in the ribs and whispered, "Bring Your Own *Bomb*, stupid. He's looking for volunteers."

Stevers didn't understand. "Yes, sir. I'd be honored, sir."

***

President Miles picked up her telephone on the first ring.

"I have Richard Alderson on the line," McDermott said.

"Thank you." She pushed line seven. "Richard, how are things going?"

"Well, it's been an exhausting couple of days, Madam President. Benjamin Netanyahu is quite a character. I honestly believe he's hoping that the United States *doesn't* intervene. There's nothing that would please him more than ordering his air force to level Tehran and Amman."

"He told me during a telephone conversation that he would not order military action until we've had a chance to respond. Has that changed, Richard?"

"It's a money game, Madam President. If you hadn't threatened to pull the plug on his foreign aid, he would have already retaliated."

"It was just a bluff." Apparently, Netanyahu wasn't aware that Kate needed Congressional approval to alter any foreign aid. "Stick close to him, Richard. If you feel he's getting an itchy finger, contact me immediately."

"Yes, Madam President."

Kate sensed more than fatigue in his voice. "Are you OK, Richard?"

"As good as I'm going to be under the circumstances."

She didn't want to burden him further, but his job was to advise. "I'm faced with a very difficult decision, and I'd like your opinion."

"Are you considering military action, Madam President?"

She wasn't sure if he was searching for a yes or a no. "I'm evaluating the need for strategic air strikes."

"For all it's worth, anything short of that and Prime Minister Netanyahu might do something catastrophic."

She was more aware of that than she wished to be. Hearing it from Alderson confirmed it. "I'll contact you right after my meeting with the Joint Chiefs."

★

CHAPTER TWELVE

After examining the confidential file titled "Strategic Iranian Targets," Kate forwarded it to the Joint Chiefs and asked them to review it prior to their meeting. She did not possess a well-spring of military knowledge from which to rationalize a strategy. Therefore, it was unlikely that the esteemed generals would recommend the same targets that she'd selected. How could they? Kate was not an Eisenhower or a Harry Truman. What had her political career taught her about military tactics? She knew a great deal about economics and the democratic process. Kate was even adept at foreign policy. But war games? All six members of the Joint Chiefs had served their country during the Iraqi War and were active during the military offensive against the Taliban regime in Afghanistan. They'd seen conflict and frontline battles. Wolfe, the senior member, had been a prisoner of war in Vietnam. McCormick had escaped from a North Vietnamese death camp. How could Kate expect to compare her strategies with those of war veterans? If ever she had to rely on her gut instincts and intuition, at what time in her life had it been more consequential than now?

When she entered the Situation Room, General Cumberland closed the top-secret folder and stopped talking in the middle of a sentence. The room was stone still. Without ceremony or perfunctory greetings, Kate sat at her place in the center of the table.

"May I have your recommendations, General Cumberland?"

He pushed his glasses higher on his nose and reopened the folder. "There are four primary targets that would pose minimum risk to nonmilitary Iranians. Two others that you may wish to consider, but with greater potential for civilian casualties."

"Outline them for us, please," Kate said.

"The main communication center in Tehran undoubtedly should be our principal target. By destroying this facility, we will prevent Ahmadinejad from relaying orders to his field commanders. It will cripple their ability to sustain any offensive or coordinate defensive measures—at least temporarily."

Kate looked at her notes. "According to my research, the facility was strategically designed and rebuilt after it was destroyed during the Iran-Iraq War."

General Cumberland displayed a surprised look. "That is correct, Madam President."

"It was constructed to withstand an air strike," Kate said. "Isn't that why it was built four stories underground?"

Cumberland removed a handkerchief from his back pocket and blotted his shiny forehead. "In theory. But we have developed highly sophisticated cruise missiles capable of penetrating its defenses."

"Will these missiles cause substantial damage to surrounding structures?"

"Minimum damage."

Kate picked up a pencil and put a checkmark next to *Communication Center*.

General Cumberland said, "The main Iranian Air Force base is located a few miles east of a city called Abadan. The

USS *Ronald Reagan*, situated in the Persian Gulf, could deploy a squadron of F-18s and wipe out the base before they had sufficient time to respond."

"Would such an attack jeopardize the city itself?" Kate asked.

Cumberland shook his head. "The base is far enough east of Abadan to ensure the city's safety."

Destroying both targets would achieve her objectives. She checked off *Air Force Base* without asking further questions.

Cumberland continued, "There are two storage facilities in the city of Shiraz, about one hundred miles north of the Persian Gulf. We believe they warehouse missiles. A barrage of ICBMs could tear the heart out of Iran's most significant firepower."

"So far, we seem to be on the same wavelength, General."

General Cumberland looked at Admiral Canfield and nodded. Canfield took a long swig of water and cleared his throat. "Madam President, there are also two factories in Qom thought to produce chemical weapons. If we are determined to end Ahmadinejad's reign of terror, these two structures should also be targeted."

It made sense, but Canfield's voice was edged with reservations. Kate remembered what Saddam Hussein had done to the Kurds during the Iraq-Iran War. She could still visualize the graphic photos printed in *Time*—mutilated bodies heaped in piles, charred skin, faces melted like wax. She could not fathom why these factories should be preserved but had an eerie feeling the admiral was going to tell her.

"The danger," Admiral Canfield said, "is that we are unable to determine how these chemical weapons will react once the facilities are destroyed. They are very unstable substances."

"What's the worst-case scenario, Admiral?" Kate asked.

"A cloud of deadly chemicals could float into space and dissipate or descend to the ground."

"Quite possibly on top of Iranian citizens?" Kate asked.

Canfield nodded.

Images of the Kurds flashed through Kate's mind. "It's out of the question."

Walter Owens tapped his knuckles on the table. "Madam President, surely the long-term benefits far outweigh the risks. This is a once-in-a-lifetime opportunity for the United States to reassert itself as a competent world leader and rid the Middle East of their dangerous chemical weapons."

"I agree, Madam President," Admiral Canfield said.

Kate was taken aback. "Am I missing something? We are dealing with lethal, volatile substances. Our objective is to disable Ahmadinejad, not to pollute the atmosphere or endanger innocent people. Walter, how would you feel if a deadly cloud of nerve gas descended on New York City?"

"With all due respect, Madam President, that's highly unlikely." He passed a black binder to Kate. "President Bush ordered an extensive study on nerve gas prior to Desert Storm. This report may change your mind."

Kate slipped on her reading glasses, opened the binder, and leafed through the two-inch-thick stack of papers.

"Considering the amount of time required to analyze this report, perhaps you would be kind enough to summarize it for us, Walter?"

Owens stood and glowed with self-importance. "Chemical weapons are stored in highly compressed cylinders. The cylinders, armed with detonators, are dropped from aircraft. But unlike conventional bombs that explode on impact, they are programmed to discharge one hundred feet above the ground. Coming into contact with the toxic cloud is almost always fatal. When it settles on the ground, however, its potency lasts for only twenty-four hours, after which it is relatively harmless."

Kate could feel her face getting hot. "So, Walter, you wouldn't mind if we filled your grandchildren's sandbox with these relatively harmless chemicals?"

"That's an unrealistic scenario," Owens said.

President Miles held up the binder. "Has anyone else reviewed this report?"

"I have," General Wolfe said. He removed the cigar from his mouth and pointed it at Kate. "Read it back in '90. It was hogwash then, and it's hogwash now."

If war monger Wolfe opposed bombing these factories, Kate thought, then the potential for catastrophe had to be unfathomable.

Frank Wallace, the other hawkish general, said, "I doubt that anyone would love to see Ahmadinejad, his chemical weapons factories, and his entire goddamn country reduced to a pile of rubble more than I, but even during war, there must be limitations on destruction. These chemicals are monstrous, inhumane. I would not wish them on my worst enemy. Besides, President Bush's report may not apply to recent innovations. God only knows if their characteristics are the same as they were over two decades ago."

"Would anyone else care to comment on these factories?" Kate asked.

There were garbled mumbles but mostly heads shaking in concert.

She surveyed the faces of the esteemed group, wishing she could delegate this supreme decision to one of them, to lift the burden from her shoulders. But she remembered the promise she'd made to herself.

"The majority opinion opposes bombing the chemical weapons factories," Kate said. She glanced at Owens and Canfield. "I concur. The other four targets are a go."

Kate looked at General Cumberland, then at General Wolfe. What was she supposed to do next? Her requisite political training had not taught her protocol for blowing up other countries.

"Well, am I supposed to sign an executive order and have it notarized?"

Cumberland smiled. "Operation Freebird is the code name, Madam President. General Wolfe, Admiral Canfield, and I will issue the necessary directives and coordinate a simultaneous attack." The general checked his watch.

"Operation Freebird will commence on November second, at fourteen hundred hours, eastern standard time. We will advise you of any and all developments, Madam President."

***

President Miles left the Situation Room and went directly to her private quarters. She shuffled into her bedroom and kicked off her shoes. She slipped her suit jacket off her shoulders, unzipped her skirt, and let both fall to the floor. It was unlike her to throw her clothes about haphazardly, but she did not have the energy to walk another step and hang them in the closet. Her brain, for good reason, was like mush, and her body felt like she'd been laboring in the coal mines of Pennsylvania.

Her bedroom was rapidly becoming her hideaway, a sanctuary of peace and quiet where she could decompress. It was the only room in the White House that ensured her absolute privacy, a secure haven of solitude.

She lay on the bed and, without forethought, reached for the telephone. Kate was filled with uncertainties and self-doubt, and a part of her longed to consult her father. Validating her decision was the curative ointment her weary conscience needed right now. How easy to dial the White Stallion Ranch. She'd never forget the number. But would a competent president, a prominent world leader, *need* to call her father? Only a cold-blooded monster could bomb another country without second thoughts and reservations. Kate had every right to feel unsettled. To search for approval from the man she respected more than any living human was only natural. The central issue, however, flowed from waters much deeper. For how long could she continue running to her father whenever her neat, orderly life unraveled? Would she ever cut the umbilical cord?

The receiver slipped from her fingers and fell into its cradle. She tried to convince her troubled conscience that Operation Freebird had been a mutual decision. The Joint Chiefs, after all, had determined that military intervention was the only logical solution. But Kate was the commander in chief. It was her finger poised on a trigger that would end innocent lives. When people were killed, torn to shreds, buildings destroyed, and the effects of her actions felt by the entire world, Kate would stand alone and assume full responsibility. Nobody would point an accusing finger at the Joint Chiefs.

Kate's decision placed Americans at risk; young pilots with families and dreams and visions of hope could be maimed or captured or killed. How would she deal with this very real possibility?

Kate forced her body off the bed and headed to the walk-in closet. Giant goose bumps covered her skin. She wrapped the terry cloth robe around her body and searched the pockets for her lucky silver dollar. Wadded up tissue. Tagamet. Peter's lighter?

Ah. She found the coin, held it tightly, and made her way to the kitchen. She felt strangely disoriented, as if she'd never been in this suite before. She snatched the bottle of Jack Daniels from the cabinet and poured a whisper of it into a tall water glass. Anymore and she'd be knocked out for hours.

I just need to take the edge off.

Other than an occasional glass of wine, Kate was a teetotaler, but at this particular moment, she required something more potent. She scuffed into the Oval Room and flopped onto the yellow sofa. She filled her mouth with the bourbon, swallowed hard, and grimaced as it burned a trail to her stomach. *Peter actually likes this crap?* Kate set the empty glass on the cocktail table and blankly gazed at the portrait of George Washington hanging above the fireplace. The muscles along the back of her shoulders twisted into a knot.

Why had Admiral Canfield and Walter Owens tried to convince her to bomb the chemical weapons factories?

She leaned back, rested her head, and waited.

***

It was almost midnight, and Charles McDermott was still at the White House. It wasn't work or dedication that kept him there; he'd done little all day except chew his fingernails and curse President Miles. Adelina had just left; her arousing scent lingered, but the stench of stale cigarette smoke overpowered it. Her visits had become more frequent. More intense. The ravishing redhead was as addictive as cocaine. And McDermott had once been well acquainted with the insidious enticement of coke. What had begun as a thoughtless indiscretion had blossomed into a torrid affair. What else could he call having sex with a married woman? He had to end it. But how? Adelina had explored every nook and cranny of McDermott's body and mind. She knew too much. He'd placed himself in a touchy situation. The Brazilian beauty knew precisely where McDermott's hot buttons were. And she'd pushed them all.

The COS gulped the last of the vodka and tried to set the glass on the corner of the cocktail table as he fell onto the leather sofa. He watched the glass wobble, then fall on the carpeting. "Son of a bitch!" He crushed a cigarette in the overfilled ashtray.

As he lay down and closed his eyes, he could see his promising career coming to a bitter end. Adelina Menendez was not the only demon in Charles McDermott's life. The peace-loving president, exalted high priestess, had decided to take military action in the Middle East. The COS had no empathy for Arab extremists, but Kate's actions could jeopardize his political future. Supposedly, he was her quintessential advisor, yet she hadn't asked his opinion. Why? He wasn't *merely* the chief of staff. Charles McDermott was the advisor to the president for policy and strategy. If bombing a foreign country did not fall under the heading *Strategy*, what did? Understandably, the Joint Chiefs had tremendous influence over her decision. But shouldn't she have consulted him? Paid him the professional courtesy? If President Miles took a fall, so did her advisor for policy and strategy. It was a package deal. And he hadn't even had the opportunity to express his opinion.

He struggled to sit up, and the room began to spin. Steadying his weary legs by grasping the armrest, he eased off the couch. McDermott took a step toward his desk and stopped. He extended his arms as if he were walking a tightrope and tried to stop his body from reeling. He reached his desk and plopped into the chair.

Adelina, Adelina, what shall I do with you?

***

As Lieutenant Kyle Stevers laced his spit-shined boots, his heart battered his rib cage like a sledgehammer. He expected that a general quarters alert would rescue him from this heinous nightmare at any moment. But the only sound he heard was a pounding on the door. As if standing in front of Commander Bradley, preparing for a zone inspection, Stevers instinctively snapped to attention. He grasped the handle on the metal door and pulled it open.

Wes Travis, displaying the most authentic Elvis Presley sneer Stevers had ever seen, stood in the doorway. Stevers's six-foot-three frame towered over his best friend.

"It's zero hour, hotshot," Travis said. "Ready to kick some butt?"

For four years, he'd waited for this exact moment. Now that it was upon him, Stevers wanted to crawl into his bunk, throw the covers over his head, and weep like a lost child. But he had an image to preserve. "Let's go blow up some bad guys."

They walked single file down the long, narrow corridor, their heavy steps echoed in the air like rhythmic beats on a metal drum. When they reached the circular stairway, they climbed two flights to the main deck. The brisk wind whistled hauntingly. The thick air felt heavy in Stevers's lungs. Ready to make history, a dozen fighter planes, their wings glistening in the bright moonlight, sat quietly along the perimeter of the runway. Armed with radar-activated missiles and smart bombs, six Stealth bombers had already taken off, prepared to level the Iranian Air Force base. The more nimble, swifter F-18s would accompany the Stealths and protect them from an air attack. *Lizzy Borden* was first in line. Stevers and Travis had named their F-18 only weeks ago. Walking side by side, they approached *Lizzy*. Their flight helmets were tucked securely under their arms. Commander Bradley stood adjacent to *Lizzy*, his neatly creased trousers waving in the breeze.

They stopped and saluted.

Bradley nodded. "Lieutenant Stevers, Lieutenant Travis, make us proud, gentlemen."

Stevers could never remember Bradley's voice sounding so benign. Did the commander actually call him by his surname?

They climbed into the cockpit. Stevers snugged his body into the gunner position, and Travis settled in behind him as navigator. Stevers flipped switches and toggles and fired up the engines. With fastidious detail, they went through their regimen and checked every control, every gauge. Stevers signaled a thumbs-up to the flight safety officer, and he waved them forward. The engines whined, and *Lizzy* inched her way to the edge of the runway. Both pilots secured their helmets and let their oxygen masks hang loosely. The canopy slowly lowered over their heads. Stevers couldn't help but feel that a glass coffin had just entrapped him. His nauseous stomach heaved bile into his mouth.

The FSO waved the white flag.

Stevers yanked on the throttle, and *Lizzy Borden* screamed down the runway. She was airborne in less than ten seconds. One by one, fighter planes ascended off the deck of the *Ronald Reagan* and thundered into the night sky. Led by *Lizzy Borden*, twelve F-18s in a V-formation cruised toward Abadan at an altitude of twenty thousand feet.

"It was brotherly of you to volunteer my services," Travis said to Stevers. "This is the one we've been waiting for."

Stevers looked at the wrinkled photo of Debra and Todd taped to the dash. "Yes, indeed," Stevers said. A few years ago, he'd fantasized about a mission like this. But as *Lizzy Borden* raced through the dark sky, all he could think about was whether or not he'd live to see his wife and son again.

Twelve minutes after takeoff, the F-18s rendezvoused with the Stealths, and the fighter planes maintained visual proximity to the bombers.

The Stealths slowly began their descent.

The sky was cloudless, an inky dome as black as soot. Stars were scattered across the heavens like salt sprinkled on black tile. For a moment, Stevers forgot where he was. His mind journeyed to another dimension, and he was absorbed into a world of soothing peacefulness. He'd had episodes of retreat before, periods of disconnection from reality, particularly at times of great stress. But never had he wandered during conditions demanding such painstaking concentration. Unlike daydreams or fantasies, this world was three-dimensional. He could see Debra, touch her, feel the contours of her warm body against his. Debra's sweet breath filled his senses with joy and excitement.

"Hang on to your nuts!" Wes Travis yelled.

Stevers jumped, adrenaline coursed through his veins, and he grudgingly returned from his momentary lapse. It took a moment for him to reorient himself with a world much less appealing. Stevers watched in utter disbelief as, one by one, the Stealth bombers released their first round of smart bombs and RAM missiles. For twenty, perhaps thirty seconds, Stevers neither heard nor saw anything. It was as if time had stopped. But then, like a Fourth of July fireworks display, the ground lit up with one burst of fire after another.

Stevers checked his coordinates.

The hits were dead-on.

As the bombers cruised past their target and repositioned for a final attack, six Thunder fighters—Iran's most sophisticated fighter planes—emerged from nowhere. The sky was peppered with flashes of light and rumbling explosions. Out of the corner of Stevers's eye, he saw one of the Stealths explode into a ball of orange fire.

He yelled into his mask, "Thunder fighters at three o'clock! Intercept! Intercept!"

With his wingman maintaining his position, Stevers led the counterattack. He wiped the sweat out of his eyes and rested his anxious finger on the trigger. Stevers checked the heads-up display and tried to lock one of the Thunder fighters in his sites. The Iranian pilot's evasive maneuvers were the best Stevers had ever seen. The Thunder fighter swerved, twisted, sharply turned left, trying to elude *Lizzy Borden*. Stevers steadied his hand and tried again to lock on his target. The heads-up display went berserk. He squeezed the red launch button, and a Sidewinder missile under *Lizzy*'s right wing ignited, burst forward, and chased the twisting and turning target. Stevers watched the helpless fighter explode into a cloud of red flames. He knew it was time to leave, but the Stealths were unable to complete their second hit. He wanted to be certain the mission was completed.

"Let's unload on these bastards!" Stevers yelled.

Stevers's wingman, Lance Wentworth, said, "No can do, hotshot. The base is history. We've done our job. Let's get the fuck out of here."

"No!" Stevers shouted. "Follow me, Lance. The rest of you maintain your formation. And watch your asses!"

To further destroy the air force base, Stevers and Wentworth maneuvered into position while the other ten F-18s continued their battle with the five remaining Thunder fighters. As Stevers locked the air force base in his sites, ready to squeeze the launch button, a thunderous explosion rocked his plane. At first, he thought he'd been hit, but when he looked to his right, he saw his wingman's plane engulfed in a ball of fire.

"Lance has been hit!" Stevers yelled.

He'd barely spoken the words, and Stevers watched in horror as Lance Wentworth's F-18 tumbled out of the sky. He clenched his teeth and pounded his fist on the dashboard. "This is for Lance, you motherfuckers."

He launched a Maverick missile, and it thrust toward its target. Just as he was about to pull back on the stick and join his fellow pilots, an antiaircraft missile tore into *Lizzy*'s left wing. The F-18 tilted to its right and rolled out of control, rapidly losing elevation. He grabbed the throttle with both hands, but the plane would not respond. Stevers looked to his left and saw half of *Lizzy*'s wing shredded off.

"We have to eject! We have to eject!" Stevers screamed.

Travis grasped the eject lever. "Let's do it!"

Lieutenant Kyle Stevers snatched the picture of his wife and son, stuffed it inside his jacket, and closed his eyes. He pulled the eject lever, and his body catapulted into the ominous Iranian sky.

***

When the telephone rang, Kate was still sitting on the yellow sofa in the Oval Room, restlessly sleeping in an upright position. She lifted her head and cranked it from side to side, hoping to get the knot out of her neck. She lifted the receiver. "This is President Miles."

"Madam President, it's Charles. I have information regarding Operation Freebird."

Kate felt her heart thundering. This was not a conversation for the telephone. "Meet me in the Oval Office in twenty minutes."

Kate had no time for a shower and was not interested in sporting a chic business suit at four a.m. She brushed her teeth, took a swig of Listerine, and threw on a pair of wool slacks and a cotton sweater. She dragged a comb through her hair and touched up her makeup. Without a thick coat of concealer, she could not hide the puffy bags of flesh hanging under her red eyes.

Kate entered the West Wing and found McDermott and Toni Mitchell waiting for her outside the Oval Office. McDermott was sitting on the corner of Emily's desk, and Toni Mitchell was pacing the floor. Kate studied the chief of staff's eyes. His stoic expression didn't yield a clue. McDermott and Mitchell followed Kate into the Oval Office. The president sat on the striped couch; the chief of staff and secretary of state sat opposite her. McDermott looked haggard, like he hadn't slept in days. But it was more than that. His cheeks were sunken in, and his glassy eyes were severely bloodshot. McDermott and Mitchell remained silent.

"Maybe you'd like to tell me what the hell's going on?" Kate was raw with impatience and full of dread.

McDermott folded his hands. "Just gathering my thoughts." He glanced at Toni Mitchell. "For the most part, Operation Freebird has been an overwhelming success, Madam President."

Kate curled her hands into fists. "'For the most part' doesn't give me a warm-and-cozy feeling. Would you care to elaborate?"

"We believe that all communication between Ahmadinejad and his field commanders has halted," McDermott said. "The two warehouses have been completely destroyed, and the air force base is no longer operational. A handful of fighter planes evaded our attack, but for all practical purposes, the base can be referred to in the past tense."

Kate knew there was more. "American casualties?"

"We lost two F-18s and one Stealth." McDermott's face was ghost white. "Five airmen are confirmed dead. Two MIA. Their plane was hit and on fire, but before the plane went down, another pilot watched the two airmen eject. We can only assume at this juncture that the two pilots parachuted to Iranian soil."

"God forgive me." Kate closed her eyes for a moment, her mind illuminated with an obscure image of the dead pilot's faces. "Has Ahmadinejad or the Iranian ambassador issued a statement?"

"Not yet, Madam President," McDermott said.

"How about our allies?"

"Not a word," Mitchell said.

There were more pressing issues to discuss, but Kate was still puzzled why Admiral Canfield, rarely known to be militarily aggressive, had pushed for the United States to bomb the chemical weapons factories. "Do either of you know anything about Admiral Thomas Canfield?"

McDermott said, "I did a thorough background check on all members of the Joint Chiefs for President Rodgers."

"Walter Owens was pressing for me to bomb two chemical weapons factories in Iran," Kate said. "Admiral Canfield agreed. Seems out of character for the admiral, doesn't it?"

McDermott said, "Admiral Canfield lost his only son during the Middle East war. An antiaircraft missile shot down Lieutenant Canfield's F-16 over Baghdad. The admiral has no love for Arabs."

Kate now understood. "Charles, contact Richard Alderson. Find out how Prime Minister Netanyahu has reacted." Her voice was unsteady. "See if there's word on the two missing pilots, Toni."

***

With an empty duffel bag securely tucked under his right arm, Joseph Angelo Vitelli left his suite at the Grand Cayman Hotel and strolled down Main Street toward the Island Bank. It was an unusually hot day for November, but the Caribbean breezes felt exhilarating. The excessive sweat drenching his linen slacks and silk shirt was more from nerves than the tropical sun. How often does an ex-chef walk into a foreign bank, hand them an empty duffel bag, and leave with five million dollars of unmarked American currency? He guessed only a lotto winner could relate to his windfall. Considering the number of multimillionaires living in America, five million dollars might not be a fortune by US standards, but in a country like Italy, a prudent man could live like a king. And that's exactly what he intended to do.

He walked past quaint sidewalk cafés, tiny gift shops, brick buildings. People were sipping espresso, spreading jam on toast, buttering croissants. He could smell the salty sea air.

At ten fifteen a.m., Vitelli pushed open the door and entered the bank. He tried to remain inconspicuous, but with an empty duffel bag stuffed under his arm, he couldn't have felt more obtrusive if a flashing red beacon were mounted on his head. While he nervously waited for the next-available banking officer, his foot bounced up and down and the loose coins in his pocket jingled. A middle-aged woman with mocha-colored skin acknowledged him with a nod. She held up her finger as if to say, *One minute.* He spotted the nameplate on her desk. Cybil Curtis. He gazed around the bank. The floors were black-and-white marble. The walls were covered with rich mahogany. He watched two men painstakingly polish abundant brass railings to a lustrous shine. He guessed that he was not the first American to withdraw a huge amount of money from this bank. More than likely, to some of the bank's depositors, five million dollars was a pittance.

Cybil Curtis hung up the telephone and stood. "How may I assist you?" she said. He found her light accent charming. Vitelli had always thought a woman's British accent was sexy, but a man's grated on his ears like fingernails dragging across a blackboard.

"I'd like to make a substantial withdrawal."

"Please have a seat." Cybil hit some keys on her computer. "May I have your account number, please?"

Vitelli had memorized it. "US3-45213-225."

She entered the number. "How much would you like to withdraw?"

"I wish to close the account."

Obviously, accustomed to similar transactions, Cybil didn't flinch. "Are you aware of our withdrawal fee?"

He'd suspected there'd be a catch. Vitelli remembered an HBO movie. A Swiss bank had charged a mafia don 20 percent for withdrawing his laundered money. Vitelli didn't think his money was laundered but guessed that the Island Bank would still reach into his knickers. "How much?"

"Five percent."

Two hundred fifty thou? Ouch. "I wasn't expecting to pay *that* much."

Her wide mouth formed a smile. "I wish there was something I could do"—she glanced at the monitor—"Mr. Crandall, but our bank is quite rigid on this policy. Shall I proceed?"

"How long will it take?"

"How would you prefer the funds?"

Feeling like a two-bit hustler, he laid the duffel bag on her desk. "In cash. American currency."

She glanced at the duffel bag. "The only way that much money will fit in such a bag is if they are one-thousand-dollar bills. Is that OK?"

Vitelli didn't really care if they loaded a Brinks truck full of silver dollars. "That's fine."

"We should be able to complete this transaction within the hour."

I'll be filthy rich in sixty minutes? "Terrific!"

"May I see two forms of identification, both with a photo ID, please?"

He handed her the Maryland driver's license and the passport given to him when he left Washington.

"There's a lounge on the second level, Mr. Crandall. Make yourself comfortable, and I will contact you when I've completed the paperwork."

Vitelli shook her velvety hand, then trotted up the stairs. He'd expected a couple of sofas, a TV, perhaps, and maybe even refreshments. The lounge was like the Taj Mahal family room. Leather sofas and chairs, cherry desks with computers, a sixty-inch television, a full-service bar, and two ravishing hostesses. He ordered a Bloody Mary and munched on appetizers he wished he had the recipe for.

This is a bank?

A wave of guilt prickled his conscience.

It wasn't as if he'd discharged a 9mm into Rodgers's chest or plunged a knife in his gut. All he'd done was remove some wine and replace it with…What? Vitelli had liked President Rodgers. Admired him. But five million dollars could tarnish even the purest soul. Unsettling feelings swept through him. His father's favorite proverb kept replaying in his mind.

What goes around comes around.

He tried to dismiss it, but it was locked in his conscience.

After Vitelli chugged three cocktails and felt a bit giddy, gorged himself with hors d'oeuvres, and thoroughly enjoyed an explicit fantasy about the hostess with Beyoncé legs, Cybil Curtis strolled into the lounge. Vitelli followed her down the winding staircase to her desk and planted his woozy body in the plush armchair.

She handed him a Montblanc pen and several forms. "Please sign these documents where indicated by the X."

Vitelli was tempted to read what he was signing, but why should he care what Mr. Crandall signed? As long as he walked out the door with a duffel bag full of money, he'd sign Crandall's death warrant if necessary. By tomorrow evening, he'd be sipping a glass of Chianti in Pesaro and breaking bread with long-lost relatives.

He scribbled his signature on the forms, gave them to Cybil, and she handed him the blue duffel bag. Unable to resist, he unzipped it and peeked inside. He gaped at the bundles of neatly wrapped bills and forced his lungs to take a breath of air. Grover Cleveland had never looked so handsome!

Cybil Curtis extended her hand. "Best of luck, Mr. Crandall. If you wish, I can arrange a security escort for you."

Overflowing with alcohol-induced courage, he said, "That's not necessary. Thank you for your assistance."

He left the Island Bank and awkwardly jogged north on Main Street toward his hotel. Bent forward from the weight of his windfall, and still quite light-headed, he looked like the Hunchback of Notre Dame. He entered the lobby, rode the elevator to the fifth floor, and staggered to his room. He'd never been superstitious but felt inordinately uneasy staying in room 513. He closed the door, turned the dead bolt, and secured the chain. Vitelli, face flushed and head spinning, stepped over to the king-size bed, unzipped the duffel bag, and dumped countless bundles of thousand-dollar bills on the forest-green comforter. He stood mesmerized for several moments. That it was all his seemed incomprehensible. He bent over and started stuffing bundles back into the duffel bag.

The floor behind him squeaked.

Before his tipsy body could react, someone firmly gripped his ponytail and yanked him upright. His head snapped backward, and his eyes felt like they'd been jarred loose from their sockets. He reached back and felt a sweaty hand grasping his hair, but before he could swing around or evoke a rational thought, something cold and sharp dragged across Vitelli's neck. It felt as if the skin had been burned with a blowtorch. Panic did not strike immediately. It wasn't until a rush of warm blood flooded his shirt and gurgled in his throat that horror overwhelmed him. Unable to draw a breath, he clutched his neck with both hands and gasped for air. His fingers frantically groped at his throat, and he could feel cleaved flesh, his bare windpipe. Like a distant church bell, his ears began to chime, and the room spun out of control. Vitelli's eyes rolled back, and he fell to the floor. He lay helplessly convulsing, like a fish gulping its last breath. He opened his eyes for a blurry moment and met his killer's icy stare. Joseph Angelo Vitelli had indeed signed Richard Crandall's death warrant.

What goes around comes around.

It was his last earthly thought.

Jack Miller haphazardly stuffed the rest of the money in the duffel bag and dashed out the door.

CHAPTER THIRTEEN

Firmly gripping his parachute harness, Lieutenant Kyle Stevers descended toward the ground. Gusts of wind had pushed him laterally, away from the raging fires and billowing clouds of iridescent smoke. But the turbulent air kept changing directions, whirling him around like a fallen leaf. Certain his arrival would be less than welcome, he struggled with the blustery wind and tried to maneuver away from the destruction. As the ground, illuminated by an ice-blue moon, came into clear view, Stevers prepared to land textbook-style—the same way he had dozens of times. But sand was tricky. If he miscalculated, hit the ground too hard, or twisted his ankle, he doubted that the Iranian soldiers would feel much compassion for him.

He bent his knees slightly so that his legs would act like springs and cushion the impact. Then, as his boots touched the ground, he squatted and rolled his body, left shoulder first.

He felt a twinge in his right knee, more like a crunching.

God no! He'd heard this sound before.

Stevers remembered the knee injury he'd sustained as a high school halfback. He could only hope that this injury was not as serious. The last thing he needed was to be stranded in enemy territory with a five-day supply of food, three liters of water, and a bum knee. He stood up slowly and carefully flexed his knee. He could feel discomfort but little more than when he'd squatted with too much weight during a workout.

Stevers closed his eyes and bowed his head. "Thank you, Lord." He hadn't spoken to his Creator in a long time. Soon, he thought, they were going to get reacquainted. His teeth were chattering, but he was unsure if it was due to the chilly desert air or because he was more terrified than he'd ever been in his life.

In the distance, Stevers could see the still-burning air force base. He estimated that he was five or six miles away and was thankful he hadn't touched down closer. Strolling across the barren flatlands wearing an American pilot's uniform would make him easy prey for Iranian troops. He unharnessed his parachute, removed the shovel from his backpack, and dug a hole in the sandy earth. Not wanting to assist the Iranian's hunt for him, Stevers buried the parachute and covered the evidence of his landing the best he could. His right knee reminded him that he needed to treat it with utmost care.

He'd lost visual contact with Wes Travis only moments after they'd ejected. He hoped, with fading optimism, that his best friend had landed safely and not too far away. The full moon was both friend and foe. Its illumination would guide him, help with his search for Wes. But it also made it easier for an Iranian search squad to flush him out.

He removed the Beretta M9 from its holster and ejected the clip. Armed with a full clip and only eighteen additional rounds, Stevers was not in a position to ward off a formidable attack. But at least he wasn't helpless.

Using cupped hands as visors just above his eyebrows, he shielded his eyes from the moon and forced his pupils to dilate to their maximum. He slowly rotated, studying the level terrain, searching for anything moving. Stevers had until sunrise to find Wes and outline a plan for survival. Once the sun lit the landscape, Iranian troops would hunt for him with relentless determination. Stevers removed the compass and map from the knapsack and began his quest.

Kate leaned forward, rested her palms on the windowsill, and stared out the triple windows, past the dying rose garden. She could see a battalion of protestors stomping down Pennsylvania Avenue. From where she stood, she couldn't hear the hooting and hollering or the poetic chants of disdain. Nor was she able to read their hand-painted signs. But the *Post* had been kind enough to display the maligning words on the front page. MILES THE MURDERER. REMEMBER IRAQ. IRANIANS ARE PEOPLE TOO. She dug her fingernails into her palms.

Kate was particularly annoyed when a group of pro-choicers—protesting in favor of third-trimester abortions—joined forces with the antiwar demonstrators. She couldn't fathom what common bond these two groups shared. Except that perhaps the only prerequisite required to protest was an antiestablishment spirit. One group believed that it was acceptable to abort six-month-old fetuses. The other was infuriated because people had been killed in Iran. That two groups with such dramatically contrasting ideals could even occupy the same *hemisphere*, let alone protest side by side, seemed like the ultimate hypocrisy.

Kate expected Richard Alderson's call at any minute and gave Emily explicit instructions to interrupt her no matter what.

McDermott, General Cumberland, and Toni Mitchell came into the Oval Office. As they discussed a dozen different scenarios of how Iran might react and what their response would be, they listened to CNN. It was like a game of chess, but the wooden pieces had been replaced with flesh-and-blood human beings.

Cumberland said, "I learned during the long battle in Iraq that CNN's sources for breakthrough news are often more reliable than our own. Don't be surprised if they make an announcement before we hear from Mr. Alderson."

"It's damn frightening," McDermott said, "that network news could be more efficient than the CIA."

Mitchell said, "CNN reporters were knee-deep in enemy territory during the Iraqi conflict and in Afghanistan. I even remember our first air strike against Baghdad in April of '91 during Desert Storm. It seemed unimaginable to be watching a war on cable TV while sitting in my living room munching popcorn."

In the background, Kate heard, "This is a special report from CNN Senior Correspondent Max Farman."

McDermott picked up the remote and increased the volume.

Farman, standing in front of the American Embassy in Amman, adjusted his tie and looked into the camera. "This is Max Farman, reporting live from Amman, Jordan. King Abdullah has just made a startling announcement denouncing the actions of President Ahmadinejad, calling his attack on Tel Aviv 'a blatant attempt to implicate Jordan and to further sabotage peace efforts between the United States, Israel, and other Muslim nations.'"

General Cumberland groaned. "Abdullah apparently has inherited his father's diplomatic charisma. I'm surprised he's not asking for American citizenship."

Farman continued. "The visibly emotional king, his eyes often filled with tears, further said he 'cannot endorse military action against a fellow Islamic country, but empathizes with America's delicate position and understands their aggressive posture.' He has ordered Iranian troops out of Jordan at once and has issued a letter of apology and sympathy to Prime Minister Netanyahu and all Israeli citizens. CNN will keep you updated as reaction to King Abdullah's bold statement unfolds. This is Max Farman reporting live from Amman, Jordan."

McDermott turned down the volume.

"What do you think?" Kate asked.

Cumberland said, "He's trying to save face. Ahmadinejad must have seduced him in some way. Now that their little affair is over, King Abdullah's pulling up his skivvies and heading for the hills. He crawled in bed with Ahmadinejad; now he's trying to cover his ass by crying rape."

"I think you're wrong," Mitchell said. "Ahmadinejad may have duped him to get his troops into Jordan. But I don't believe that King Abdullah conspired to bomb Israel."

"Frankly," McDermott said, "at this juncture, King Abdullah's innocence or guilt is inconsequential. Iran's reaction is the only issue." The COS lowered his voice. "Ahmadinejad's silence concerns me. Either the son of a bitch is convinced that we mean business or he's plotting retaliation."

Kate considered their opinions. McDermott was correct. Only Ahmadinejad's next move mattered. "We have no choice but to sit tight." She swiveled in her chair and glimpsed out the window at the growing number of protesters. Their timing could not be worse.

***

For almost a week, Guenther Krause had been navigating the floors of his tiny hotel room, waiting for the telephone call that would change his life. He bitterly understood how cabin fever could drive a man insane. He was certain that one more Whopper or order of fries or bucket of greasy KFC would cause his digestive system to completely shut down. On top of everything else, he'd been lighting one cigarette off another.

Trying to preserve his sanity, Guenther found some peace strumming his six-string acoustic guitar. He wasn't very good—never would be—but could play enough chords to make music. Since he was a little boy, he'd wanted to be a musician, but God hadn't blessed him with any natural talent. And of course, if there had been any chance that one day he'd be a fair guitarist, all hopes were lost because he had had to keep his guitar hidden from his father, so practicing was nearly impossible.

When he wasn't playing his Yamaha, he spent way too much time clicking through the TV channels with nothing to watch but soap operas, old movies, and the propaganda of local and nation-wide news broadcasts. With limited cable, he couldn't even watch Animal Planet. Guenther viewed one news segment and learned about the Middle East crisis; he watched it long enough to fear that the president might cancel her lecture. Then what?

Were his brothers testing him again? Was this some kind of perverse initiation? Hadn't he proven his worthiness and courage when he'd strangled Rabbi Herzhaft, right after the old man began a movement against the Disciples of the Third Reich? All Guenther wanted was to point his gun at President Miles, squeeze off seven rounds, and watch her head explode. Was that too much to ask? If the president postponed her lecture because of the Middle East crisis, surely he'd lose his mind!

Guenther peeked through the blinds for the hundredth time in the last hour. He didn't know what he was looking for. A Corolla parked next to Guenther's rental car. A young couple got out of the car. An attractive blonde and a...? Guenther couldn't even *think* the word!

The tramp musta been raised by hogs.

If his mission weren't so vital, he'd show them a thing or two about proper conduct. The cotton-picker? He'd slit his throat ear to ear and watch him bleed like a pig. And the bitch? Bone her to death. It was more than the whore deserved.

Unable to look at them without feeling uncontrollable rage, Guenther turned his head. A sudden dizziness caused the room to spin. He fell on the bed and squeezed his eyes shut. He could feel his lungs constricting as if someone were twisting them like a wet washcloth.

"I should'na looked out the window."

For years, Guenther had tried to understand why his mother never said anything about his scarred stomach. She had to have noticed. How could she have slept in the same bed with a man who had brutally abused both of her sons? Exploring every logical answer, he finally realized that she, too, lived in constant fear. Guenther remembered the heavy makeup concealing her black-and-blue eyes. Often, her lips were puffy, compelling evidence that she *had* confronted his father. He could, perhaps, forgive his mother for allowing Jurgen Krause to use her two sons' kidneys as punching bags and their bellies as ashtrays, but he'd *never* forgive her for...

Guenther grasped his head with both hands and shook it violently from side to side.

The slow-motion video began to play. He saw his mother lying on the bed. Her legs were wrapped around...

"No! Leave me be!"

He clenched his fist and repeatedly punched himself on the side of his head, trying in vain to dislodge the image. His eyes began to water, and snot dripped from his nose. He could see her clearly now.

Etta Krause's blonde hair hung off the side of the bed. Her milky-white skin glowed in the candlelight. Oh, God, how beautiful she was! The black man, slick as a wet seal, kissed her wildly, thrusting deep inside her. Guenther pressed his palms against his ears. He could not bear to hear her pleasurable moans. He'd just been released from Maplewood, had only been home for a week. He could never remember how long he'd watched them; the acrobatic fury went on forever. He'd tried to tear his eyes away, but he'd stood in the doorway, frozen. Watching. Feeling his gut turn inside out.

Why, Mother? Why with a...?

The telephone rang. He hadn't gotten a call since receiving instructions where to pick up a special package.

Guenther wiped his face with his sleeve and reached for his cigarettes. He shook one from the pack and lit it. Then he shuffled toward the nightstand; the burning cigarette hung off his lower lip and a swirling plume of blue smoke trailed behind him.

"Yes," he said. His voice was shaky. He waited for the only comment that would prevent him from slamming down the receiver.

"Nice day for a white wedding," the unfamiliar voice whispered.

"I'm listening."

"Security problems. No one will be allowed into the auditorium without first walking through a metal detector. Wrap the gun in a plastic bag. Go to the literary lecture tomorrow night at seven p.m. During the lecture, go to the men's room and securely tape the bag inside one of the toilet reservoir tanks with duct tape. The tank doesn't fill to the top, so tape it to the upper edge of the porcelain. Any questions?"

"She ain't gonna cancel, is she?"

"As of yet, no."

"How will I know if she does?"

"I'll be in touch."

Guenther dropped the phone on the bed and went to the window again, forcefully separated the blinds, and twisted them out of shape. The young couple removed the last piece of luggage from their trunk and strolled arm and arm toward the back stairway of the hotel.

"Ain't that sweet."

Guenther hurried into a pair of jeans, pulled a sweatshirt over his head, slipped into his sneakers, and reached for the Redskins cap. He grabbed his keys, stuffed his wallet into his back pocket, and entered the hall. As he slowly made his way toward the stairway, the young couple opened the steel fire door and walked toward him.

"Mornin', folks." He pulled open the fire door, cranked his head, and looked over his shoulder. Ebony and Ivory entered the room next to his. He'd been careless. He'd looked Ebony square in the eyes. Smiled at Ivory. He just might have to take drastic measures.

***

Filling his mouth with the warm canteen water, Stevers limped along the sandy terrain, unsure where he was headed. He had plenty of water, but soon the Iraqi sun would make it difficult for him to drink it sparingly. During survival training, he'd been taught never to challenge the desert sun, to walk during evening hours. But terrified that the moonlit landscape, abundant with uneven surfaces, might cause him to turn an ankle—an additional injury that would ensure his demise—he defied sound judgment and journeyed in daylight.

He sat on the ground and rested his back against a huge rock. There was no need for him to wander aimlessly. Preserving his energy was just as imperative as conserving food and water. He needed a plan for survival.

Stevers slipped the knapsack off his back, unzipped the front pocket, and removed a map. He unfolded it, laid it on the ground between his spread-eagle legs, and studied it. Abadan was just east of the air force base—perhaps three miles. Under the circumstances, it wasn't a city he wanted to visit. He seriously doubted that the Iranian military would welcome him with bands playing "The Star-Spangled Banner." Looking at the map more closely, Stevers estimated that the Kuwaiti border was about ten miles east of his current position. He felt certain he could find refuge there. If he could maintain a pace of three miles per hour, and rest only when necessary, he would likely reach the border in about four hours. But with the bum knee, he had no idea how often he'd have to rest.

He looked at his once spit-shined boots, now dull and dirty. They reminded him of his own deterioration. His luster had been gone for a long while. He'd gotten lazy since his tour of duty began on the *Ronald Reagan*, almost eighteen months ago. What happened to the high-spirited young man with the rock-hard body? He wanted to hold the Navy accountable for his apathetic attitude, but a little voice in his conscience told him otherwise. If he had any hope of surviving this ordeal, trudging his way to the Kuwaiti border, somehow he'd have to resurrect the once-determined, disciplined Kyle Stevers from the dead.

He swiped a black fly off his head.

It was now more apparent than ever that Lieutenant Kyle Stevers might never see Debra or Todd again. He could not afford to think about such a devastating possibility right now. Stevers stood and stretched. He bent forward and touched his toes. His joints snapped and cracked, and a dull throb blossomed in his knee.

Ten miles.

He snatched the knapsack, flipped it around his back, and slipped his arms through the straps. He removed the compass from his leather flight jacket and held it between his thumb and index finger. He headed east, focusing his eyes on the horizon, hoping he'd reach the Kuwaiti border before he ran out of food, water…and time.

***

Kate was discussing the Middle East crisis with McDermott when her intercom buzzed.

"Mr. Alderson is on line seven," Emily said.

"Hello, Richard. I hope you have good news for me."

"Ahmad Habib wants to meet me on neutral territory."

"For what purpose?"

"His communication said, and I quote, 'to circumvent further consequences.'"

"Consequences for whom?"

"I'm assuming the United States and Israel."

"Where does he want to meet?"

"Riyadh, Saudi Arabia."

"Has the king agreed to this?"

"Yes, Madam President."

"How do you feel about this, Richard?"

"My bags are packed. All I need is your blessing."

"Would you excuse me for one minute, please?" Kate pushed the mute button and looked at McDermott. "Habib wants to meet with Richard in Riyadh."

McDermott stood and folded his arms across his chest. "It's a positive gesture, but…Alderson may be in over his head."

"In what regard?"

"I'm not so sure he's a potent negotiator."

"Then who should mediate, Charles?"

"The secretary of state."

She was surprised at how unreservedly he answered.

"Richard, I'm going to dispatch Toni Mitchell to Riyadh. She will be our official representative, but I'd like you to accompany her during the meeting with Ambassador Habib."

The telephone was silent for a moment. "I understand, Madam President."

She hoped he did. "Is everything OK with Prime Minister Netanyahu?"

"He's not going to do anything stupid, if that's what you're asking."

"I'd like to conference with the secretary of state and you prior to the meeting. I'll advise the Joint Chiefs so we can outline a detailed strategy."

"It's important we cover all the bases," Alderson said.

"That's exactly what I intend to do." She unconsciously crossed her fingers. "Any word on the missing pilots?"

"I expect Habib will be the first to tell us."

"I'll speak with you soon," Kate said.

She set down the receiver and remembered a battered face she'd seen on the cover of *Newsweek* many years ago. She couldn't recall the brave pilot's name, but she never forgot the terror in his black-and-blue eyes.

"Are you OK, Madam President?"

McDermott's words startled her. "No, as a matter of fact, I'm not." Her head was pounding. "Would you locate Toni Mitchell for me, please?"

⊷ ★ ⊷

CHAPTER FOURTEEN

It was an invigorating notion, one that Guenther Krause reluctantly dismissed. To deviate from his plan, even for such a worthy venture, was a risk he was not willing to take. No matter how appealing, he forced himself to resist the temptation. Nonetheless, he fantasized about the things he wished he could do to Ebony and Ivory.

To Guenther, there was a greater satisfaction than the pleasure derived from exterminating inferior ones. The begging, the hopeless pleas for life at the exact moment before death, made Guenther feel godlike. When he'd killed the rabbi, he could have been compassionate and ended his life quickly. But there was no joy in mercy. The rabbi's pathetic whimpering had produced sheer joy. Guenther had watched the self-righteous old man die slowly; he'd reduced him from a holier-than-thou preacher to a sniveling, spineless coward. During this first eradication of an inferior one, Guenther discovered that the power over life and death was the greatest of all mortal pleasures—a transcendental orgasm beyond definition.

Guenther pressed his ear to the wall and tried to decipher Ebony and Ivory's conversation. Their words were garbled, but Ivory's pleasurable moans were unmistakable. Hers was a quivering, almost painful cry. A horrible image crept into Guenther's thoughts. *Mutter.* He knew what Ebony was doing to Ivory; he'd lived this nightmare before. He pressed his ear harder against the wall. To be reminded of his mother was unbearable, yet he was unable to stop the intrusion into his neighbors' private world. He could see the thrusting, Ebony slamming between Ivory's spread-open legs, his demon seed searching for her fertile egg. Another misfit could be conceived. The procreation of an inferior breed. How could a loyal Aryan do nothing?

Currents of rage gushed through Guenther. His hands curled into fists, and his fingernails dug deep into his flesh. He could not imagine despising his mother more than at this moment. Guenther had found a way to forgive his mother for neglecting his brother and him, for allowing his father to abuse them. But he could not live with his mother's disgrace. Etta Krause had tarnished the purity of Guenther's white blood by giving herself to a black man. For this, he could never forgive her. He buried his face in the pillow; his guttural scream was audible only to him.

For how long could he lie to himself? His life on Earth would soon be over. Moments after he killed the president, Secret Service bullets would tear into his flesh and turn his organs into oatmeal. So why worry about cleansing the world of two more misfits? Why not accept this unexpected windfall as a divine gift? To deal with these inferior ones could only endear him to his Aryan god. Perhaps his noble deed would redeem his mother's wanton behavior.

A door slammed. Guenther jumped off the bed, tiptoed to the door, and opened it enough to poke his head in the hall. Ivory was strutting her way to the exit door. Her blonde ponytail rhythmically swayed to her stride. Her plump ass wiggled with purpose, just begging for something only Guenther could give her.

Guenther sat on the bed and scratched the back of his head. How was he was going to do it?

He put on his Levi's, stuffed the Colt in front of the jeans, and slipped on his red flannel shirt, letting it hang out to conceal the gun. He stepped into the bathroom, rinsed his face with cold water, checked his smile in the mirror, and headed for the door. Before he stepped into the hall, he put on his Redskins baseball cap. To his delight, the corridor was empty. Guenther was happy they occupied the room next to his. He tapped his room key on the door. The door swung open, and Ebony's six-foot-six torso towered over him. His head was shaved clean as an eight ball, and he was wearing a white tank top and orange Syracuse University sweatpants. His deltoids were deeply cut, isolating them from his well-pumped triceps. His dark skin was as waxy as a semisweet chocolate bar.

"Howdy, neighbor," Guenther said. "My telephone ain't workin'. Any chance I can use yours to report it?"

Ebony stepped to the side. "No problem." His voice was deep, gravelly. He extended his hand. "My name's Jerome."

Guenther would have preferred to stick his hand in a meat grinder. "Bill Thompson. Appreciate you lettin' me use your phone."

Jerome's huge hand swallowed Guenther's skinny fingers. The big man jerked his arm like he was pumping water from a well. Guenther pulled his hand away and as inconspicuously as possible wiped it on his jeans. Keeping his back toward Jerome, he walked into the room and listened for the door to close, then Guenther turned around. "You here alone?"

"You said hello to my wife and me in the hallway, remember?"

Wife? Should'na told me that.

"Oh yeah. Your wife's real pretty. Where she at?"

"She ran to the liquor store. I've been offered a professorship at Georgetown, so we want to celebrate. But not enough to shell out eighty bucks for a bottle of hotel champagne."

"Congratulations."

"What brings you to Georgetown?" Jerome asked.

Guenther looked into the man's slick-black eyes. "Gonna assassinate the president in a couple days."

Jerome let out a resonant guffaw. "That's a good one, Bill." His eyes widened and locked on Guenther's face.

Ain't sure if I'm jokin', huh?

Jerome's pearly smile melted to a catatonic stare; his shiny brown cheeks blushed red. Guenther waited for him to make a move.

Still standing in the foyer, Jerome leaped for the doorknob and yanked hard. Guenther tore the Colt from his jeans and, with one fluid motion, pulled back the slide and pointed the gun at Jerome.

"Open that door, motherfucker, and I'll decorate the walls with your black brains."

The doorknob slipped from Jerome's moist fingertips, and the metal door clicked shut. Sweat trickled down his forehead into his eyes. He blinked furiously. "All I've got is thirty or forty dollars, Bill. Take it. Take my credit cards."

"My name ain't Bill, and I don't give a rat's ass about your fuckin' credit cards. I ain't no common thief."

"What do you want?"

"I wanna meet your...*wife.*"

***

Kyle Stevers estimated that he'd covered close to four miles. A few mouthfuls of water sloshed around in his canteen; he'd already drunk two of the three reserve bottles. He'd made better time than expected, but his right knee was swollen and inflamed, and he was certain his feet were covered with blisters. He'd found four ibuprofens in his first aid kit and swallowed them with barely enough water to prevent them from lodging in his throat. The anti-inflammatory might have helped if he were able to sit down and elevate his leg for a while, but that was a luxury he could not afford.

Along the way, the only sign of life he'd noticed were striped snakes and lime-green lizards. He hadn't seen an Iranian soldier, civilian, car, truck, or aircraft. It was like being stranded on the moon. Although the sun had not been as intense as he'd expected, he buried all nonessential items that would slow his pace. He tore the legs off his pants just above the knee, stuffed one in his back pocket, and wrapped the other around his head to protect it from the sun. Only food, water, flight jacket, first aid kit, knife, and shovel remained in his knapsack. He tried to pick up the pace, pushing his body to its limit. But his throbbing knee had suddenly grown to nauseating pain, so the best he could do was shuffle along and pray he didn't throw up. In this barren desert, every horizon looked the same. As he hobbled along, Stevers checked the compass often to be sure he was headed toward the Kuwaiti border. After thirty more minutes, at a snail's pace, Stevers could no longer endure the pain. He almost fell onto the hot sand. With great care, he extended his legs. By gripping the back of his thigh and pulling it toward his chest, he tried to bend his right knee. He'd hardly moved it before the stabbing pain became nearly unbearable. Keeping his right leg straight was the only position that yielded minor relief. He had to find a way to immobilize his leg.

Stevers craned his neck and searched the landscape. The sandy soil did not offer any extraordinary solutions. He remembered an emergency technique he'd learned in basic training. He removed the shovel from the knapsack, unfolded it, and laid it on the ground beside his right leg. The concave blade appeared to be the same contour as his thigh. Keeping the shovel parallel to his leg, he rested the back of his thigh on the curved blade and positioned the handle behind his right calf. Using the shovel as a splint, Stevers tore the extra pant leg into strips and secured it to his leg in three places. He rolled to his stomach, pushed up his torso, bent his left knee, and struggled to stand. He took several steps, swinging his right leg like a pendulum as he walked. The makeshift brace would slow his already snaillike pace, but by keeping his leg rigid, he hoped to reduce the pain and minimize further damage.

He struggled forward, often dragging his right leg, other times swinging it. He focused his thoughts on Debra and Todd, trying not to think about his knee, hoping he could will the pain to subside.

A strange sound broke the desert silence. A whining. A thumping. He swiveled around. In the distance, he could see what he believed was a helicopter heading toward him. He surveyed the landscape. There wasn't a tree in sight. Only miles of flat, sandy earth. He considered running, but how could a gimp outrun a chopper? For an instant, he thought about digging a hole in the loose soil and burying himself. If he exposed only his nose he could breathe. He looked back at the helicopter. It was closing in quickly. Stevers dropped his knapsack on the ground and gripped his holstered weapon with his right hand. He used his left hand as a visor and shielded his eyes from the sun as he watched the helicopter's rapid approach. As the chopper came into clear view, he could see a tricolor rectangle painted on the side of the hull. Red, white, and green. Islamic emblem in the center.

The Iranian flag.

He covered his eyes as the chopper kicked up a swirling sand storm. It hovered for a minute just above his head, then descended to the ground, twenty yards away. The engine stopped whining, and all Stevers could hear was a slowing *wop-wop* sound. He opened his eyes and watched four soldiers charging toward him as if he'd just caught a punted football. They pointed their rifles his way. Now, of course, he regretted his decision to walk during daylight hours.

Brilliant strategy, Lieutenant.

For a fleeting moment, foolhardy heroics nearly compelled him to draw his weapon. But in his mind's eye, he could see the picture of Debra and Todd stuffed in his back pocket. He placed his hands behind his head and prayed they wouldn't open fire. If he had to die for his country, he wanted it to be on American soil.

***

Following Carl Kramer's strict orders to forward any calls related to the White House directly to him, his assistant buzzed Kramer on the intercom and told him a police captain was calling.

"What's he want, and how did he get to *me*?"

"It has to do with the White House, and he said it was urgent."

Just what I need today. "Go ahead and put him through." Kramer cleared his throat. "Carl Kramer speaking."

"Mr. Kramer, Captain Teddy Daniels ringing you up from the Grand Cayman Islands. You in charge of the CIA, mate?"

"I'm deputy director." Kramer recognized the Cockney accent. Daniels was a Brit.

"We've found an American. His throat was slit ear to ear—execution style. Lad's got two names."

"What do you mean, two names?"

"A bloody mystery. The young chap had two Maryland driver's licenses. Could be Richard Crandall or Joseph Vitelli."

"Why did you contact the CIA?"

"The bloke had a White House ID. Should I be chatting up a different agency?"

"No, Captain Daniels. You've done the right thing by calling me." Kramer chose his words carefully. "Is there anything else I should be aware of?"

"We found a passport and three airline tickets. One to Miami. Miami to New York. And one from New York to Rome, Italy. All one-way."

"Any suspects or witnesses?"

"Not a bloody clue."

"What will you do with the body?" Kramer asked.

"Unless next of kin pay for his transport back to the US of A, I'm afraid he'll be cremated. Not much room for cemeteries on the islands."

Kramer knew that Vitelli's only family was somewhere in Italy. "Have you contacted anyone else?"

"Just you, mate."

"I can't explain why he had an alias, but the man's real name is Richard Crandall. If you release information to the media, please be sure you use his proper name. If there *is* a living Joseph Vitelli, we wouldn't want to write a premature eulogy, would we?"

"What shall we do with the lad's body?"

"He has no family. Have it cremated."

Kramer could tell by the silence that Daniels was taken aback.

"If you need to phone me," Daniels said, "you can ring me up at police headquarters in George Town."

Kramer scribbled the number on a legal pad. "Please call me immediately if *anyone* contacts you regarding Mr. Crandall's murder."

"Be happy to, mate."

Kramer expected the police captain to say good-bye, but he could hear heavy breathing.

"I do have a bit of a pebble in my shoe, Mr. Kramer. Why did the White House ID identify him as Vitelli? Seems a bit daft."

"Mr. Crandall may be the only one who can answer that, Captain."

After a long silence, Daniels conceded. "Have a cheery good day."

Kramer couldn't dial the number fast enough.

"*Washington Post*, how may I direct your call?"

"Tommy Luciano, please."

As he waited for the call to be transferred, sweat trickled down Kramer's forehead. Tommy was one of those journalists who didn't always walk a straight line—the kind of reporter Kramer relied on for "special" assignments.

"Newsroom. Luciano speaking."

"This is Carl Kramer."

"Long time no see. Got something juicy for me?"

"I need a favor, Tommy—just between you and me."

"It's not going to put me in the slammer, is it?"

"No. But it might make you a hero."

"I'm listening."

***

Guenther Krause made himself comfortable on the king-size bed. He propped a pillow against the headboard and rested his back. He wondered why Ebony and Ivory's mattress was firmer than his. Did black professors get some kind of preferential treatment? Ebony sat in the corner of the room on the plaid love seat. Pools of sweat dripped off his shiny skin. Ebony had been silent since

Guenther had said he'd wanted to meet his wife. Guenther could tell by his twisted facial expression that Ebony's thoughts were raw with fear. He had good reason to be frightened.

When Guenther heard a key click in the door, he jumped up and stood with his back against the wall, positioning his body perpendicular to the entryway. When Ivory entered, he concealed his body from her line of vision. He pointed the Colt at Jerome. "A big smile, tar baby."

The door opened. "Found a chilled bottle of Moet, sweet-heart," Ivory said.

Guenther listened for the door to click shut. The room filled with a sickening-sweet perfume smell, as if a ten-dollar-an-hour hooker had just come in. Unable to see Guenther with her peripheral vision, she walked toward Jerome holding the bottle out in front of her.

"You look like you've seen a ghost," she said.

"Boo-hoo," Guenther yelled.

The woman pivoted around. Her eyes were fixed on the Colt.

"Scream and I'll blow your fuckin' face off!"

The champagne bottle slipped from her fingers. She covered her mouth with both hands and muffled a yelp. The bottle bounced on the carpet, spun around like a bowling pin, then rolled under the bureau. She gaped at her terrified husband. He shrugged his shoulders and clutched her hand.

"Ain't that cute. Ebony and Ivory. Just like the song."

"My *name* is Joanne."

Ah, the bitch is spunky. "As long as I got the gun, your new name is Ivory. Or would you prefer White Bitch?" He shook the Colt at Jerome. "And your hubby's name is Ebony. Got it?"

Guenther checked his Timex. To allow ample time to hide the gun in the toilet reservoir before the lecture began, he had to be in the auditorium by seven p.m. A lot could happen in three hours. He was glad he'd bought some duct tape to secure the gun to the toilet reservoir.

He reached in his jeans pocket and pulled out his room key. "Hey Ivory, fetch me the gray duct tape on the bathroom vanity. If you ain't back in two minutes, I'm gonna stick this gun up Little Black Sambo's ass and blow his guts all over the room. Got it?"

She reached for the key, but Guenther closed his fingers around it. "Two minutes is all you got."

She snatched it from his hand and looked at Guenther as if he were a cockroach needing to be stepped on. He knew exactly how to tame feisty bitches. The scent of her perfume reminded Guenther of the blue-haired women at the bingo hall his mother'd taken him to when he was young. The old hags loved to mess his hair and pinch his cheeks red and tell him what an adorable little boy he was. If they could only see him now, he thought, they'd be turning over in their graves.

The second hand swept past ninety seconds. She walked back in the door and handed Guenther his key and the roll of tape. He handed the duct tape back to her and wiggled the gun at Ebony. "I want your tar-black ass in that chair. And face it toward the bed."

The man swiveled the wooden chair and sat down. Guenther shook the gun at Ivory. "Tape Ebony's legs to the chair. Nice and tight."

She unwound the gray tape in circles and taped his right leg, then his left.

Guenther watched her closely. "Ain't enough for this big boy. Don't be stingy with my tape." He didn't want to underestimate

Ebony's strength. "Now his arms. All the way around his body. Tape him to the chair real good."

He let her wrap the tape around his body until he was certain Jerome couldn't move.

"Now tape those big lips."

Ivory tore a six-inch piece and gently placed it over his mouth. Guenther checked the tape and made certain the muscular black man was securely immobilized.

She stood next to her husband and gripped his shoulder. Her face was as pale as skim milk. "What do you want from us?"

Guenther looked at her purple Georgetown sweatshirt. Her Guess jeans were skintight, cutting deeply into her, leaving little for his imagination. "We're gonna play a little game of Q&A. If you tell the truth, Ebony lives. If you don't, he eats a bullet. Got it?"

She looked at Jerome, apparently searching for guidance.

"Are your boobs real, or did Dr. Silicone give ya them?"

"*What?*"

"Your tits. I wanna know if they're *gen*-u-ine."

"You're *disgusting!*"

Guenther pointed the Colt at Ebony. "Are they?"

"Of course they are."

"With that baggy sweatshirt and all, you might be fibbin'. And a fib is a lie where I come from."

She glanced at her husband.

He shook his head.

"Go fuck yourself," the blonde said.

Guenther stormed toward Ebony, flipped the gun in the air, and caught it by the barrel. He smacked the side of Jerome's head with the handle. Jerome closed his eyes and let out a muffled moan.

Guenther clenched his teeth. "I *ain't* playin' with ya."

She crossed her arms, grabbed the elastic band at the bottom of the sweatshirt, and turned it inside out over her head. Guenther's eyes opened wide. Either she was wearing a Wonder Bra or the Booby Fairy had been generous.

"Lose the bra."

She hesitated, and Guenther cocked his arm.

"OK! OK!" She reached behind her back, unsnapped the lace bra, and let it fall to the floor. Her breasts were full, like generous scoops of vanilla ice cream. Her pink nipples were youthfully erect.

"You a *real* blonde?" Guenther asked.

"What the fuck does *that* mean?"

"Don't you understand English? Where did the blonde locks come from, God or Clairol?"

"It's natural."

"How do I know you ain't lying?"

"I can't prove it."

"If it's real, then you got a blonde pussy." Guenther grinned. "Show it to me."

Jerome's biceps flexed and veins sprouted on his forearms. He rocked the chair from side to side, and his oversized eyes glared at his wife.

Guenther again walloped the side of Ebony's head. "If you don't sit still, Ivory is gonna eat a bullet. Now, behave. Just like your granddaddy did in the cotton fields."

She loosened her belt, pulled down her zipper, and wiggled the jeans over her curvaceous hips. She unlaced her sneakers, kicked them off, and stepped out of the jeans.

"I ain't got x-ray vision."

She squeezed her eyes shut and tears leaked from the corners. She hooked her thumbs inside her pink bikini panties and slid them down her legs.

"Well, I'll be damned. Ain't no lying going on in this room. At least not yet." Guenther tossed the Redskins cap on the bed. "You a virgin?"

She peered at Guenther with wild eyes. "What kind of a sick fuck are you?"

Ebony rocked the chair again, wiggling and twisting like a man covered with bees. Guenther ripped the tape off his mouth, and the man's face contorted. He pressed the gun to Ebony's trembling lips and jammed it into his mouth.

"Wanna know how sick I am?" Guenther clicked off the safety, and Ebony's teeth chattered on the steel barrel.

"Please!" she yelled. "Don't hurt him."

"I asked if you was a virgin."

"How *could* I be? I'm married."

"That don't mean jack-diddly. The Virgin Mary didn't give any to Joseph."

She fell to her knees and folded her hands in prayer. "I beg you. *Please*, don't do this."

Guenther pointed to the bed. "Lay down. Time for Dr. Dick to give you an exam."

For a moment, she hesitated. Her chin hung to her chest. Guenther stuffed the gun deeper into her husband's mouth. Ebony coughed and gagged. Whimpering in breathless gasps, Ivory labored to stand, then moved toward the bed. She fell on her back, pressed her inner thighs firmly together, covered her breasts with her forearms, and folded her hands over her pubic hair. She looked like a naked mummy. Guenther stood over her, his eyes surveying her critically.

"Don't be bashful," Guenther said. "Give me a look at those big titties and that tight little pussy of yours."

She looked at her husband and slowly moved her arms to her side.

Her sandy-colored pubic hair was trimmed to a narrow V. Under her left breast, he noticed a strawberry birthmark. The blonde hair, vanilla-cream skin, and radiant blue eyes made her look like an angel. The gun fell out of his hand, and it bounced on the bed. He unzipped his jeans and slid them and his boxers to his ankles. He placed his hands between her knees and spread her legs. For several minutes, Guenther was lost, frozen like a deer staring at bright headlights. Ivory was beautiful. And she deserved something special. Guenther crisscrossed his arms, grabbed her ankles, and turned her over to a prone position.

Glancing to his left, he met Ebony's wide-eyed look of horror and knelt between her thighs. With clawlike hands, he grasped her hips and forced her up on her knees. "Lemme show you how a real man docs it."

CHAPTER FIFTEEN

After brainstorming with the Joint Chiefs, considering every conceivable scenario that Ambassador Habib might bring to the negotiating table, Kate locked herself in her private office to concentrate on strategy and insulate her thoughts from distractions. While preparing for her conversation with Mitchell and Alderson, Kate took a moment and coordinated a conference call with Debra Stevers and Marcia Travis, the MIA pilots' wives. The English language did not offer sufficient words for her to clearly express her regrets. She invited them to the White House, believing it was unlikely they'd accept. They thanked her, graciously and with a sincere air of appreciation, but chose to stay with their families. Kate tried to encourage them, promised to exhaust every resource to ensure their husbands' safe return. But by the skeptical tone in both their voices, Kate could tell that her attempt to embolden their spirits had failed.

The intercom buzzed, and Kate snatched the receiver. "What *is* it?"

"You asked not to be disturbed, Madam President, but Carl Kramer says it's urgent he speak with you. Shall I instruct him to come back later?"

For Kramer, Kate would make an exception. "Send him into my private office."

Kramer softly knocked, peeked around the door, and eased his way inside. If network television ever decided to resurrect the old *Dragnet* series, Kate thought, Kramer—stocky body, out-of-style brush cut, drab clothing, sedate demeanor—would make a perfect modern-day Sergeant Joe Friday.

He sat in the chair to the left of the president, crossed his legs, and leaned forward. "Joseph Vitelli was murdered in the Grand Cayman Islands."

It took several deep breaths for Kate to grasp Kramer's announcement. "My God in heaven." A familiar pain throbbed in her temples. "How? Why?"

"His throat was slit. No suspects or clues. He had a bogus driver's license, passport, and plane tickets to Rome. All under a phony name."

"What does it mean?"

"Don't need to enlist Sherlock Holmes. Vitelli had something to do with President Rodgers's assassination, and somebody wanted to silence him."

"Give me a name," Kate said.

"Jack Miller."

"*What?*"

"I don't know how he's involved, but he's up to his eyeballs. Mr. Miller—if that's even his real name—coincidentally worked for the Chicago Police Department. In the *scuba* squad."

Kate remembered the jellyfish poison.

"He's recently had assignments in Topeka, Kansas, and Long Beach, California," Kramer said. "But there are no records indicating who dispatched him or what the nature of his business was."

Kate knew he was in Long Beach interrogating Wendy Marshall, but why had he visited her hometown? "What do you make of it?"

"At this juncture, I'm not sure."

Kate tried to clear her tangled thoughts. "I can believe that Joseph Vitelli might have been coerced into poisoning President Rodgers and perhaps that Miller harvested the poison. But I can't imagine that Miller acted on his own volition. What possible motive could *he* have?"

"I'm certain there's a mastermind, Madam President. Someone who profited from President Rodgers's death."

She knew the innuendo was unintended, but still, it was like a left jab to her head. "I gained more than anyone, Carl."

"I didn't mean to—"

"I understand." She wasn't sure Kramer did. "We have to confront Jack Miller."

"That might not be possible," Kramer said. "He conveniently resigned a few days ago."

Kate almost laughed. "Interesting coincidence."

"For obvious reasons," Kramer said, "I did not want to involve the department, so I asked a private investigator friend of mine to do some leg work for me on the hush."

"Is he reliable?"

"I'd trust him with my life."

She remembered that the DCI had given President Rodgers the suspect bottle of wine. "Any dirt under Ellenwood's fingernails?"

Kramer coughed into his hand and shook his head. "As head of the CIA, he's right in the thick of things." He fixed his stare on her. "And so am I."

"We're in an exclusive club, Mr. Kramer."

The corners of Kramer's eyes twitched to a smile. The room suddenly felt like a sauna. Kate slipped off her suit jacket and let it rest on the back of the chair. "Think we can locate Miller?"

"I'll do my best," Kramer promised.

"Please keep me posted. And, Carl...Watch your behind."

"I learned to grow eyes in back of my head a long time ago, Madam President."

***

Not one of Kyle Stevers's captors had spoken to him. At first, this seemed strange. Then he realized that none of them could speak English. He'd repeatedly asked about Wes Travis, but all they did was look at him with a peculiar stare and shrug their shoulders.

Stevers glanced out the helicopter window and could see what remained of the Iranian Air Force base. The main building had been reduced to heaps of charred bricks and twisted metal. Scattered about, he could see disfigured desks, crushed file cabinets, and mangled chairs. With enormous anxiety, Stevers studied the smoldering piles of rubble, wondering how many Iranians might be buried alive, gulping their last breaths of air. As the helicopter descended, Stevers could see a metal building that had survived the air strike.

When the soldiers captured Stevers, he was terrified they'd forcefully remove the shovel splinted to his right leg. But they handled him compassionately and seemed only concerned with confiscating his weapon, knapsack, and dog tags. He'd been taught that Iranians were savages, but Stevers was beginning to believe that military propaganda had painted a distorted picture. He'd thought that seeing the destruction from such a close proximity would garnish his spirit of patriotism. Instead, it nauseated and disgraced him to be an American. Was he supposed to feel like a hero? How impersonal and calculating to have flown

his F-18 twenty thousand feet above and fire his missiles at targets and human beings he knew nothing about. He hadn't realized until this moment that to murder people simply because he
was ordered to contradicted everything he believed in. What did
he know about Iranian culture? What made him and his fellow
Americans judge and jury? The Iranians had to be enraged; they
had every right to be. Yet they hadn't hurt him. What did their
quarrel with Israel have to do with Lieutenant Kyle David Stevers?

Stevers—for no apparent reason except the Iranians' behavior—felt safe, removed from harm's way. This was a dangerous
attitude for a prisoner of war. Maybe, he thought, it was the "calm
before the storm." It was risky to let down his guard. But until
the Iranians did something to threaten his safety, he'd remain as
polite and cooperative as his patriotic ethics allowed.

The helicopter landed fifty feet from the steel building. Two
soldiers, young enough to be in high school and skinnier than
pencils, assisted him out of the chopper. His kneecap felt like it'd
been replaced with hot charcoal. With one soldier on each side
supporting his weight, they helped Stevers hobble to the building.
He could no longer move his injured leg without paying a painful price; he dragged it along the ground as if it were a dysfunc-
tional prosthetic limb. The soldiers led him through an expansive
building. He gazed up at the fifty-foot ceiling. A warehouse, he
guessed. Maybe the one used to house the planes his fellow pilots
and he'd destroyed.

The soldiers escorted him to a small square room with corru-
gated-steel walls. Two metal chairs sat side by side in the middle
of the room; a narrow table in the corner reminded Stevers of a
massage table. There were no windows in the room; the only light
came from a bare bulb hanging from the ceiling. It could not have
been more than sixty watts. The bulb swayed to and fro, casting

creepy shadows along the wall. The room was damp and smelled like oily rags. One of the soldiers gestured, and Stevers supposed they wanted him to sit down. He carefully sat on one of the chairs and extended his braced leg forward.

When the soldiers left the room, the younger one with the two-week beard and curly black hair looked over his shoulder and smiled at Stevers just before the door closed behind him. It was nine parts sinister, one part curious. His stomach growled, and for the first time since landing on Iranian soil, Stevers felt hungry. More like ravenous. He heard voices from the other side of the door. Doors slamming. Engines starting and stopping. Brakes squealing. The door swung open, and two men walked in. One looked like an officer. He was dressed in a military uniform, remarkably well-groomed, and his cap had a havelock draped around the back. The other man's complexion was pallid. He was wearing a doctor's white smock and carried a black leather bag. Stevers thought it strange that anyone living in a desert could be so pale.

"My name is Dr. Aziz." There was a trace of accent, but his English was perfect. "This is Colonel Bajraf."

"Lieutenant Kyle Stevers, United States Navy."

The doctor looked at Stevers's extended leg. "Have you been injured?"

"It's my knee. I think it's serious."

"Dr. Aziz will look at knee," Colonel Bajraf said. "Get on table."

The colonel grabbed Stevers's right arm, stuffed his hand into his armpit, and helped him to stand. The colonel's grip suggested that he was a powerful man. Stevers braced his palms on the edge of the table, cautiously lifted his body into a seated position, then slid back so his splinted leg rested comfortably. He noticed four straps hanging from the table.

"May I examine your knee?" Dr. Aziz asked.

"It feels like it's on fire."

From his black bag, the doctor grabbed an unusual-looking pair of scissors and cut the strips of cloth securing the shovel. He grasped the heel of Stevers's boot, gently lifted his leg, removed the shovel, and allowed the back of his leg to rest on the table.

He carefully poked and prodded the area around the knee cap. "Does this hurt?"

Stevers grit his teeth, and his body cringed beneath the doctor's touch. "Yes. Everything hurts." It felt as if Aziz were pushing hot knives into his knee.

"Can you bend your knee?"

"Not without feeling as if I'm tearing something inside."

"Roll to your left, please."

With the doctor's help, Stevers struggled but was able to position his body as the doctor requested.

"I am sorry for the discomfort, but I must check your range of motion. When my exam is completed, Colonel Bajraf will arrange to have you flown to a hospital in Abadan. Your knee must be x-rayed."

Stevers's glance met the colonel's cold stare. Something didn't feel right. He'd destroyed their air force base, slaughtered their people, and they treated him like a comrade?

"Doctor, has anyone found my copilot?"

"He was more fortunate than you. Perhaps Colonel Bajraf will allow you to see him."

"Where is he?"

Dr. Aziz and the colonel exchanged words in their native tongue.

"He's resting," the doctor said.

The doctor gripped Stevers's ankle with one hand, held the back of his right thigh with the other, and slowly bent his knee.

"Holy fucking shit!" Stevers clutched his calf and stopped the doctor from bending his leg any further. "Please. You're killing me, Doctor."

"I am concerned," Aziz said. "Ten degrees causes extreme pain. You require more sophisticated medical attention than we can offer here, Lieutenant. Bending your leg beyond its comfortable range may result in irrevocable damage."

Again, the two men spoke in a foreign tongue.

"Are you hungry, Lieutenant?" Dr. Aziz asked.

"Starving."

"Our culture is quite different than yours. Do not expect hamburgers and french fries. After you eat, the colonel will arrange for you to be transported to a hospital."

"Can I see Lieutenant Travis?"

"Perhaps," Aziz said.

The men left Stevers alone. He wished he could understand Persian or whatever language they were speaking. Or maybe not.

***

After extensive deliberation with Toni Mitchell and Richard Alderson, to prepare them for their meeting with Ahmad Habib, Kate decided to have a peaceful dinner with her father. They sat quietly in Kate's private dining room. Trevor barely touched his steak, and Kate used her butter knife to play with her garlic-and-cilantro mashed potatoes.

"Is the steak not to your liking?" Kate asked.

"It's delicious, honey. I guess I'm more tired than hungry." He pointed to her plate. "You're not doing so well, either."

"Whenever I slaughter people, I lose my appetite. Must be a quirk in my personality." She wanted to ask his opinion, but his silence spoke volumes.

"Was the air strike solely your decision or predicated on the Joint Chiefs' recommendation?"

"There were points of contention, but we all agreed that military intervention was necessary."

"Then why are you bearing the burden of responsibility?"

"Because I pushed the button. I should have continued pursuing a diplomatic remedy."

"The die is cast, Kate. You made the only decision possible."

"Then how come I feel like throwing up every time I think about it?"

"My sweet, lovely, compassionate daughter. Your conservative measures prevented a full-fledged war. You saved hundreds, perhaps thousands of lives. No one can predict how Ahmadinejad or Prime Minister Netanyahu will react, but so far, you've prevented mass destruction and a bloodbath."

"The 'so far' part is what worries me." He had no idea how much his encouraging words lifted her spirits. Although this was neither the time nor place, there was a nagging question she'd wanted to ask him for years. Why Kate chose this particular moment eluded her.

"Are you disappointed that I haven't given you grandchildren?"

He stared at her with saucer-like eyes. "Is there something you're trying to tell me?"

"Heavens no, Daddy. Just a hypothetical question."

He gave her a thoughtful glance. "I can't say for sure, but I suppose it could be fun."

The telephone rang. Kate jumped, and her fork fell to the floor. Could it be Secretary of State Mitchell so quickly? Martin, one of the service staff, knocked twice and peeked his head through the slightly open door.

"Sorry to interrupt you, Madam President, but you have an urgent telephone call."

Kate yanked at her left earring and almost tore her lobe. She rubbed her ear and lifted the cordless lying next to the dinner plate. "President Miles."

"This is Toni, Madam President."

Kate looked at her father, and he immediately stood up. She realized he misunderstood her gesture. She shook her head and motioned for him to sit back down.

"Did Ahmad Habib live up to his dubious reputation?" Kate asked.

"The pilots are alive. Supposedly, neither is seriously injured."

"That's fantastic news."

"If we meet their demands, it is. President Ahmadinejad has agreed to stop all military action against Israel and promises to return our pilots unharmed—if we meet three conditions."

"I'm listening."

"First, we must withdraw our battleships and aircraft carriers from the Persian Gulf and the Red Sea. And sign an agreement prohibiting their return unless unanimously approved by the United Nations."

"Other than their endorsement for the United States to launch a military offensive against Afghanistan after the September eleventh terrorist attack, the United Nations has never agreed on *anything* unanimously," Kate said.

"I think that's the method to his madness. Second, we cannot initiate future military action against Iran unless a declaration of war has been issued by the United States Congress."

Kate took a gulp of ice water. "Ahmadinejad has done his homework."

"The last one is the coup de grâce, Madam President. Within sixty days, we must withdraw our troops from Kuwait, Saudi Arabia, Iraq, Egypt, and Turkey. Their return is prohibited unless there is a valid declaration of war against an Islamic nation."

"Did you tell Habib that he and his leader should seek psychiatric counseling?"

"Wanted to. I told him that Ahmadinejad's demands were outrageous and unrealistic, and the likelihood of the United States considering them was less than remote."

"His reaction?"

"If we do not comply within seventy-two hours, our pilots will be publicly executed as war criminals. He said they would send graphic videotapes of their execution to the media."

Kate dipped her fingertips in the ice water and rubbed her flushed cheeks. "I'm going to convene the Joint Chiefs at once. I'll have directives for you as soon as possible."

"There's one more thing, Madam President: Habib also said that it's imperative we watch CNN news at eight p.m., eastern standard time."

"For what purpose?"

"He wouldn't tell me."

Kate sculpted the mashed potatoes with her butter knife. "Clarify your position for me, Toni."

"Richard and I have discussed it extensively, and our opinions differ. To surrender to extortion, under any circumstances, would result in disastrous consequences."

"And if our unwillingness to comply is a death sentence for the pilots?"

"If we modify our Middle East military objectives in any way, our worldwide credibility and *thousands* of lives will be at risk. Besides, we have a strict policy that prohibits us from negotiating with terrorist groups. Technically, of course, Habib represents Iran as a nation. But nonetheless, we're dealing with a terrorist mentality. To acknowledge any ultimatum would show a sign of weakness on our part."

Toni's words struck a sensitive chord in Kate. "I'll speak with you shortly."

Kate set down the telephone, put her elbows on the table, and rested her chin on her folded hands. Her eyes were misty. She gazed at her father and shook her head. "Do you suppose it's possible that I was an executioner in a prior life?"

***

Kyle Stevers stuffed the unidentified ground meat and rice combo into his mouth as if it were an aged Omaha steak. He tried not to think about what he was eating, hoping it wasn't some old decrepit camel. It seemed unlikely that this backward-ass country had free-range cattle or pigs roaming the desert. As the gamy flavor grew more unpalatable, he dropped the spoon and wished he had some Rolaids. He had no perception of time, but it had been awhile since the doctor and colonel had left him. Resting his back against the wall and extending his leg was the only comfortable position for his injured knee, so he remained on the massage table.

Stevers scratched his two-day stubble. What he wouldn't give for a warm shower and shave, to change his sweat-stained clothing. But this wasn't exactly the Ritz. Any sane man would feel delighted just to be alive; he could only feel guilt. For the first time since landing in Iran, Lance Wentworth's double-dimpled smile crept into his thoughts. Stevers had convinced his wingman to play a deadly game. He could feel a lump growing in the back of his throat. He squeezed his eyes shut and tried to rid his mind of the haunting image. But there was nowhere to hide from the vivid video of Lance's plane engulfed in flames. His stupidity, his reckless heroics, had cost Lance his life. Stevers had widowed Samantha and forced his two daughters to grow up without their father. For what? So one day—assuming he survived whatever the Iranians were planning for his sorry ass—he could bounce his grandson on his lap, point to a map of Iran, and tell a tale of how Grandpa beat the crap out of the bad guys?

Careful not to move his leg, Stevers reached behind his back and slid the picture out of his pocket. He tilted it toward the dim light so he could see Debra and Todd clearly.

Voices came from the other side of the door.

Stevers pressed the picture to his chest. The door squeaked open. Wes Travis stumbled in. Stevers had trouble clearly seeing his best friend's face. Something was terribly wrong. Colonel Bajraf pushed the butt end of his rifle into Wes's back and forced him to step further into the room, directly under the light. The bare bulb illuminated the surface of Wes's face and grotesquely exaggerated his features.

"Sit!" the colonel ordered.

Wes Travis collapsed onto one of the metal chairs. His left eye was swollen shut, his right cheek bloody red, and his lips puffy and black-and-blue. Either he'd had a disastrous landing, which Stevers thought unlikely, or the Iranians had brutally beat him.

Three soldiers charged into the room and rushed toward Stevers.

The colonel pointed his rifle at Stevers. "Down on table!"

Stevers slid his butt forward and lay on his back.

The fucking straps.

The tall soldier with a missing front tooth stuck the barrel of his rifle in Stevers's face.

The colonel said, "No move."

Stevers clutched the picture in the palm of his hand and tried to conceal it. One soldier secured his arms to the nylon straps and pulled them tourniquet tight. The other wound rope around his left ankle and tied the other end to the leg of the table. Lieutenant Stevers knew why they hadn't secured his injured leg.

Colonel Bajraf sauntered to the table.

The soldiers stepped away. The short one with the beer gut sat next to Wes and pressed his rifle to Wes's bruised cheek. It was the first time Stevers had gotten a good look at the colonel. His swarthy complexion was covered with pockmarks. His eyes were wide set, beady, black as obsidian glass.

The colonel whispered in Stevers's ear, "Now we play."

Bajraf gently laid the butt end of the rifle on Stevers's swollen right knee. It felt more like the colonel whacked it with a hammer. A shock wave of pain radiated into Stevers's shin. He arched his back like an Olympian wrestler. Holding the end of the barrel, Bajraf flipped the butt over and forced the twisting rifle handle to bounce on Stevers's knee. Stevers gripped the edge of the table with his bound hands, dug his fingernails into the wood, and unconsciously crumpled the snapshot of Debra and Todd. The colonel was toying with him, and the pain was unbearable. How would he endure the pain when the colonel got down to serious business? Stevers, panting like a woman about to give birth, groaned, but he refused to give the colonel the satisfaction he sought. Nausea overwhelmed him, and his mouth filled with sour saliva.

"What the *fuck* do you want from us?" Stevers shouted.

"In time, Lieutenant."

Stevers again prayed to the god he hadn't spoken to in years. The colonel set his rifle against the wall. He grabbed Stevers's right ankle with one hand and gripped the heel of his boot with the other. He looked at Wes Travis and grinned. Slowly, he pushed Stevers's foot and forced his knee to bend.

Stevers screamed uncontrollably. His guttural cry echoed in the metal room, and his head snapped from side to side. It felt like his knee had been torn open. The snapshot slipped from his fingers and tumbled to the floor.

"Stop! Please stop!" Wes yelled. "I'll do it. I give you my word."

Stevers moaned in agony. He didn't care what it was Wes had to do. The only thing that mattered at this moment was stopping the colonel. If his partner had to kiss Ahmadinejad's ass on international television, give him a blow job, piss on the American flag, Stevers didn't care. Bajraf held his ankle and kept his knee at a twenty-degree angle. Stevers teetered toward unconsciousness. How much more could he endure?

The colonel let go of his leg. Stevers slowly tried to lower it, but it wouldn't move. He felt an intense throbbing, as if blood were gushing inside his knee. Bajraf bent over, picked up the mutilated photograph, and gawked at it with wild eyes.

"Your wife good fuck-fuck?" The colonel rubbed the photograph obscenely against his groin and gyrated his hips. He laughed hysterically. Sneering at Stevers, Bajraf licked the photograph. "She taste good." He tore it into tiny pieces, and like confetti, sprinkled them on Stevers's head.

Stevers growled through clenched teeth. "I'm-gonna-cut-your-fucking-heart-out!"

"We see how brave you Americans are," Bajraf said. He grasped Stevers's boot again and violently pushed, forcing his knee to bend to its maximum range. Something crunched in Stevers's knee, and what he felt was more than pain. His mouth hung open, and he vomited all over his chest. He coughed and gagged and tried to scream, but all he could do was moan. He turned his head and looked at Wes's horrified face. His ears popped, and the room began to whirl. His eyes lost their focus, and he could hear garbled words. Lieutenant Kyle Stevers, in his last moment of consciousness, thanked God for his temporary hiatus from hell.

**

When Craig Coleman approached the late-model Corolla, he looked at the rear side window for a valid parking permit. *Ah*, he thought, *bushwhacked another moocher*. Did they really think he was that stupid? If they didn't want to get caught trying to horn in on a free parking space, they should have wedged their car in the thickest part of the lot, not isolate it in the farthest corner.

Coleman parked the red Chevy Tahoe—with GEORGETOWN UNIVERSITY SECURITY painted on the doors—three spaces from the Corolla. He grabbed his flashlight, the yellow pad of citations, straightened his hat, and hopped out of the Tahoe. He moseyed over to the light-blue Toyota, stood behind the car, and shined the flashlight on the license plate so he could write a ticket. He glanced up from the yellow pad and focused his eyes on the rear window. Something wasn't quite right. He shined the flashlight toward the window, and Coleman's six-battery Eveready sliced through the fog and spilled into the car. Either it was the strangest-looking headrest he'd ever seen or somebody was defiant enough to be sitting in the front seat. He didn't know if they had balls, or they were just plain dumb.

He tiptoed to the driver's door, shined the light through the foggy side window, and tapped on the glass with his knuckles. The man didn't move. He tapped again with the butt end of the flashlight. Nothing. *The son of a bitch must be drunk*. Slowly, Coleman lifted the door handle, expecting it to be locked. More than likely, he'd have to call the cops. The door clicked. Not wanting to startle the man, he was careful not to swing it open too quickly.

No telling how a drunk or cokehead might react if he scared the crap out of him. With the door slightly ajar, Coleman shined the light on the side of the man's face.

As if a rattlesnake were springing toward his head, Coleman backpedaled and almost fell to the asphalt. "Mother of *mercy!*"

It was not necessary for Coleman to shake the man's shoulder or nudge him with his flashlight; the black man was dead. There was a gaping hole in the side of the man's head, bigger than a golf ball. Two cigars, Dutch Masters bands around the ends, were sticking out of the man's eye sockets. He shined the light on the man's legs. A naked blonde woman—with blood-stained hair and a nose looking as if it had been hit with a sledgehammer—lay with her head on his lap. Her dead eyes were wide open, almost staring at Coleman. The security guard covered his mouth and could feel vomit inching its way to his throat. The woman's breasts had been hacked off.

He ran to the Tahoe, panting, out of breath, his heart pounding furiously. He grabbed the two-way radio and called the main security office.

CHAPTER SIXTEEN

"Remember what I told you," Trevor said. "Objectively listen to the Joint Chiefs. But in the end, Kate, you must follow your instincts."

The president buttoned her suit jacket, brushed her hands across the front of her skirt, and tugged on each sleeve. She kissed her father on the cheek and picked up a faint smell of Old Spice.

"Sorry I have to leave, but I need some time to review my notes before the meeting."

His cologne was like a memory-enhancing drug. Its scent always evoked flashbacks of her childhood. As if it were yesterday, Kate could almost feel the metal tools clicking on her teeth. Dr. Westin, seventy-two years old, had hovered over her like a mad professor. How could *any* six-year-old not be terrified? Kate's repeated cries for her father had done little but annoy the elderly dentist. Maria Martinez had held her hand and wiped away the tears. The soft-spoken Latina woman explained to Kate that her father was away on business. Kate did not understand what business was. But it must have been more important than her first dentist appointment.

"Are you OK, sweetheart?" Trevor asked.

"A little jittery."

"I'll be waiting for you."

"Could be a long evening, Daddy."

"I'll manage. The Presidential Suite isn't exactly a Motel 6."

No matter how dismal the situation, he could always make her smile. She kissed his cheek again.

She took three steps and stopped. "Why didn't you spend more time with me when I was a child?"

He set down his coffee and shrugged his shoulders, a look of sadness in his eyes. "I've been waiting thirty-five years for you to ask that question. Are you sure this is the right time?"

She didn't answer, but her eyes welled with tears.

Trevor stood and walked toward her. He stuffed his hands into his pockets like a schoolboy standing in front of an angry principal. "It wasn't a plan, Kate. It just happened."

"We didn't need the money."

"I got on the corporate merry-go-round and couldn't get off." He touched her cheek with the back of his hand. "It couldn't have damaged you that severely."

"How do you know what I feel in my heart?"

"From a Kansas ranch to the White House is quite a leap. I must have done something right."

She thought about that for a minute. "If you could go back, would you do things differently?"

"Spend more time with you?"

She nodded.

"All I know"—he swallowed hard and his eyes filled with tears—"is that I love you with all my heart. Always have. Always will."

She wasn't sure if she felt love or anger or regret. Maybe a little of each. It was a conversation far too important for the limited time. She had more to say but left him standing in the dining room.

As she walked through the halls of the White House, the air was oppressive, like a humid Kansas evening in mid-August. The usual cheery glances and respectful nods were now hidden by glares of uneasiness. Everyone was on edge. Kate had quickly learned the paradox of the presidency. When the Executive Office made a favorable decision, Kate's advisors were credited for their divine wisdom. If they blundered, however, Kate was chastised for incompetent leadership. It was a lonely job.

She entered the Situation Room, first to arrive, and sat in the chair with the presidential seal embossed on the seat back. Kate shook her reading glasses out of their leather case and opened the folder. She'd studied the notes a dozen times, yet some intuitive urge compelled her to consider them one last time. Despite wearing a wool business suit, Kate felt like the air-conditioning was set at fifty degrees. Lately, she'd be covered with goose bumps one minute, and the next her armpits were wet. *Menopause?* She shuddered at the thought. Her periods had become sporadic—she'd even skipped a month occasionally—and the severe cramps were reminiscent of her teenage years. Something was going on; something she wanted to deny. She'd blamed this anatomical phenomenon on her stressful life, but for how long could she continue to deny that the symptoms meant more?

And so, while she waited for the Joint Chiefs, Kate's ambivalent life unfolded with poignant clarity. To most of the world, she was the president of the most powerful nation on Earth, a woman to be revered for her unprecedented accomplishments. But in her mind's eye, she envisioned herself a childless woman, estranged from a husband she never should have married.

The door opened. One by one, the Joint Chiefs marched in. It was like a procession of shiny brass buttons and chest decorations. Then, like an ominous cloud, Walter Owens emerged. His shirt was barely tucked in enough to cover his portly midsection, and his tie was four inches too short. Perhaps clothing manufacturers didn't make neckties long enough to span his portly belly?

Sitting next to such an esteemed group of military officers, Kate couldn't help but believe that Vice President Owens had to feel completely out of place. She studied his round face and Andy Rooney eyebrows. She did not like anything about this man. In fact, she loathed him. Even in the most diabolical creatures, Kate could find a morsel of good. But in Walter Owens, she had not uncovered one redeeming quality. As everyone adjusted themselves in their chairs and exchanged small talk, Kate cleared her mind and counted heads.

Owens leaned forward. "Have you prepared your speech for the Georgetown lecture?"

World War III was looming over the horizon, and Owens was concerned about the *lecture*? "Under the circumstances, I haven't given it a second thought."

He looked at her with owlish eyes. "Dean Whitney is very enthusiastic. Standing room only, he told me. A departure from the craziness in the Middle East is just what you need, Madam President."

She counted to ten. "We'll discuss it later, Walter."

Kate surveyed the eager faces of the Joint Chiefs. She did not sense, as in the past, an air of overflowing male ego. The men looked attentive, anxious to hear her speak. Did it result from their concern with the international crisis, or had she earned some respect? Perhaps, Kate thought, she had broken down a barrier, bridged a gap between machismo behavior and feminine credibility. Today's meeting, no doubt, would either augment their confidence in her or forever tarnish her image as a competent leader.

"Gentlemen, thank you for meeting with me on such short notice. Recent developments in the Middle East require our immediate response. President Ahmadinejad has given us an ultimatum: Our troops, battleships, and aircraft carriers must be removed from the Middle East, and he has demanded that we sign an agreement ensuring that we will not engage in any further military action against Iran without a Congressional declaration of war. If we do not comply, our Navy pilots will be publicly executed."

Chewing on his unlit cigar, General Wolfe chuckled. "It's comforting to know that we're dealing with such a reasonable man."

Kate refused to dignify his comment with an answer.

General Wallace said, "Back in '91, shortly after our first air strike on Baghdad, Saddam tried the same tactics. He agreed to release four captured pilots if we did not interfere with his occupation of Kuwait. He actually expected us to turn our heads while he raped, pillaged, and slaughtered his neighbors."

General Wolfe slammed a fist on the table. "George W. showed those sand lizards what Americans are made of. And that's *exactly* what we should do, Madam President."

Kate was in no mood for a debate, so she let the comment slide. She did have quite a different opinion of former president George W. Bush and the invasion of Iraq. But this was not the time or place to enter into that conversation. "I thought when we bombed the communication center, the air force base, and the two warehouses, we *did* show them what we're made of."

"Perhaps Ahmadinejad needs a more convincing demonstration of our military might," General Wallace suggested.

General Cumberland stood, his high forehead glistening under the bright lights. "The Iranian president is well aware that we will not comply with his demands. We do not, under any circumstances, negotiate with terrorists. But by asking for outrageous concessions, he's hoping that we will compromise. And if we do, it will be a huge victory for him."

General Wallace asked, "Madam President, have we confirmed that Iran has actually captured our Navy pilots?"

"Ahmad Habib insisted that we watch CNN at eight p.m. I'm certain it has something to do with the pilots."

Admiral Canfield said, "Navy pilots are well prepared for this sort of situation, Madam President." His lips tightened to a narrow line, and he blinked several times. "I lost a son during the Middle East war, and no one is more sensitive to an impasse like this than I. But the welfare of our pilots cannot influence our response. We must react in the best interest of the United States and our allies."

Kate prepared herself for a grueling evening.

They exchanged strategies and opinions for ninety minutes, but Kate had made up her mind long before she'd entered the Situation Room, and none of the Joint Chiefs had changed her position.

At seven fifty-nine p.m., Walter Owens turned on the television.

"This is CNN Senior Correspondent Paul Carrow. Ladies and gentlemen, what you are about to see is an unedited videotape given to us by the Iranian government. We caution you: it may be disturbing, so please watch it at your own discretion."

The television screen went black for an instant. A young man's face slowly came into focus. His right eye was swollen shut, and his nose looked broken. Kate held her hand over her mouth and silenced a gasp.

"My name is Lieutenant Wesley L. Travis. I am a pilot in the... United States Navy..."

His speech was labored, his words slurred like he'd been drugged.

"Please do not be alarmed by my appearance. My facial injuries were sustained when I ejected from my aircraft."

Kate felt like her rib cage was shrinking.

"I speak for myself and my fellow pilot, Lieutenant Kyle Stevers. We do not endorse...the atrocious actions of the United States of America. I denounce my country for engaging in an unjustified act of war against a peaceful nation."

"This is a travesty," Walter Owens grumbled.

Travis continued. "Madam President...I implore you...Please cease and desist from any further military action against Iran. Comply with President Ahmadinejad's modest requests. We have been treated kindly by the Iranian people. But any further acts of aggression will ensure our justifiable execution." As if he were looking for a cue, Travis's eyes glanced at something to the side of the video camera. "Please wish our families well. Thank you."

Paul Carrow's face appeared on the screen.

"Turn it off," Kate said to Walter Owens.

Admiral Canfield said, "This is a clever ploy, Madam President. We cannot be seduced by this melodramatic performance. The Iranian president wants us to abandon rational solutions. He's hoping this contrived video will encourage us to make an emotional decision. I assure you, an Iranian soldier held a gun to Lieutenant Stevers's head while Lieutenant Travis read the script."

"So should we forget about the pilots and their families?" Kate asked.

"'They might already be dead, Madam President,'" General Wallace warned. "We have no idea when that video was made."

Kate thought the decision to bomb Iran had been a difficult one. But seeing Lieutenant Travis's battered face, imagining what he and Lieutenant Stevers may have already gone through, made everything flesh and blood. She hadn't seen the faces of the Iranian soldiers killed during the air strikes. But now she'd looked into the blue eyes of a potential victim, an American, and it weighed on her conscience. Flashbacks from the September 11 bombing of the World Trade Center raced through her mind.

"First, I'd like to thank you for your invaluable input and support. You've helped make my decision more palatable. I am going to instruct Secretary of State Mitchell to deliver a counter-ultimatum. I will not, under any circumstances, negotiate with Iran. As General Cumberland pointed out, the United States of America has a strict policy prohibiting us from negotiating with terrorists. And I intend to uphold this policy. Ahmadinejad hides under the guise of his presidency, but he is a terrorist in every sense of the word. And terrorists, by nature, are cowards. So we must expose his cowardice by standing firm.

"There are two separate issues to consider: our commitment in the Middle East and the lives of the pilots. This is what I propose. We will agree to sign a document proscribing further military action against Iran, providing they remain a peaceful nation. Any threat to a neighboring country nullifies our agreement. They must cease and desist any production of WMDs, including chemical weapons, and they must allow the United Nations to periodically inspect Iran's nuclear facilities, to be certain their enrichment program is for the production of energy, not bombs. We will *not*, however, remove our troops or ships from the area and will continue with military support for our allies. If President Ahmadinejad does not release the pilots to the Saudi government in forty-eight hours, we will coordinate a massive air strike against an undisclosed, heavily populated Iranian city. The bloodshed will be on his hands."

The group sat frozen, staring at their president as if she were an alien being. At first, Kate guessed that either they were thinking about impeachment proceedings or trying to figure out where to locate the nearest straitjacket. She could hardly believe what she'd just said. How could she expect the Joint Chiefs to understand? General Wolfe stood and turned toward the president. He smiled and began to applaud. The rest of the group stood and joined the ovation.

Cheering. Clapping. Whistling.

Kate didn't feel that she deserved their adulation, but the overwhelming support moistened her eyes and helped solidify her decision.

***

For Richard Alderson, Toni Mitchell, and Ahmad Habib to meet, King Al Sabah graciously offered a private room in his 86,000-square-foot palace. The king's overt hospitality, uncharacteristic of years past, amused Mitchell. She'd been around Washington politics for nearly twenty years, long enough to remember how his predecessor, King Fahd, had opposed United States involvement in Arab affairs. But having a hostile lunatic like Ahmadinejad for a neighbor, Mitchell thought, can convert even the most vehement anti-American country into a dedicated ally.

Mitchell sat next to Alderson and gazed around a room decorated more lavishly than anything she'd ever seen. The palace was like something out of a Walt Disney cartoon. Mitchell, whose austere heritage was well rooted through three generations of middle-income ancestors, had formed a rigid aversion to ostentatious wealth. In the spirit of capitalism and free enterprise, she could almost digest the unimaginable wealth of a Bill Gates. But *obscenely* wealthy, arrogant, and self-absorbed Arabs, like Al Sabah, offended Mitchell. Because nature had been kind and enriched barren deserts with unlimited reserves of crude oil—a natural resource used to bleed the Western world—radical Arabs, many supporting terrorism, became filthy rich. This did not sit well with Mitchell. Consequently, facing the king and accepting his benevolence with sincere appreciation had been enormously difficult for the secretary of state.

Alderson was still sulking. He had been for the last hour. Mitchell elbowed his arm.

"You haven't said anything about the president's decision."

"That's because I'm still numb," Alderson said.

"You don't agree with her?"

"If it works, I'll join her fan club. If it blows up in her face, I'll draft my resignation letter."

Mitchell was astonished with his disloyal answer. Before joining him in Riyadh, she had not interacted with him one on one. Now she clearly understood how his seditious mind worked. She'd always believed that a leopard showed his real spots during the darkest hours. Alderson was now clearly showing his.

Alderson's eyes scalded Mitchell's face. "So tell me, do *you* think the president is acting responsibly?"

"Military strategy is not an exact science. She weighed every conceivable option and chose the best one."

"Thank you for that little lesson in military tactics. Need I remind you that I am a retired Army colonel?"

"OK, *Colonel*, what would you do if you were in her shoes?"

He tugged at his collar. "I wouldn't threaten to blow up an entire Iranian city."

"You're sidestepping the question, Richard."

He looked at her with that condescending gawk men get when a woman challenges their manhood. "I haven't had the luxury of meeting with the Joint Chiefs and examining every possible solution."

"Well, President Miles has," Mitchell said. "And her decision is based on hours of strategic deliberation. Whether we agree with her or not, Richard, we have a responsibility to facilitate her directives with our unconditional support."

"So you ate a bowl of patriotic Wheaties this morning and decided to take out your aggressions on *me*? Why are you getting in *my* face?"

"Because this is not a situation for lukewarm advocates. Mr. Habib is as shrewd as they come. If we are unable to convince him that our position is immutable, if he even sniffs uncertainty in our resolve, Ahmadinejad will call our bluff. We must deliver a convincing performance."

He poked his index finger on the walnut table, and his cheeks filled with blood. "I'm on *this* side of the table, Ms. Secretary of State, remember?"

"Richard, I respect you, but I must ask that you remain silent during our negotiations."

Alderson launched up so quickly he almost knocked over his chair.

"What the fuck gives you—"

The double doors swung open. Habib and his entourage made their grand entrance. The ambassador strolled toward the table with casual style, as if he were meeting a fellow countryman for afternoon tea. Mitchell was not impressed with his appearance. He looked like a peasant dressed in a business suit. On certain men, Mitchell found facial hair quite sexy. But Habib had an unruly beard that looked like a rat's nest.

Alderson, his face still feverish, was standing. The secretary of state eased up. Habib bowed toward Mitchell, hardly acknowledging her, then offered his hand to Alderson.

Ahmad Habib sat opposite Richard Alderson; one of his henchmen sat across from Toni Mitchell. The other four Iranians remained near the entranceway. Habib, Mitchell thought, could pass for Yasir Arafat's twin, minus the headgear. He had wide-set eyes and a prominent nose. He was an unattractive man—ugly, actually. His fingernails were meticulously manicured. Perfect hands for a Palmolive commercial. The young man accompanying Habib was handsome; he looked more Hispanic than Middle Eastern.

As in their first meeting, Habib directed his conversation toward Alderson, overtly ignoring Mitchell. "Has your government agreed to our requests?"

She wanted to teach him a basic lesson in etiquette, but there were more important things for a sexist pig to learn today. "We have a counter-proposal for President Ahmadinejad," Mitchell announced.

"Any alternative is unacceptable. I made that clear during our first meeting."

Mitchell glared at Habib. "Then perhaps you have wasted your time coming to Riyadh."

For the first time since entering the room, Habib's coal-black eyes met Mitchell's.

With her peripheral vision, she could see Alderson peering at the side of her face. She hoped he was wise enough to keep his mouth shut. Silence was a powerful negotiating tool, one she'd learned in the business world. Once you play your hand, you sit silently until your opponent responds.

Habib toyed with his wiry beard. In their native tongue, he and his escort exchanged words, apparently unaware that the secretary of state was fluent in several Arabic languages.

"President Ahmadinejad insists on hearing unfavorable news immediately," Habib said.

"Please outline your counter-proposal."

"Ambassador Habib," Mitchell said, "the United States of America will not allow you to use our Navy pilots as pawns during these negotiations. They must be released, unharmed, at once. If you comply, the president will sign a formal agreement with the United Nations prohibiting us from engaging in military intervention against Iran. Providing, of course, your country coexists with other nations in a peaceful manner and your government immediately stops its development of nuclear and chemical weapons of mass destruction. We will not, under any circumstances, de-escalate our military forces in the Middle East."

Habib sat forward and rested his elbows on the table. "Your president has not acknowledged *any* of our requests?"

"They were beyond reason," Mitchell said. "Surely you did not expect us to comply."

"Your government has no legitimate right to threaten Iran."

"How have we threatened you?"

"Iraq is still occupied by American troops, and there are American bases surrounding us in other Middle East countries. Our waters are infested with your battleships and aircraft carriers. They pose a constant danger to our national security."

"Mr. Habib, the United States has never engaged in an act of war against Iran."

"I strongly disagree. My country has not, in any way, initiated military action against the United States, yet your president savagely destroyed our air force base, crippled our communication center, and demolished warehouses filled with food for our people. George W. Bush invaded Iraq many years ago without justification or the endorsement of the United Nations. Your military destroyed Iraq and slaughtered tens of thousands of innocent Iraqi citizens. How can you sit across from me and claim that your military presence in the Middle East does not pose a threat to my country? Perhaps I should show you photographs of Iraqi citizens with their bodies torn to pieces."

"And perhaps I should show you photographs of mangled Israeli citizens."

In Persian, Habib told his escort that the American woman was a formidable opponent. The escort suggested they lift the woman's skirt to see if she had testicles.

Toni Mitchell, her face flushed red, could not figure out how she stopped herself from digging her four-inch heels into the escort's groin, but she silently applauded her self-control.

"Why does our dispute with Israel concern your government?" Habib said. "The United States has not been appointed guardian for the entire world."

"Mr. Habib, your semantics are amusing, but they do not detract from the central issue. My country will not maintain a passive position toward any nation that infringes upon another country's right to exist as a sovereign state."

"Ms. Mitchell, I thought perhaps your president would acknowledge Iran's independence, but that is not the case. Instead, you wish to insult us. I can speak freely for President Ahmadinejad. Your terms are unacceptable to my government. Unless your president agrees to our original proposal, the execution of your Navy pilots is imminent. Their blood will be on your president's hands."

"I am also authorized to speak for President Miles. You must immediately release the pilots to the Saudi government before we can continue with any further negotiations. If they are not delivered to the American Consulate here in Riyadh in twelve hours, the United States of America will launch a massive military offensive against an undisclosed Iranian city. And I caution you, Ambassador Habib, our president's intention is to reduce every structure to a pile of smoldering ashes."

Habib's eyes narrowed to a squint, and his lower lip began to tremble.

Toni Mitchell fixed her eyes on Habib's and maintained a stern expression. "Ambassador Habib, I don't know how much you know about President Miles, but I can assure you, she is more than what your culture perceives as a stereotypical woman. In fact, she has completely ignored the advice given to her by the Joint Chiefs of Staff. She's a loose cannon, Mr. Habib, high-strung and frightfully unpredictable. There is no telling what she's capable of."

"Your president would kill *thousands* of innocent Iranian citizens?"

"That's entirely up to your president."

In their native tongue, the escort said to Habib, "We must consult President Ahmadinejad at once."

Mitchell expected Habib to respond in Persian and that his comment might reveal what he was thinking. Instead, the ambassador and his escort stood as if on cue. He did not offer his hand or utter another word. He turned and left the room, and his entourage, like baby ducklings, followed him out the door.

CHAPTER SEVENTEEN

Kate was sitting alone in her private office, brooding over the sanity of her military strategy, when Emily buzzed her.

"The secretary of state is on line seven." Emily's voice, usually cheery, epitomized the heavy air hanging over the White House. Kate guessed that everyone except the Joint Chiefs and perhaps her father—although he hadn't offered nor had she asked for his opinion—concluded that their new president was stark raving mad.

McDermott and other concerned Cabinet members had offered—almost insisted—to accompany her while she waited for Mitchell's call. But Kate, in no mood for insincere encouragement or camaraderie, needed to ride this emotional wave alone. She stared at the telephone, partially wanting to answer it, mostly wishing she could ignore it. In the next few moments, her name could be indelibly etched in history books. Whether as heroine or assassin would soon be determined.

Kate had not been able to erase Lieutenant Travis's battered face from her mind. But it was not his physical appearance that troubled her. His piercing eyes had delivered a reticent message:

Ignore the script, Madam President. Please save my life.

His desperate appeal was well hidden, but Kate could clearly see past the smoke screen and recognize the young pilot's plea. As her father had suggested, she'd ignored conventional wisdom and listened to her instincts. Had she gambled with American blood? Lieutenants Travis and Stevers might already know whether Kate Miles was their savior or executioner.

Expecting Mitchell's words to be explosive, Kate lifted the receiver as carefully as she might a time bomb. She forced a swallow and moistened her scratchy throat. "Hello, Toni."

"Is that you, President Miles?" Toni Mitchell said.

"I've been fighting off a cold." Her voice was raspy. "How did the meeting go?"

"At first, not well. When I warned Habib that you were prepared to level one of Iran's most populated cities, I managed to capture his undivided attention."

"And his reaction?"

"He stormed out of the room, quite upset."

"Was he upset because I ignored Ahmadinejad's demands or because he believes my threat is legitimate?"

"I'm not sure, Madam President. I tried to deliver a compelling statement. As you requested, I made it clear that you were highly unpredictable and that your goal was to completely level a key city."

"Did you portray me as a crazy woman with her period?"

"With all due respect, I painted a grim picture of you. Mr. Habib left the meeting believing that the president of the United States is high-strung and perfectly capable of excessive military force."

"Do you think he was convinced enough to influence Ahmadinejad?"

"I couldn't read him, Madam President, but I believe we should prepare for a dramatic response."

"How are you and Richard holding up?"

"Edgy. The waiting drives you mad."

"Are you comfortable remaining in Riyadh?"

"The Saudi government has been extremely gracious. I am welcome here for as long as necessary."

"Then we have no choice but to sit tight."

"The moment I hear anything, I'll contact you, Madam President."

Kate swiveled in the chair and looked out the window. Once again, she saw the insolent black crow perched on the white birch. He had returned to taunt her.

"Thank you for delivering my message to Mr. Habib. It must have been quite difficult for you."

"That's my job." The line was silent for a moment. "Madam President, if Iran does not release the pilots, are you fully prepared to initiate a massive air strike?"

She'd asked herself that question a dozen times. "Let's just pray that I'm not faced with such a decision, Toni."

***

Kate ignored the greetings and encouragement of her service staff and rushed to her bedroom. She locked the door, lay on the bed, and curled into a fetal position. In less than twelve hours, either Iran would release the pilots or Kate would be facing the most crucial decision of her life. The moment she'd chosen to grandstand Ahmadinejad, Kate had placed herself in an irreversible situation. She had moved a chess piece and could no longer rescind that move. Kate could only hope that a glimmer of reason was suppressed somewhere in Ahmadinejad's twisted thinking. The Iranian president had never played such a deadly game with a woman from the western hemisphere, and Kate's entire strategy relied completely on his unfamiliarity with the temperamental female mind. If her instincts did not betray her, and if

Toni Mitchell had convinced Habib that Kate was truly capable of initiating a massive air strike, Ahmadinejad, true to his past cowardice behavior, would not call her bluff.

Kate tried in vain to distract herself from the same menacing thoughts. But nothing could rid her mind of the impending impasse. Ahmadinejad's silence was like slowly burning splinters under her fingernails. Mitchell had been right: the waiting drives you mad. She did not wish to be alone, but thought it prudent. After all, the president of the United States had an image to uphold. As the leader of the most powerful nation in the world, she did not have the luxury to expose her weaknesses or any emotion that diluted her strength. She wanted to be embraced, needed to feel consoling arms around her, urgently desired to escape from this solitary purgatory, if only for a moment. But Kate did not summon her father. Nor did she call her advisors. The president of the United States was determined to triumph over this relentless demon herself.

***

Carl Kramer snatched the telephone on the first ring.

"Sorry to bother you, mate," Captain Teddy Daniels said, "but I've stumbled upon something I think might interest you."

Kramer did not utter a word.

"A banking officer at the Island Bank rang me up. Name's Cybil Curtis. Smashing woman. She saw the clip in the *Cayman News* 'bout the young bloke murdered in the Grand Cayman Hotel. The day Mr. Crandall met his destiny, he withdrew five million dollars cash from the bank. Ms. Curtis handled the transaction. Not sure what it means, my friend, but whoever ended Mr. Crandall's holiday helped himself to the loot."

"Any leads?" Kramer asked.

"Not a bloody one."

"I appreciate the call," Kramer said.

"I'll ring you up if I hear anything more. Good luck, mate."

***

At four a.m., Kate's telephone rang. It startled her more than woke her. Not too many weeks ago, when McDermott had called her in the middle of the night and announced that President Rodgers was dead, it had changed her life. This particular phone call had the capacity to change it even more. She nervously combed her fingers through her hair and lifted the receiver.

Her voice was unsteady. "President Miles."

"Sorry about the time, Madam President," Toni Mitchell said. "Hope I didn't wake you."

"I'd have to be sleeping in order for you to wake me, Toni."

The secretary of state's hesitation, Kate feared, was not a good omen. She leaned on an elbow. "Has Ahmadinejad responded?"

"The pilots have been released."

It was as if every tense muscle in her body had suddenly turned to jelly. Kate hopped off the bed. With the cordless phone in her hand, she whirled around the bedroom like a Munchkin in *The Wizard of Oz*. Thankfully, no one was there to witness her temporary insanity. "Please tell me that they haven't been seriously injured."

"Lieutenant Travis—the pilot who was on CNN—sustained superficial injuries, but Lieutenant Stevers's right knee is in pretty bad shape and needs to be treated by an orthopedic surgeon."

The timbre in Kate's voice was brimming with an upbeat tone. "Assure the pilots that they will receive the best medical attention available. Tell them that we will notify their families immediately. As soon as they're physically able, I would like to invite them to the White House."

"Lieutenant Travis asked me to apologize to you, Madam President. The Iranians did not give him a choice. Had he refused to participate in their political propaganda, he was afraid they would torture and kill both of them."

"Be sure he understands that we never doubted his patriotism." Kate snatched her lucky silver dollar from the nightstand and pressed it to her heart. "Has the Iranian government issued a statement?"

"Not a word. Ahmad Habib contacted the Saudi ambassador several hours ago and made arrangements for the pilots to be flown to Riyadh. Having dealt with the Iranians in the past, I did not want to call you until I saw the pilots with my own eyes."

"What do you think is going on?"

"Either Ahmadinejad is planning some form of military retaliation or he's looking for a shrewd way to save face."

"The waiting game never ends," Kate said.

"Would you like Richard and me to remain here?"

Kate contemplated the question. "Will it be beneficial?"

"Perhaps I should fly to Israel and meet with Prime Minister Netanyahu before I come home. Assuring him face-to-face of our continued support might help reinforce our commitment in the Middle East."

"Why don't you have Richard accompany you? He has a rapport with the Prime Minister."

Mitchell hesitated. "I would prefer to go alone, Madam President."

Kate did not question this request. "Then instruct Richard to fly back to Washington. Contact me when you arrive in Tel Aviv."

"Madam President, I'm proud to be part of your administration. Your actions were gutsy. I just wanted you to know that."

"Thank you, Toni. Your support means a great deal to me. Have a safe flight."

***

McDermott and Riley walked into the Oval Office at nine fifty-five a.m. The chief of staff again looked like he hadn't slept in days. His haggard appearance was becoming mainstream. Riley's swanky look never wavered: double-breasted Armani suit, hair impeccably groomed, and signature Chiclet smile. They exchanged good mornings with the president and sat opposite her.

"Have you made arrangements for the pilots at Bethesda?" Kate asked McDermott.

"Dr. Morris has assured me that they will be treated like war heroes."

"They *are* war heroes," Kate said. "As a matter of fact, as soon as the pilots have recovered, I'd like to invite them and their wives to the White House for an intimate dinner and a private award ceremony."

"Ceremony?" McDermott said.

"I think both Lieutenants Stevers and Travis deserve a commendation for their heroism. Would the Distinguished Flying Cross Medal be appropriate?"

McDermott smiled. "It's a bit over the top, but—"

"Then make it happen, Charles."

McDermott nodded.

"How did the media respond to your statement, Mr. Riley?"

"Not even the most naive citizen believed Lieutenant Travis's comments were not scripted. Everyone suspected it was a ruse. Based on the media's response, I believe the headlines will be positive. Your Georgetown lecture could not have come at a more favorable time."

She'd forgotten about the lecture.

"Bill and I have discussed it at great length," McDermott said. "Your lecture will attract tremendous media coverage. You're a national hero, Madam President. We feel strongly that this is the perfect opportunity for you to introduce the Healing of America bills. Your remedies in the Middle East have endeared you to Americans. You have their ear. Now is the ideal time to reinforce your political posture and clearly define your administration's objectives."

"I might be a hero today, but if Iran chooses to do something crazy, my prowess will be short-lived."

Riley said, "That's why you have to ride the wave for as long as you can. Opportunities like this don't come very often. If you handle this lecture strategically, the benefits will be enormous. You've just disarmed an international time bomb. Now you can tell your fellow Americans how you're going to fix the nation. It's a political utopia, Madam President."

Kate wasn't yet ready to face political critics or millions of Americans and discuss her Healing of America bills. "I've barely caught my breath, gentlemen, and I'm supposed to stand in front of the world and outline the Healing of America bills? At this point, I'm not yet comfortable that the crisis in the Middle East is resolved. Can we postpone for a few days?"

"That would be unwise, Madam President," Riley said.

"You have to strike while the iron's hot," McDermott said. "It doesn't get any hotter than this." McDermott leaned forward and rested his elbows on the desk. "Madam President, Bill and I will spend the rest of the day helping you organize your speech. We will not let you walk into that auditorium unprepared. I promise."

Kate studied McDermott's persuasive eyes. "OK, you've convinced me. Let's get to work, gentlemen."

★

CHAPTER EIGHTEEN

Deputy Director Kramer hesitated outside Ellenwood's office and sucked in a quivering breath. He'd reviewed the questions carefully because the "Silver Fox" did not react favorably to interrogation. Any stammering and the DCI was aptly capable of twisting the query around and placing Kramer on the defensive. He was a shrewd old bastard. To be sure that the heat of the moment did not distract him, Kramer had written down his questions on three-by-five index cards. He flipped through them one last time, moving his lips as he read. He folded the cards in half and stuffed them into his jacket pocket. The DCI's door was slightly ajar. Kramer pushed it open as he gently knocked.

"Hi, Boss." He stepped into the office. "Can you give me a couple of minutes?"

Ellenwood looked at his watch. "Make it quick. I'm meeting Owens for dinner before we head over to Georgetown."

"Georgetown?"

"The president's speech. Wouldn't miss it for all the tea in China. I hear it's going to be a pisser."

Kramer closed the door, ambled toward his desk, and sat in front of Ellenwood.

"You're welcome to join us, Carl."

"No time. The president has backed me in a corner because I've made little progress with the assassination investigation."

"Anything I can do?"

"You can answer a few questions for me."

The DCI steepled his fingers and set his elbows on the desk. "What's on your mind, Carl?"

"I need some information on Agent Jack Miller."

Ellenwood's forehead furrowed. He sat silently for a moment, and Kramer could see his jaw pulsing. "Mr. Miller is no longer an agent."

"I'm aware of that. Explain to me, please, why he was exempt from the department's policies and procedures."

Ellenwood removed his glasses, held them up to the light, and wiped them on his white shirt. "Hiring him was a mistake. That's why he's no longer with the CIA." He set down the glasses and rubbed his eyes.

"His assignments haven't been documented in the system. Where did he get his orders?"

"Don't push this one, Carl."

"*I'm* not the one pushing. Miller's activities have raised suspicions with the president, Victor, and *I'm* the one in the hot seat."

"He no longer works here, and that's all you and Miles need to know."

Kramer's face got hot. "Don't dismiss me like a fucking child."

"Then don't act like one."

Kramer took a deep breath. "Victor, I don't want to place myself in a compromising—"

"Then leave it the *fuck* alone."

Kramer wagged his index finger at the DCI. "I'm not gonna do that, Victor. Not until you tell me what's up with this guy."

"Mr. Kramer, forget that I'm your boss, and take some advice from a friend: if you don't forget about Miller, it's going to bite you in the balls—hard."

Ellenwood wasn't budging. Not yet. Kramer folded his arms across his chest and lowered his voice. "How do you expect me to pacify the president?"

"Give her a good fuck. It might be just what the frustrated bitch needs."

Never had he heard Ellenwood speak with such blatant disrespect. At least not directed toward the president.

"Thanks for your time." It was the most sincere voice Kramer could muster.

The DDCI left Ellenwood, went into his office, and locked his door. He waited fifteen minutes to be sure Ellenwood had left, then he made a follow-up phone call to Private Investigator Jake Carson.

"Jake? Carl. What's the scoop on Jack Miller?"

"You mean, Jack *Mueller*?"

***

Guenther Krause received the final telephone call. Never again would he have to hear the phrase *Nice day for a white wedding*. He sat on the bed in his underwear and studied the diagram of the auditorium. Although he'd tried to deny it, he had hoped that the president would have resigned and that his assignment would be aborted. From the start, he had understood that his was a suicide mission. Although his loyalty to the cause was uncompromising, he wasn't ready to die.

Lingering thoughts of Ebony and Ivory fractured his concentration. After he'd finished with them, he removed their driver's licenses, credit cards—all forms of identification—from their bodies. Killing his hotel neighbors had been a risky yet gratifying adventure. He had been very careful removing their bodies from the hotel and placing them in their car. Their room was only a few steps away from the backdoor exit, and their Corolla was parked in a spot close to the door. Fortunately, his brothers had put him up in a second-class hotel. After midnight, the place was like a morgue. Guenther figured that by the time the police identified their mangled bodies and traced them back to the hotel, the president's lifeless corpse would be lying on a slab in the morgue. And more than likely, unless through some divine intervention, Guenther Krause would be lying beside her.

In less than two hours, if everything went as planned, Guenther Krause would alter the future of the world. To be a hero, to be eulogized by his brothers as a great patriot for the cause, would fulfill a desperate longing. In his mind's eye, he'd gone over the plan a dozen times, until it was embedded in his memory bank. But now that the moment of self-resolve was looming, a pang of uneasiness overshadowed his enthusiasm. Guenther had no doubts about ridding the world of an inferior one; she was a swine and deserved to be slaughtered. But what if he failed? He could not foresee the actions of the Secret Service, had no idea how many would accompany her, nor did he know where they would position themselves. Not even his contact in Washington knew. How could he be certain that he'd get a clear shot? The window of opportunity, Guenther deduced, might last for only five seconds—five heartbeats to draw his weapon and discharge as many rounds as possible before the Secret Service restrained him or blew his brains out.

Guenther hopped off the bed and stood erect in front of the full-length mirror. He closed his eyes, sucked in several full breaths of air, and tried to stop his heart from racing. He held out his hands and spread his fingers. Why was he trembling?

Guenther slipped into his jeans, pulled Ivory's oversized Georgetown sweatshirt over his head, and laced up his sneakers. He slid the admission ticket and college ID into his back pocket, and put on the Redskins cap. Ivory's pink panties were sitting on the corner of the bed. He snatched them off the comforter, pressed them to his face, and inhaled their arousing scent. For good luck, he stuffed the panties in his front pocket and scurried out the door.

***

After trying on several outfits, most of which were heaped on her bed, Kate was uncertain which would be most appropriate for such an important event. Finally, and with great reservation, she selected a conservative charcoal-gray business suit and her favorite silk white blouse. She finished her ensemble with a white pearl necklace, matching earrings, and black pumps. Late in the afternoon, Kate'd had her hair cut and slightly restyled. The cut was not a radical departure from her conservative hairdo, but in spite of Emily's comment that she looked chic, Kate wasn't sure she liked it this short or if it was becoming of the president.

McDermott accompanied her to the main entrance of the White House, where two limousines waited. "You look exceptionally stylish this evening, Madam President,"

McDermott said. He hustled to keep pace with her. "Your new hairdo becomes you."

"Thank you, Charles."

In spite of several unresolved issues, Kate had grown fond of McDermott. She did not believe the malicious rumors she'd heard about him. Most were either untrue or overly exaggerated.

She could not deny that he was a bit egocentric, and he often displayed a giant chip on his shoulders, but he held one of the most influential and prestigious jobs in the world. How could anyone in this capacity not be high-strung?

"So you think I've got a chance at winning over the conservative crowd?"

"They're going to make you an honorary alumnus," McDermott said.

"I wish I were as confident as you and Mr. Riley."

"Trust me, Madam President, tonight you're going to make history."

There was something unsettling in his voice.

To outline the security plan, Albert Cranston, director of the Secret Service, rode with Kate and McDermott in the presidential limousine. A second limo carrying eight agents led the way to Georgetown University.

Cranston said, "Before you go into the building, Madam President, we'll make sure that everyone is seated and the main lobby is secured." He pointed to the diagram. "You'll enter the auditorium through the west entrance. Mr. McDermott and four agents will accompany you as you make your way down the aisle to the stage. When you reach the first row, Charles and you can sit with Walter Owens and Victor Ellenwood until Dean Whitney introduces you. When your speech is finished, leave the stage using the steps on your left, and the agents will escort you down the east aisle to the exit."

"There's a rumor that a photo of me is adorning every Iranian post office with a *Wanted Dead or Alive* banner hanging over my head. Should I be on the lookout for suspicious-looking characters?"

Cranston chuckled. "No one, not even the Pope, enters the building without proper ID or going through a metal detector. As an extra security measure, we'll walk everyone through a second detector before they can enter the auditorium, and we'll randomly frisk anyone even remotely suspicious. You'll be as safe as the gold in Fort Knox."

"Evidently, you've never seen *Goldfinger*, have you, Mr. Cranston?"

"There's nothing to worry about, Madam President," Cranston assured her. "You concentrate on your speech, and we'll take care of everything else."

She clutched his forearm and smiled. "By the way, Albert, I owe you a long-overdue apology."

He shook his head and looked at her with curious eyes. "For what?"

"For acting like a madwoman the morning I thought I'd been poisoned."

"That's perfectly understandable, Madam President. Under the circumstances, I think you maintained your composure quite admirably."

"It may have been understandable, but it was inexcusable. I'm sorry."

***

To retrieve the Colt .45 he'd hidden in the toilet reservoir and to secure an aisle seat so he'd get an unobstructed shot at the president, Guenther arrived at the auditorium ninety minutes before the speech was scheduled to begin. Hopping up the front steps of Saint Thomas Hall two at a time, Guenther was surprised at the number of people waiting to go through security. It looked like Kennedy Airport on Christmas Eve. He adjusted his cap and straightened his prized sweatshirt. He yanked open the door and waited for his turn. After what seemed like an eternity, a uniformed security guard motioned for him to step forward. Two men in dark suits stood adjacent to the black security guard.

Ebony boys are everywhere, Guenther thought.

"May I see your identification, please?"

Guenther reached in his back pocket and handed the man his student ID. The security guard studied the laminated card, looked Guenther up and down, then fixed his eyes on the baseball cap.

"A Skins fan, huh?"

"Always been my team."

"Been to any games?"

"A couple."

"How'd you get tickets? Every game was sold-out during preseason."

Guenther's palms began to sweat. "My uncle's got connections."

"Lucky you." He returned the ID and handed Guenther a plastic container. "Would you empty your pockets of any loose change, keys, anything metal, remove your cap and shoes, and walk through the archway."

He followed the instructions and stepped through the metal detector. He tried not to get distracted, but when Guenther caught a hint of Ivory's scent still on the sweatshirt, he smiled. He wondered if the security guard could smell her.

The security guard gave Guenther a once-over. "May I have your admittance ticket, please, Mr. Thompson?"

He reached into his back pocket and handed him the ticket. The security guard tore it in half, scribbled something on the stub, and gave it to Guenther. "Show this to the security guard at the entrance to the auditorium. And enjoy the lecture."

"I'm sure I will."

As Guenther approached the auditorium, he could see a funnel of frenzied people—many more than he'd anticipated—crowded around the main entrance. He'd gotten past the first security check without delay, but for some reason, a terrible bottleneck had developed. The muscles along the back of his neck tightened. Would he have enough time to recover the gun and secure an aisle seat? He had no idea how many people had already entered. As he anxiously waited, Guenther's stomach rode a nauseating roller coaster.

***

At seven thirty-two p.m., the executive limousines pulled up to the west entrance of Saint Thomas Hall. Four Secret Service agents filed out of the lead vehicle and waited by the steps. The other four agents remained posted around the president's limo.

Cranston looked at his watch. "It's going to be about a fifteen-minute wait, Madam President. Four agents and I will go inside and check things out. I'll leave you with Charles and return when it's time for you to go in." Cranston stepped out of the car, and the agents followed him into the building.

"Would you like me to help you fine-tune your speech?" McDermott offered.

"I've never been good at reciting speeches verbatim. They flow much better when I follow a loose outline and improvise as I go."

Kate could not think of anything to talk about, and it appeared to her that the COS was lost in his own private thoughts. She picked specks of lint off her skirt. Peter, she remembered, loved the way she looked in this suit. Not even during the Middle East crisis had he called. Things had eroded so far beyond any chance of a reconciliation perhaps a permanent remedy was the only thing that made sense. And the truth was that she did not really miss him. It was just a matter of time before some nosy journalist, trying to get inducted into the reporters' hall of fame, rekindled the rumors about her separation from Peter.

McDermott's voice thundered into her deep thoughts. "Madam President, I haven't had the opportunity to speak with you one on one, but I wanted you to know that I admired your courage during the Middle East crisis. I must be honest, though. I, like most of the world, did not endorse your resolutions without tremendous reservations. But, as the saying goes, 'all's well that ends well.'"

"I hardly think that anything has ended. But thank you, Charles. I appreciate your candor."

Again, there was silence.

This was not the most ideal time for a delicate discussion, but Kate had been avoiding this conversation far too long. "Charles, while we have a few minutes, we need to talk about Adelina Menendez."

His face filled with blood. "We all have our little vices, Madam President."

"She's a vice you'll have to do without. If you don't remedy the situation, both Adelina and you will be placing yourselves in a very precarious situation."

"I've been trying to handle it, but—"

"She's married, Charles, and it's inappropriate."

He looked like a whipped puppy. "I'll handle it, Madam President."

***

As he hustled down the auditorium aisle, Guenther elbowed his way through the unruly crowd. Most of the aisle seats had already been taken. He jogged to the men's room as quickly as he could without causing unnecessary suspicion. He shoved the door open with clenched fists, stomped over to the last stall, and pushed his palms against the door. From the other side of the metal door, Guenther heard an irritated voice.

"This one's occupied, buddy."

He went to the sink, removed his cap, turned on the faucet, and doused his flushed face with cold water. Guenther cranked two feet of brown paper towel, wiped his hands, and blotted his face. His eyes focused on his reflection.

Time to separate the soldats *from the* huhns, *Guenther*.

A chill crawled through his body. Standing behind him, he could see a blurry image of the Grim Reaper. Honing his sickle, his lipless smile and lifeless eyes heckled him. But as Guenther studied the mirage more closely, his father's twisted face was superimposed over the skull. Was his *vater* trying to warn him? He gripped the sink with both hands and squeezed his eyes shut to avoid looking at his father's mocking grin. Failure was no longer his nemesis. The enigma of death was what horrified him most. Guenther Krause was ill-prepared to meet his Aryan god. And not until this moment did he fully comprehend this.

The toilet flushed. A belt buckle rattled.

For a fleeting moment, Guenther considered defecting. But where would he hide? The Disciples would hunt him down and kill him slowly. Painfully. He'd spend the rest of his life looking over his shoulder, unable to trust anyone. And even if he could evade his comrades, where could he hide from his god? Was it not better to die a quick death as a hero? Guenther Krause had come too far to betray God, his brothers, or himself.

An older man, Yul Brenner–bald, came out of the stall. With casual style, he moseyed to the sink, seemingly unaware of Guenther, and scrubbed his hands thoroughly enough to perform brain surgery. Guenther could not risk entering the same stall with the old man still hanging around. Wouldn't he wonder why Guenther hadn't used one of the other seven stalls? In no particular hurry, the man shook the water off his hands, pumped the lever on the paper towel dispenser, and meticulously dried his hands.

The bathroom door opened.

Two young men walked in. The short one, tugging at his zipper, hustled to the urinals. The other made a beeline for the last stall. Guenther wanted to tackle the son of a bitch but stopped himself. He gritted his teeth so fiercely that his jawbone ached. If not for the imperative nature of his mission, he'd kick the door in, grab the porcelain cover off the toilet reservoir, and crush the asshole's fucking skull. He heard the man's stream of urine splash into the toilet bowl.

Flush.

The man stepped out of the stall.

Without washing their hands, the young men left the bathroom. Yul Brenner followed them out the door. Without delay, Guenther dashed for the stall, closed the door, and turned the thumb lock. Carefully, he removed the reservoir cover and straddled it across the toilet bowl.

He heard someone enter the bathroom. Heavy footsteps. Two, perhaps three people were talking. Somebody stepped into the stall next to Guenther. He heard him fumbling with his belt.

Zip.

He plopped onto the toilet seat.

Quietly, Guenther tried to yank the duct tape loose, but it was stuck to the porcelain. He pulled harder. The plastic bag ripped open and the gun tumbled out of the bag and sank to the bottom of the tank with a clunk.

"Are you OK, pal?" the stranger in the next stall asked.

"I'm fine." *Mind your own fucking business!*

Guenther pushed his sleeve up to his elbow, reached in, pulled the gun out of the cold water, and hurriedly wiped it dry on the front of his sweatshirt. Would cold water adversely affect the ammunition? Guenther imagined the horror he'd feel if he pointed the gun at the president, pulled the trigger, and heard the quiet click of the hammer. He did not have enough time to remove the bullets from the magazine and wipe them dry.

He carefully replaced the reservoir cover, gently pulled back the slide on the Colt, loaded a round into the chamber, locked the safety, stuffed the gun into the front of his pants, and covered it with the sweatshirt. He rushed out the door, brushed past a young man, and hurried to the west aisle.

The auditorium was buzzing with activity; people flocked to vacant seats as if it were a game of musical chairs and the top prize was one million dollars. Guenther bolted down the west aisle and checked every seat on both sides. Not one end seat was available. Reluctantly, he sprinted to the east aisle. He did not believe that he could endure her speech without vomiting, and by sitting in the east aisle, he would be forced to wait until she exited the auditorium before he'd get a clear shot. What other choice did he have? He searched every row, craning his neck, frantically looking for an end seat.

No aisle seat.

Desperate and fraught with anxiety, Guenther pulled out a wad of money from his front pocket. He peeled a fifty-dollar bill off the roll and fought his way back to the west aisle. Surely he could find a starving student who could use fifty bucks. For a moment, he stopped and tried to imagine whether it would be more advantageous to shoot her as soon as she walked in or just before she reached the stage.

People stampeded by him like startled cattle.

Guenther figured that by the time the president reached the stage—shaking hands and greeting people as she walked—the Secret Service agents would be less alert. He'd have a better chance of surprising them when the president was closer to the front of the auditorium. Guenther spotted a young woman sitting on an end seat in the sixth row. He genuflected on the floor beside her and smiled. With his fingertips, he held the fifty-dollar bill and flashed it in front of her face.

"Wanna sell your seat, miss?"

***

Albert Cranston opened the limousine door. "It's time, Madam President."

Kate, McDermott, Cranston, and four Secret Service agents marched into Saint Thomas Hall. Their heavy footsteps clicked on the marble floors and echoed in the air. With the exception of armed security guards posted at all three exits, the main lobby leading to the auditorium was unoccupied. Until this moment, Kate hadn't felt nervous. But when Cranston opened the double doors at the back of the auditorium, and Kate heard the thunderous applause, whistles, and enthusiastic cheers over the hum of the college band playing their rendition of "Hail to the Chief," her heart hammered against her rib cage.

Two agents led the way, two followed Kate, and McDermott lagged slightly behind. Cranston remained at the back of the auditorium, waving his arms, pointing toward the stage, yelling orders into his headset. Displaying her warmest smile, the president began her promenade down the aisle. Hands reached out to her as if she were the Messiah.

***

Guenther recognized the swine immediately. It made him ill, but he forced himself to applaud. He stood on his tiptoes and strained his neck trying to see the number of Secret Service agents. He counted five.

Two additional agents stood shoulder to shoulder at the front of the aisle, their eyes meticulously examining the crowd. Guenther's plan was to wait for the last agent to pass him, so he was out of the agent's line of vision, and then shoot the president in the back of her head. But there was a problem. The two agents waiting for her at the front of the aisle would surely see him draw his weapon; they were less than ten feet away. How could he initiate this plan without one of the agents spotting him?

The president meandered down the aisle, shaking hands and exchanging salutations with all she passed. While he anxiously waited, Guenther noticed a young man several rows back wearing a Redskins baseball cap. He reached up to adjust his own cap and realized he'd left it in the men's room.

I'm gonna save a bullet for you, you thieving bastard!

He did not hold a sentimental attachment to the baseball cap, of course, but Guenther, as part of a sacred ritual, had shaved his head completely bald this morning, exposing his prized swastika tattoo. It had been a risky, perhaps foolish move, making him more vulnerable. But nothing was more important than the pride he held in his membership to the brotherhood, and to expose the swastika to the world exemplified and venerated that pride. As long as his head remained erect, Guenther believed, few people were tall enough to see it. But really, did he need another concern to compromise his concentration?

***

"It's so delightful to see you, President Miles!" The young woman vigorously shook Kate's hand.

"Thank you for coming," Kate said.

Kate had never felt so invigorated. The effervescent smiles. The urgency to touch her hand. The enthusiasm and kind words were overwhelming.

"Pleasure to meet you," Kate said. "Hope you enjoy the evening. Thank you. Thank you."

She tried to touch as many hands as possible, to make eye contact and say hello. But she could only greet those people seated near the aisle. She turned and looked at McDermott, who was trailing behind the agents. She thought it odd that he was not walking closer to her and partaking in this historic event. He'd been right. She had not yet given her speech, and everyone adored her. Kate expected the crowd to be dominated by faculty and alumni, but the auditorium was jammed with eager young faces. Nothing could please her more than to make a positive impact on the impressionable minds of America.

***

Guenther slowly slipped his hand under the sweatshirt and gripped the Colt. He rested his thumb on the safety. The Secret Service agents, paving the way for the president, were twenty feet away. The tall, lean one, with curly red clown hair, made eye contact with Guenther. His stare was more meddlesome than it should have been.

Guenther released the gun, removed his hand, and began to applaud again. The agent looked away. Guenther had to reevaluate his plan.

He lifted his chin to be certain that the curious agent, now only five feet away, could not possibly see the tattoo. The agent studied Guenther's face. The moment the agent walked past him, he'd have to yank the Colt from his jeans, click off the safety, and unload as many rounds as possible into the president's chest. He knew that shots to her head would be fatal, but the agents' suspicious looks forced Guenther to abandon the original plan. Besides, the president's jerky movements made her head a difficult target. If he unloaded the entire magazine into her chest, she couldn't possibly survive. This was the only logical strategy. Because Guenther was holding his chin up, his eyes were drawn to a man sitting in the first row of the balcony. The man looked directly at Guenther with binoculars. Then, as if in a frenzy, the man dropped the binoculars and began speaking into his headset. He pointed Guenther's way.

The two agents in front of the president were almost perpendicular to Guenther. President Miles was barely ten feet away. Guenther gave the agent in the balcony a quick glance, then looked at one of the agents waiting at the front of the aisle. Suddenly, the agent waved his arms and pointed to Guenther.

One more step, you swine!

Panic stricken, Guenther tore the Colt .45 from his jeans. His thumb fumbled for the safety as he raised his arm and cocked his elbow. He closed one eye and pointed the gun at the president's chest. Sweat poured off his head, trickled into his opened eye, and blurred his vision. He swiped the sweatshirt sleeve across his face and tried to steady his aim.

***

Charles McDermott spotted the agent frantically waving his arms and pointing to the tall student with the shaved head. He watched the man lift his Georgetown sweatshirt. A spotlight, fifty feet above the man, reflected off a shiny metal object in front of the man's jeans, and a beam of light flashed into McDermott's right eye, causing him to squint.

The flash of light lasted for a split second, enough time for McDermott to realize that the young man with the shaven head was pointing a gun at President Miles. Without forethought, McDermott lunged forward. With outstretched hands, he reached for the top of Kate's shoulders and firmly grasped her wool blazer. He spun the president around and positioned his body between the gunman and her. He was not thinking about heroism or consciously trying to sacrifice his life for the president; his reaction was involuntary. Seconds after his body shielded Kate, McDermott heard a thunderous explosion. With the force of a sledgehammer, hot lead ripped into McDermott's left arm, cleaved his triceps, and tore into his rib cage. His chest was ablaze, and the impact from the bullet spun him around like a puppet.

***

Kate, unable to comprehend what was happening, felt whoever was grasping her shoulders release her. She turned and watched Charles McDermott collapse to the floor. As her mind scrambled for a lucid thought, a frantic agent put his arms around her torso, bear hug style, and forced her to the floor. She saw McDermott lying on the floor, his body motionless. Someone had tried to kill her. Thoughts of David Rodgers flooded her mind. Everything seemed so surreal.

***

In a flurry of utter chaos, Guenther did not realize that the president was lying on the floor. He squeezed the trigger a second time. The bullet whizzed by a student's head, and the panic-stricken woman covered her ears with both hands and screamed wildly. Having no other choice, Guenther aimed at the agent blanketing the president. If he emptied the clip into the agent's back, one bullet might find its way into the president's body. What else could he do? Out of the corner of Guenther's blurry eye, he spotted two frantic agents, their outstretched arms reaching for him.

He hesitated a moment too long.

One agent, his grip like a silverback gorilla's, grabbed his arm. Guenther swung his right arm and smashed the gun into the agent's face. The agent's nose squirted blood, and he fell to the floor with his hands covering his face.

An army of agents sprinted toward Guenther, their pistols drawn, pointed at him. He now realized that he had failed.

Guenther fell to his knees and stuck the barrel of the Colt deep into his mouth. Time seemed to stop. The harried crowd was moving in slow motion, their deafening screams hushed to whispers. A million images flickered in his mind. He saw his mother's pretty face. His father's snarl. Ebony and Ivory. But foremost in his mind was his brother Derrick's sweet smile. For the first time in many years, Guenther Krause's eyes filled with tears as he pulled the trigger.

‐➤ ★ ◄‐

CHAPTER NINETEEN

Kate was uncertain how she'd gotten into the backseat of the limousine. After the assassination attempt, everything seemed disjointed. It felt as if she'd been in a state of suspended animation. She remembered hearing a chorus of screams, seeing people ducking, crawling, running in every direction, and McDermott lying in a pool of blood; the front of his white shirt was stained with a red spot as big as a dinner plate. Her ears were still ringing from the gunshots, and she felt certain she would throw up. When the agent had knocked Kate to the floor, her right knee hit first, bearing all her weight. The injury hadn't bothered Kate immediately; delirium and bedlam overshadowed any possibility of feeling pain. But now, as the rush of adrenaline began to lessen, Kate could feel a severe twinge throbbing inside her knee. The rest of her body still felt numb.

Groups of spectators gathered outside Saint Thomas Hall, and a small crowd clustered around Kate's limousine. Six Secret Service agents kept them at bay. People were talking with their hands, flapping their arms, pointing at her limo. Through the deep-tinted side window, Kate watched in disbelief as two paramedics swiftly wheeled McDermott out of the building. An IV hung from a long pole attached to the gurney. McDermott's face was covered with an oxygen mask, and he appeared to be unconscious. As she watched them place McDermott in the ambulance, she opened the door and tried to get out, but a stabbing pain in her injured knee warned her to remain seated. The light bars across the top of the ambulance lit up, the engine roared, and sirens blared as the red-and-white van squealed its tires and sped off.

Albert Cranston opened the rear door and slid next to Kate. "Are you all right, Madam President?"

"I don't know. Ask me tomorrow. How is Charles?"

"Don't know yet. He's lost a lot of blood."

"Dear God." She clutched Cranston's shoulder, almost piercing his jacket with her fingernails. "Take me to the hospital, Albert."

"Madam President, Dr. Weinberg has summoned an orthopedic surgeon to the White House. Both are waiting for you. The doctors will check your knee and give you a thorough exam. If they feel it is necessary, I will rush you to the hospital immediately."

"Albert, take me to the hospital—*now!*"

***

When the president's limousine pulled under the emergency room carport, a flurry of people flocked around the car like groupies trying to get a look at their favorite rock star. Sixteen Secret Service agents held the crowd back the best they could, but more than one hundred people were pushing and shoving, attempting to see the president. Cranston helped Kate out of the backseat. Journalists were yelling questions and poking microphones in Kate's face. She delicately put weight on her right leg, but her knee buckled. Cameras flashed in Kate's eyes, and she shielded them with her forearm. She felt like a notorious criminal.

Cranston waved his arms like a traffic cop, and a young Asian man in a green surgical outfit jogged toward them pushing a wheelchair. Kate was rushed past the gauntlet of people, through the automatic doors, and into a private examination room. While the agents remained outside, managing the curious onlookers, Cranston spoke briefly with the receptionist. Kate understood why Cranston had tried to discourage her from coming to the hospital. She knew the scene would be a media frenzy. But at this particular moment, McDermott's welfare took precedent over everything.

Kate tried to stand, but a spasm of pain forced her to remain seated. She grabbed her knee and gently rubbed it. Cranston helped her up, and she carefully lifted her body onto the examination table in the center of the room.

"He saved my life, Albert."

"I know."

"Please see what you can find out."

"I'd rather not leave you."

"I'm fine."

Cranston instructed two agents to stay with Kate and reluctantly left the room.

"Is there anything we can do for you, Madam President?" Tom Walsh asked.

"Say a prayer for Charles McDermott."

Walsh eyed the other agent and they both bowed their heads as if they were honoring the president's request.

***

Wearing a white lab coat and a stethoscope draped around his neck, a baby-faced man, almost pretty, entered the examination room. He looked too young to be a doctor, Kate thought. He adjusted his tortoise-shell glasses and smiled.

"I'm Dr. Hawkins, President Miles." He looked to be a head taller than Kate. "I am terribly sorry that we're meeting under such unfortunate circumstances. How are you feeling?"

She did a half sit-up and supported her torso with her elbows. "What can you tell me about Charles McDermott?"

"As I understand it, several physicians are treating him in Trauma Two. He's been stabilized, but I am unable to comment on his current condition."

"Listen to me very carefully, Dr. Hawkins. With all due respect, I don't want any first-year residents anywhere near him. Who must I speak with to ensure that the doctors who treat Mr. McDermott are absolutely top-notch?"

"I assure you, Madam President, he's being treated by extremely competent physicians."

"Competent is not good enough, Doctor. I want the best people on staff. The best people in the country. Doctors who can walk on water."

"Madam President, four physicians—including the chief of surgery—are attending to Mr. McDermott right now. He could not be in better hands."

"If I seem a little pushy, Doctor, it's because Mr. McDermott's well-being is very important to me. I must be certain that he's receiving uncompromising care."

"I fully understand your position, Madam President, and I promise, Mr. McDermott is surrounded by highly qualified medical professionals. Arguably the best in the world. Now, may I examine your knee?"

***

When Victor Ellenwood entered his office, Carl Kramer was sitting on the leather chair waiting for him.

"Dammit, Carl, you scared the shit out of me."

Kramer stood up and stalked over to the DCI. His face was inches away from Ellenwood's. Kramer peered into his eyes. "That's what I'm trying to do."

Ellenwood turned his back on Kramer, slipped off his topcoat, neatly placed it on a wooden hanger, and hung it on the coat tree.

"You look like a man with a mission, Mr. Kramer. If this is going to be another grand inquisition, save your breath."

"Let's talk about Jack Mueller."

Ellenwood glared at the deputy director in a way Kramer had never seen. He wasn't sure if he saw terror, anger, or defeat in Ellenwood's bloodshot eyes. The DCI's long silver hair, ordinarily well groomed, looked like he'd been in a windstorm. Ellenwood lumbered to his desk and sat down, almost falling into the chair. He slouched forward. "So you know about Mueller?"

"Enough to end your career."

"My letter of resignation will be on the president's desk in the morning—assuming that my fucking car doesn't explode."

"What the hell is going on, Victor?"

"I've been complicit in Rodgers's assassination. But that shouldn't be news to you, Carl. Your head's been wedged up my ass for a couple of weeks."

"I'd like to hear your side of it."

"I swear to God, it was not my intention to be part of this insanity. I had no choice but to look the other way, Carl. That makes me just as guilty as the assassins, doesn't it?"

"And what about the assassination attempt on President Miles? Were you sitting on the sidelines on this one too?"

"As *God* is my judge..." Ellenwood's hands were trembling like an alcoholic going through withdrawal. The DCI's shoulders curled forward, and he swallowed with a painful grimace. His eyes welled and his voice was shaky. "I was horrified when they assassinated President Rodgers, but my hands were tied. They had me right by the balls and wouldn't let go. The bastards *assured* me, *convinced* me, that President Miles would resign. I swear to you, I *never* thought they'd try to kill her too." The DCI pressed his palms against his eyes and shook his head. "Twenty-seven years, Carl. What the *fuck* am I going to do?"

"Victor, I don't know what to say."

"I didn't really give a shit about myself. But my grandchildren…" Ellenwood glanced past Kramer's face and focused his eyes on a distant object. He massaged his temples with his fingertips. "Things are not as they appear. You, me, the president—we're all fucking pawns."

***

While Kate sat on the examination table trying not to jump, Dr. Hawkins poked and prodded her knee.

"Nothing more than a contusion, but I'd like to get a series of x-rays and an MRI. I can give you something for the pain, if you wish."

"As long as it's not a shot—I *hate* shots! And don't give me something that will make me drowsy."

"I'll have a nurse bring you some extra-strength ibuprofen right away."

The doctor departed, and Kate asked the two agents to give her some privacy.

She lay on her side, curled into a fetal position, and wedged her clasped hands between her knees. Her arms sprouted goose bumps. The room was cold but not enough for her to tremble so uncontrollably. Maybe her thermostat was on tilt again? Lying quietly, she could almost taste the antiseptic odor hovering in the air. Hospitals had such a sterile smell. More offensive than clean.

Kate rolled on her back, sat up, and supported her body with arms stretched behind her. For the first time since the assassination attempt, Kate was coherent enough to fully comprehend the evening's dramatic events.

"Somebody tried to kill me," she whispered.

Kate could hardly swallow. It felt as if insects were crawling on her skin. The sedative powers of shock, merciful and humane, had temporarily numbed her emotions. But suddenly, the harsh reality of what almost happened dominated her thoughts. Unfamiliar rage assaulted her mind. Kate wanted to scream like a maniac, hurl something across the room, anything to release the welling currents of anger surging through her. A lunatic had pointed a gun at her with intentions of ending her life. She pivoted on her butt, carefully bent her knees, and let her legs hang off the side of the examination table. Kate pressed her palm to her breastbone and could feel her heart hammering.

Why did this stranger try to kill her? And what gave him the right to threaten her?

Even at times of irrational behavior, Kate was not a violent person. But at this particular moment, she wished that the assassin were alive. In all her civilized grandeur, she wanted to hurt the bastard. Her hands curled into shaky fists, and her fingernails dug deeply into the white sheet covering the table. A quick death had been far too merciful. He had swindled her out of the sweet rapture of revenge. Who was this monster? Could it be that the same people who conspired to kill President Rodgers had targeted her as well? Or perhaps Ahmadinejad had not quietly and submissively gone away. Maybe he was the mastermind behind the whole assassination attempt. From what she knew about him, she had little doubt that he was perfectly capable of such an act. But today was not her day to die.

A light knock on the door interrupted her thoughts. Albert Cranston entered the room. He looked at Kate with haunted eyes.

"Please don't tell me Charles is…"

"They're taking him into surgery. The bullet's very close to his heart."

"What does that mean?"

"It doesn't look good, Madam President."

"Is he going to die?"

"That's not a question I can answer right now."

"Then who can answer it?"

"Not even the doctors."

"Who's performing the operation?"

"Dr. Stuart Blackman."

"What do you know about him?"

"He's the chief of cardiothoracic surgery. Supposed to be one of the best in the country."

"He better be."

She eased her body off the table and limped over to Cranston. "Talk to the chief administrator and ask if he might accommodate me until Charles gets out of surgery. Perhaps there's a waiting room or lounge where I can have some privacy and not have to worry about the press or noisy staff members."

"Madam President, I urge you to let me escort you to the White House. I'll leave explicit instructions for Dr. Blackman to contact you the moment Mr. McDermott is out of surgery. You're not going to help him by placing yourself in an uncomfortable situation."

"I'm not leaving this hospital, Mr. Cranston. Would…you… *please* talk to the chief administrator?"

"Yes, Madam President."

***

Kate was sound asleep when Cranston shook her arm. "Sorry to bother you, Madam President, but—"

"Is Charles OK? Is he out of surgery?" Her eyes were half-open, but her body jittered like she'd drunk two pots of Italian espresso.

"There's no word as of yet. Carl Kramer would like to see you if you're up to it."

She rubbed her eyes and surveyed the unfamiliar twelve-by-twelve room. There was a soda machine humming in the corner, a Bunn-O-Matic coffeemaker sitting on a table, wooden chairs with powder-blue vinyl seat cushions. The cocktail table was covered with magazines. *People. Time. Reader's Digest.*

Kramer shuffled in. He looked like he'd been wearing the same suit for a week. His five o'clock shadow was about eight hours shy of a beard. He sat next to her on the plaid sofa.

"Madam President, I am unable to find the appropriate words—"

"It wasn't necessary for you to come to the hospital, Carl."

"Is there anything I can do for you? Are you OK?"

"My knee's banged up, but I'll be fine."

"I haven't been able to catch my breath since I heard," Kramer said. "Any word on McDermott?"

"He's in surgery."

Kramer's knee bounced up and down, and he nervously scratched his stubble. "I have some rather disturbing news. I would have waited until morning, but...Do you need a few minutes, Madam President?"

"It's been a rough day." She reached for the ceiling, stretched her arms, and rotated her knotted neck. She covered her mouth and yawned. "What's this all about, Carl?"

"Victor Ellenwood has made a startling confession."

"A confession to what?"

"He had prior knowledge that President Rodgers would be assassinated. But he did not intervene because he claims he was being blackmailed."

"Victor could have prevented David's death and did *nothing*?"

"Yes, Madam President."

"Who is powerful enough to blackmail the director of central intelligence?"

"I pressed him, but he's too frightened to tell me. My guess? Jack Miller. His real surname, by the way, is Mueller. The missing bottle of wine that allegedly killed President Rodgers, the wine that *Victor* had given him, well, the blackmailer threatened that if Victor did anything heroic, the FBI would miraculously find the half bottle of poisoned wine and the hypodermic needle. And guess whose fingerprints would be found on both?"

"Victor's?"

"Precisely."

"Did Victor know there would be an attempt on my life?"

"He was told you'd resign. Vehemently swears they assured him you would not be harmed."

Kate's half-awake brain rushed with a dose of adrenaline. "You said Miller traveled to both Topeka and Long Beach and that there was no record of what he was doing at either place?"

"That is correct."

"He was in Topeka privately speaking to my husband. Check the date of Miller's trip to Kansas, and I'll bet it was a day or two before October twenty-sixth. Miller must have scared the daylights out of him because when Peter returned to Washington, he tried to convince me to resign."

"Do you know why Miller was sent to Long Beach?" Kramer asked.

"He was interrogating one of my old college friends. Probably hoping to dig up something incriminating. Miller must have tipped off the *Post* right after Peter and I secretly separated. He hoped to create a scandal."

Kramer said, "Miller's questionable activities and the fact that he once worked for the Chicago Scuba Squad could be a relevant detail."

"It may fill in a few blanks, yet it doesn't explain who killed President Rodgers or who tried to kill me and why." Kate did not want to divulge her Ahmadinejad theory. Not yet, anyway.

Kramer blinked nervously and swiped his hand across his forehead. "I haven't told you everything yet, Madam President. You've been so involved with the Middle East—"

Albert Cranston popped his head in the door. "Sorry to interrupt, Madam President, but Dr. Blackman would like to have a word with you."

She held up her index finger. "Hold that thought, Carl." Kate carefully stood and tried to brush the wrinkles out of her skirt. Her knee awakened with a dull throb. She fluffed her hair the best she could and attempted to make herself look presentable. The doctor walked in and removed his green surgical cap. His black hair was thick, slightly graying at the temples. His green eyes smiled as he extended his hand toward the president. She noticed his cleft chin.

"I'm Dr. Blackman. It's a pleasure to meet you, President Miles."

Terrified of what the doctor might say, Kate could feel her heart flutter in her upper chest.

"Mr. McDermott is a very fortunate man. A few millimeters to the left and the bullet…Well, there's no reason to speculate. He's lost a great deal of blood, but he's a fighter, and his vital signs are strong. I expect a complete recovery."

Kate closed her eyes for a moment. She grabbed Dr. Blackman's hand. "From the bottom of my heart, I thank you, Doctor."

"And I thank *you*, Madam President. It's about time this country had a leader of your caliber. I'm honored to meet you."

"I appreciate your kind words." She took a deep breath. "May I see Charles?"

"He's in recovery. I don't expect that he will require a stay in intensive care, so you can visit him when he's taken to his room. About two hours, I'd guess. Expect him to be quite sedated."

When the doctor left, Albert Cranston came back into the room and handed Kate a cellular telephone. "Your father called the White House. He should be calling you directly in about thirty minutes."

"Does he know I'm OK?"

"Yes, Madam President."

Cranston left the room and closed the door behind him.

Kate sat next to Kramer. She squeezed her eyes shut and could feel her throat tightening. "Sorry, Carl. It's just that…" The emotions had reached a point beyond Kate's ability to suppress them. Her eyes welled with tears, and a few trailed down her cheeks.

Kramer held her close and gently rubbed the center of her back. His embrace was like a healing ointment. He handed Kate a handkerchief. She blotted her eyes and blew her nose.

"I'll buy you…a new one, Carl." Her voice was still quivering. "You were telling me there are more pieces to the puzzle?"

***

After Kate and Kramer finished their conversation, the DDCI went back to the White House. He told the president that he wanted to contact Private Investigator Jake Carson, to see if he'd uncovered any additional data on Jack Miller/Mueller. Kate tried to sleep, but menacing thoughts whirled through her mind. When she'd spoken to her father, he promised to be on the next flight out of Phoenix. She tried to discourage him, asked him not to come back until the convention was over. But her father insisted he'd see her by nightfall.

Cranston knocked on the door and pushed it open. A nurse stood behind him. "Madam President, Mr. McDermott is in his room," Cranston said.

Forgetting about her knee, Kate stood up quickly and almost fell backward.

The stubby nurse rushed toward Kate. "Would you like a wheelchair, President Miles?"

"How far do I have to walk?"

"Mr. McDermott's room is just around the corner."

"I'll be OK."

The nurse, along with two Secret Service agents, led Kate down the corridor to room 338. Kate swung open the door and limped into the private room. McDermott's bed was in the corner, near the window. She could see a dressing around his left upper arm, heavy bandaging on his chest. An IV was attached to the back of his black-and-blue hand, and an oxygen hose hung from his nostrils. He appeared to be sleeping, so she quietly tiptoed toward him. She stood by the bed and looked down at him. His eyes opened just a slit.

"You really know…how to give a lecture…Madam President. Can I be…excused from the next one?"

"You're my new best hero, Charles. You saved my life."

"I think…It's in my job description." He closed his eyes for a moment. "Did they get him?"

"He killed himself."

"Good. I hope the bastard suffered before he died."

She pulled a chair from the corner, slid it next to the bed, and sat down. "Is there anything I can do for you?"

"How about a raise?"

Kate smiled. "Dr. Blackman tells me you'll be playing tennis in no time."

"Then I suppose I should take lessons." He licked his chapped lips. "May I have some water, please?"

Kate poured ice water into the plastic glass and held it while McDermott sipped it through the flexible straw.

"Can you handle a few questions, Charles, or should I wait until morning?"

"I'm a bit groggy, but that's OK."

Kramer had asked Kate, without offering an explanation, not to disclose certain facts to McDermott. So Kate repeated most of what Carl Kramer had shared with her about the blackmail plot against Ellenwood, Miller's questionable activities, and the conspiracy to force her to resign. McDermott's eyes grew more alert with each word.

"It was Ellenwood who asked me to contact Peter," McDermott said. "*I* set up the meeting with Jack Miller. But Victor said Miller was going to persuade Peter to come home to help you get through the first few weeks of transition. I had no idea Peter tried to convince you to resign."

She did not doubt McDermott. "Remember the morning I walked into the Oval Office and you were penciling in an appointment for Olivia?"

He nodded.

"Earlier that morning, you were in your office talking on the telephone. Who were you speaking to?"

McDermott thought for a moment. "The vice president."

"Walter Owens?"

"Yes. It was his idea to send Miller to Topeka. He was deeply concerned about your state of mind."

"I'll bet he was."

"When he asked me if I thought Peter's presence would help you get settled, I told him it was just a matter of time."

Just a matter of time. She recalled those words. There were more questions, but Kate sensed it was wise to let him rest. "Get some sleep, Charles. I'll be back in the morning, and maybe then we can talk about that raise." She kissed his cheek.

"Have they identified the assassin?"

"The name on his student ID is William Thompson, but the FBI checked with the school administrator's office, and no one by that name attends Georgetown."

"Any other leads?"

"The would-be assassin had a swastika tattooed on top of his head, so that might identify him as a member of a particular gang. One thing is certain: Jack Miller's fingernails are dirty, and the FBI is utilizing every possible agent to locate him."

McDermott yawned.

"See you in the morning, Charles."

CHAPTER TWENTY

Kate returned to the White House at five twenty a.m. She tried to sleep, but her mind swirled like a carousel. Half resting and half sorting out the fragments of information she'd processed since speaking to Kramer, she forced herself to stay in bed until ten fifteen. At Kate's request, Olivia Carter notified all Cabinet members and other key advisors that the president and Kramer had urgent business, and they were asked not to disturb her—not even enter the West Wing—unless it was imperative.

Kate took a quick shower, got dressed, ate a piece of rye toast, and headed for the Oval Office. A slight limp remained, and she still favored her right knee, but the throbbing had diminished considerably, and movement no longer caused severe discomfort. As soon as Kate came through the doorway of the executive offices, Emily ran over to her like a lost child reunited with her mother.

"Oh, Madam President, I'm so happy you're all right." She put her arms around Kate and firmly hugged her.

Kate could feel a familiar lump grow in her throat. "Thank you, Emily."

"There are hundreds of messages for you. Everyone in the *world* has called and sent their regards. Wait until you see your office. Is there anything I can get you?"

"Locate Carl Kramer for me. Tell him I'd like to see him as soon as possible."

"Right away, Madam President. How about some hazelnut coffee?"

"That would be wonderful."

When Kate walked into the Oval Office, it was like entering a colorful botanical garden. Throughout the office, occupying just about every flat surface, were roses, birds of paradise, orchids, and exotic flowers she couldn't identify. Kate took a deep breath and choked back the tears. She guessed that the dike would break the moment she saw her father.

On her desk were piles of telephone messages and fax communications. She was about to look through them when her intercom buzzed.

"Have you located Mr. Kramer?" Kate asked.

"Mr. Miles is on the telephone."

Peter was the last person she wished to speak with. She forced a long, hard swallow.

"Hello, Peter."

"It's great to hear your voice, Kate. I feel so relieved. Cranston told me you were OK, but I wasn't sure if he was being honest. One TV station said you might have been shot in the leg. Is that true?"

"My knee got banged up, but it's nothing serious."

"Thank God. How's McDermott?"

"It was frightful for a while, but he'll be OK."

"Did he really save your life?"

"He pushed me out of the way and stepped in front of a bullet."

"I didn't think the little twerp had it in him. I'm gonna have to put him on my Christmas list."

Kate did not have the time or the patience to hear much of anything her estranged husband had to say. "So, Peter, what can I do for you?"

"Did you get the flowers I sent?"

Kate scanned the assortment of floral arrangements throughout the office. Then she noticed the bouquet of violet calla lilies—her favorite flowers. "Yes, I did. They're lovely."

"Glad you like them."

Silence.

"How would you feel about me flying back to DC—just so we can talk?"

"We can talk on the telephone."

"Kate, I really screwed up, and I just want the opportunity to make it up to you."

"I just don't think it's a good idea. Not at this time, anyway."

"Can I call you again when things settle down?"

"As long as I'm president, Peter, things will never settle down."

There was a long, uncomfortable silence. She remembered the day they'd first met. Pieces of their ambivalent relationship flashed through her mind.

"It's over, Peter."

"Kate, please give me—"

"I want a divorce."

For several moments, Peter was silent. "At least talk to me face-to-face, Kate." His voice quieted to a whisper.

"My attorney will contact you in a couple of weeks. I'm really sorry, Peter." She did not wait for him to say good-bye.

She set down the telephone and sat motionless for several minutes. She didn't feel regret or anger, only sorrow. Had she done the right thing? It was a question that she couldn't truthfully answer at this time.

Emily knocked on the door and stuck her head inside. "Mr. Kramer is here, Madam President."

"Tell him to give me five minutes."

She swallowed the knot in the back of her throat and inhaled a quivering breath of air. After a few moments, her pounding heart settled down, and she regained her composure.

Kramer walked in and approached Kate's desk with purpose in his step. "I think it's time to put a big piece of cheese in the rat trap, Madam President."

***

Accompanied by four Secret Service agents, Kate went to the hospital and visited with McDermott. The color was starting to return to his face, and he looked more animated than when she'd first seen him.

"There's a pile of work waiting for you, Charles, so I expect a quick recovery." Kate couldn't keep a straight face.

He shook his head and smiled. "Always the slave driver, huh, Madam President?"

"Can't run the country without my right arm." She kissed him on the forehead before leaving.

***

Carl Kramer had set up the meeting with Owens for four p.m. To review their strategy one last time, Kate met with Kramer at three thirty. Walter Owens walked into the Oval Office at three fifty-five.

Owens sandwiched Kate's hand between his clammy hands. "Madam President, thank God you weren't seriously injured. I can't tell you how horrified I was. That maniac should rot in hell. Dean Whitney sends his warmest regards." The VP shook Kramer's hand and sat adjacent to him. "How are you, Mr. Kramer?"

"Couldn't be better, Mr. Vice President."

The VP looked at his Rolex. "Should we begin or wait for Victor?"

"Victor, unfortunately, has been detained," Kramer said. "The FBI arrested him this morning and placed him under protective custody."

Owens's eyes opened wide. "The FBI arrested *Victor*?"

"As soon as we track down Jack Mueller, he'll be visiting the big house too," Kramer said.

The vice president's forehead sprouted drops of perspiration. "Who is Jack Mueller?"

"You might know him as Jack Miller," Kate said.

Owens's voice was unsteady. "Did agent Miller have an alias?"

"So you know Miller?" Kramer asked.

"We were...acquainted."

"We think you were more than acquainted," Kramer said. "We also know that it was you who recommended Miller for the CIA job."

Owens tugged at his shirt collar. "This is preposterous." He glared at Kate; his face contorted grotesquely. "Are you accusing me of something, Madam President?"

Kate glanced at Kramer.

"We'd like to hear what you have to say about your relationship with Miller," Kramer said.

Owens's eyes darted around the room. He clasped and unclasped his hands and twisted his neck from side to side. Kate thoroughly enjoyed watching the fat man squirm.

"I hadn't heard from Jack in years. Our grandfathers, best friends since childhood, emigrated here from Europe. I don't know when they changed their last name, but it must have been a long time ago because I always knew him as Jack Miller. When

Jack contacted me a few months ago and asked if I could pull a few strings to get him a position with the CIA, I thought I was doing a good deed for an old friend. I spoke with Victor, he checked the guy out, and the next thing I knew, Jack was working for the CIA."

"Why did you deny knowing Miller?" Kate asked.

"When Victor informed me that Jack was trying to blackmail him for President Rodgers's assassination, I wanted to help, but Victor told me to keep my nose out of it."

"Why didn't you come to me?" Kate asked.

Owens pulled a handkerchief out of his back pocket and blotted his forehead. "I thought about it. But my past association with Jack placed me in a very awkward situation."

"And you think by lying you're in a better position now?" Kate asked.

"Madam President, you can accuse me of acting inappropriately, but I knew nothing about Agent Miller's activities."

"You're ignoring one integral piece of information, Mr. Owens," Kramer said. "Joseph Vitelli's confession."

Owens smiled with pursed lips. "Mr. Deputy Director, are you trying to dupe me? Vitelli was murdered in the Cayman Islands. Everyone who can read the newspaper knows that. Unless you've found a way to resurrect the dead, I have nothing more to say."

"How do you know Vitelli's dead, Walter?" Kate asked. "Did Miller tell you?"

"Of course not! It was the article in the *Post*. When the president's former executive chef is mysteriously murdered, it makes front-page news."

Kramer opened a manila folder and handed Owens a copy of the newspaper article. "Perhaps you should read the article more closely."

Owens wagged his index finger at the DDCI. "I've got better things to do with my time, Mr. Kramer. I'm not interested in playing your little game of espionage any longer. Unless there is a point to this meeting, I'd like to be excused, Madam President."

Kate stood and folded her arms across her chest. "Walter, the *Post* article reports that a Maryland resident by the name of Richard Crandall was murdered while vacationing in the Grand Cayman Islands. How could you possibly know that Joseph Vitelli and Richard Crandall were the same person?"

Walter Owens snatched the article from Kramer's hand and gawked at it. His face turned scarlet red, and he collapsed in the chair. The vice president looked like an inflatable doll that had just been punctured with a knife.

"Would you care to change your position?" Kramer offered.

Owens nervously rubbed his hands together. "You have no idea what you're dealing with."

"Why don't you tell us?" Kramer said.

"Save yourself, Walter, before it's too late," Kate added.

"Hitler's mysterious disappearance at the end of World War II didn't stop the Aryan movement; instead, it served only to intensify it. They have infiltrated every segment of society. Government. Private industry. Police departments. The Supreme Court. They work beside you, live in your neighborhoods, teach your children how to read—they are everywhere, and the movement cannot be stopped."

"Movement?" Kramer said.

Owens's lower lip was trembling. "The movement for white supremacy. For over sixty years, loyal supporters of the Aryan philosophy have carried on with the dream to rid the world of inferior ones."

"That's an interesting history lesson, Walter," Kate said, "but what does it have to do with you spending the rest of your life in prison?"

"What happens to me is inconsequential. They control more than you'd like to believe, Madam President. They are getting closer every day. It could have been so easy if you weren't so damned stubborn. Why didn't you just resign?"

Kate wanted so badly to slap his face. "So—reading between the lines, here—the plan was to convince me to resign, and if that failed, kill me, which would have put you in the Oval Office?"

"Precisely. They would have gained a great deal with me as president."

"And you can sit across from me and so casually say that you had no problem with me being assassinated?"

"It wasn't personal, Madam President. You were simply in the way, and they wanted you gone."

"You keep referring to *they*, Walter," Kate said. "Who gives you orders?"

Owens fixed his stare on Kate, but sat quietly.

"This is not a time for blind loyalty," Kate said. "Are you forgetting that I'm in a position to help you? Give us the leaders' names, and perhaps I can consider leniency."

"You really don't get it, do you, Madam President? The leaders are untouchable. And they won't rest until the mission is completed." Owens stared out the window. "I have nothing more to say."

"One more question, Walter," Kate said. "Why are you giving us all this proprietary information about the so-called movement? Aren't you betraying their loyalty by telling us these things?"

"What do you think you're going to do with this information? It's meaningless. You don't know who they are, where they are, or where they'll strike next." Owens's eyes twitched to a smile. "But rest assured. They *will* strike."

"You disgust me, Walter," Kate said. "You're the vice president of the United States, for crying out loud. How could you betray your country this way?"

"You would never understand my reasons."

"Is that your final word, Walter?" Kate asked.

Owens sat silently and didn't utter a sound.

Kate and Kramer looked at each other. Kramer nodded.

Kate picked up her telephone and pushed the intercom button. "Please send them in, Emily."

Two FBI agents marched into the Oval Office and stood by the door at attention.

Walter fixed his squinting eyes on Kate. "You can stop me, but you will never stop the movement."

Kramer motioned to the agents. "Arrest the vice president for the murder of President Rodgers and conspiracy to assassinate President Miles."

Each agent grabbed an arm and escorted Owens to the door.

The vice president looked over his shoulder at Kate. "This is just the beginning."

Kate rubbed her bruised knee and limped over to Kramer. He was blankly staring at the door. "Do you think he's a madman?"

"I certainly hope so, Madam President. If he isn't, he'll likely spend the rest of his life in prison."

"This may sound crazy, but I almost feel sorry for him," Kate said. "Or maybe I just feel sorry for his family."

"You're anything but crazy, Madam President. It's an honor to work with you."

"Thank you for everything, Carl."

"I'm sorry it's taken so long to piece things together."

"What about Miller? Will we ever find him?"

"It's doubtful."

"Is Victor part of this?" Kate asked.

"Personally, I think he just got caught in the web. But that's for the FBI and DA's office to figure out."

"You realize that, even if he's vindicated, he can no longer head the CIA."

"I feel sorry for him." Kramer's voice was shaky.

"The CIA could use a leader like you, Mr. Kramer."

He looked at her with oversized eyes.

"Are you interested?"

"More than you could ever imagine."

She put her arms around him and embraced him. "Congratulations, Mr. Director."

***

"It's been a bizarre couple of weeks since I took office, Daddy," Kate said. "And the last few days have been surreal." She set the cup of tea on the saucer and stared into the blazing fire. "Is it possible that there truly is a conspiracy so widespread that it's infested all facets of our society?"

"Anything is possible, honey. Nazism, fascism, skinheads, and Muslim extremists are challenging free governments throughout the world. To what extent is a frightening question."

"How can you fight something you can't see?"

"By arresting Walter Owens and exposing his movement, you've attacked their most valued asset—their anonymity. Thanks to the media, there's a new consciousness in America. Citizens will now be more aware that antigovernment groups live and breathe and prosper. It will be more difficult for them to operate secretly. You've foiled their progress and set them back twenty years."

"Why don't I find any solace in your words?"

"Because you're an idealist. Until you mend every crack and plug every hole, you'll always be troubled. That's why history will confirm my premonition."

"And what premonition is that?"

"Katherine Anne Miles will prove to be one of the greatest presidents this country has ever seen." He held her close, and they sat quietly, enjoying the warmth of the fire.

CHAPTER TWENTY-ONE

Krieger walked into the diner and quickly surveyed the crowd. He wore a fedora low on his forehead, and sunglasses. He had summoned Miller and Hoffman to meet him at this diner without offering an explanation. Krieger hustled to the booth and sat opposite them. He kept his head down.

"It's been a long while, Jack," Krieger said. He shifted his look to the other man. "Jakob."

"We are honored, sir," Jack Miller said.

Jakob Hoffman nodded.

"The meeting had to be here," Krieger said. "I could not take any chances."

Hoffman said, "I'm sorry that—"

"You assured me that Guenther Krause would not fail," Krieger snarled. "He was supposed to be the best."

"No one was more shocked than me," Hoffman admitted.

Krieger looked at Hoffman with blazing eyes. "Mistakes like this are inexcusable. This can *never* happen again."

"I understand, sir."

"I have a new plan," Krieger said. "Did you bring the money, Jack?"

Jack Miller slid the briefcase across the table. Krieger set it on the booth beside him and opened it. He looked around the diner to be sure no one was watching. It was three a.m., and the usual drunks were gulping coffee and eating greasy bacon and eggs. Nobody seemed to care about three men making plans in a Greek diner.

From the briefcase, Krieger removed ten thousand-dollar bills. Then he reached inside his jacket pocket and pulled out an envelope. He handed the money and envelope to Jack Miller.

"New identity," Krieger whispered. "Passport, credit cards, airline tickets, and enough money so you can eat surf and turf every day."

Jack Miller opened the envelope and looked at the contents. He studied the airline tickets for a moment. "Tonga, sir? Why the South Pacific?"

"A hundred agents are hunting for you, Jack. I don't think they'll look for you on a remote island." Krieger smiled. "Besides, I hear the scuba diving's fantastic."

"Thank you, sir," Miller said. "How long should I stay there?"

"You'll be contacted."

There was silence for several minutes.

"What do you want *me* to do, sir?" Hoffman asked.

"Our business is completed, Jakob."

Hoffman's cheeks filled with blood, but he obviously knew better than to question his leader's authority. He quietly left the diner.

"He's the weak link in the chain, Jack. Can't be trusted."

"I'll handle it."

"Not all is lost," Krieger said. "Ellenwood is out of the way."

"How about Walter?"

"He was a loyal member, but he knew the risks going in," Krieger said. "I made it perfectly clear that if Miles did not resign or Guenther failed to assassinate her, Walter would have to be the fail-safe. That was the deal."

"What's going to happen to him?" Miller asked.

"Think any sane jury's going to believe his crazy story?"

Miller grinned and shook his head. "I suppose not."

"He told the president just enough for her to conclude that he must be delusional. That was part of the plan."

"Brilliant idea."

"There's another bit of unfinished business, Jack. We no longer require the services of the Menendez girl. See that somebody handles the situation before you leave the country."

"Yes, sir."

They sat quietly for several minutes.

"Tell me about your new plan," Miller said.

"First, you must congratulate me," Krieger said. "The president has appointed me director of central intelligence."

⋆

EPILOGUE

It was a recurring dream, one Kate hoped would fade with time. She could see his face. His shaven head. The swastika tattoo. Her body jumped as if a charge of electricity surged through her. She opened her eyes, rolled on her back, and peeled the covers from her drenched skin.

McDermott would be released from the hospital tomorrow, back to work in a couple of weeks. Kate had told him to take as much time as he needed, to enjoy a vacation. But true to his nature, he was anxious to roll up his sleeves and dive back into his work.

There were enormous tasks waiting for Kate. The Healing of America bills were her first priority. Congress, she believed, might view her credibility with a refreshed perspective and embrace the bills with greater objectivity. She was also faced with the difficult task of appointing another VP. At this juncture, she had no one in mind. But one thing was certain: this time she'd be wiser and more selective. Her quest to locate Jack Miller would be an ongoing mission. He was a key link to the conspiracy puzzle, and if ever apprehended, Miller could answer vital questions about the leaders of the radical movement.

There were personal issues to deal with as well.

Heaped on top of Kate's pile of things to do was an onus she'd wrestled with for most of her adult life. Now more than ever, Kate could not ignore her thundering biological clock. No longer would she allow conventional thinking to enslave her. Yes, Peter and she were going their separate ways, but she did not need a husband to conceive a child. Medical advances and contemporary philosophies had changed the whole concept of motherhood. At this juncture, she was unsure what approach she'd take, but Katherine Anne Miles was determined to be a mother before her fertile body surrendered to middle age. Of this, more than any aspect of her life, Kate was certain.

Before facing the duties of the presidency and tackling her personal agenda, Kate, mentally exhausted and physically drained, needed to remove herself from the limelight. To give herself a period of self-evaluation and much needed rest, she planned a week-long visit to the White Stallion Ranch. To spend some quality time with her father, to purge her soul of all unfinished business, of unspoken feelings, was long overdue. And of course, in between hugs and kisses and tearful reflections—and savoring Maria's sumptuous creations—Kate would find time to saddle up Breezy and follow the trail she'd ridden a thousand times as a child.

Kate reached toward the nightstand and grasped her lucky silver dollar. She fondled it affectionately and remembered how many times it had protected her when the demon of loneliness had paid her a visit. Kate had slain this demon. Never again would he torment her. She pressed the coin to her heart, rolled to her side, closed her eyes, and tried to dream a happy dream.

ACKNOWLEDGMENTS

I would like to thank the following people for their support and invaluable contributions to the creation of, *I Do Solemnly Swear*. If I've forgotten anyone, please accept my sincere apologies.

Jill Marsal, Terry Goodman, Jacque Ben-Zekry, Charlotte Herscher, Ashley McDonald, Leslie LaRue, Kaila Lightner, Justin Golenbock, Jennifer Ann Chasser, and the dozens of support people at Amazon Publishing who worked behind the scenes to make this book possible.

── ★ ──

ABOUT THE AUTHOR

Daniel M. Annechino wrote his first book, *How to Buy the Most Car for the Least Money*, in 1992, while working as a general manager in the automotive business. But his true passion has always been fiction, especially thrillers. He indulged his taste for suspense during his former career as a book editor specializing in full-length fiction. He spent two years researching serial killers before finally penning his gripping and memorable debut novel, *They Never Die Quietly*. He went on to publish *Resuscitation*, a follow-up thriller. *I Do Solemnly Swear* is his third novel. A native of New York, he now lives in San Diego with his wife, Jennifer. When not writing, he enjoys cooking, drinking vintage wines, and spending time on the warm beaches of Southern California.

15630431R00174

Made in the USA
Charleston, SC
13 November 2012